SHATTERED STREAMS

KELLY POLLARD

Mom and Dad,
thank you for your unwavering support

CHAPTER ONE

"There she is!"

Jay, beaming while holding up his phone in one hand and a fountain drink in the other, walks toward me in the baggage claim. Skipping an official greeting, he continues recording. "Little sister, age fifteen—"

"Seventeen."

"—coming to visit her charming older brother." He turns the phone around to get a closeup shot of himself. "Wait," his eyes shift from the phone to me, "since when are you seventeen?" He winks.

"Since when do you have any followers to create content for?" I shoot back.

He smirks, turning the camera toward me again. "I try not to get caught up in your generation of social media."

"Nine years doesn't separate you from my generation." I take a few steps forward to cover the lens with my hand. "What are you doing anyways?"

"Creating your very own personalized documentary of this rare visit," he answers with a smile, proud of his idea.

"And when did I agree to this?" I push his shoulder with my free hand, being careful not to remove my other hand from the lens.

Jay taps his phone to end the recording and envelops me in a hug, the greeting I've been looking forward to for weeks. "You told me over the phone you wanted a memorable summer, so I thought I'd help you out with the remembering part."

"I want to remember it in my head, not on a screen," I clarify, pulling away. I tend to leave the BeReal and Snapchat selfies to my friends back home.

"You'll thank me later. Oh." He lifts his hand with the fountain drink. "This is yours."

"Raspberry iced tea?" My eyes widen and Jay nods. "Thank you!" I suck on the straw as if I'd just flown in from a deserted island, not my home two hours away. It's still cold, soothing my dry mouth and throat as I gulp it down.

"Whoa, Aves, take it easy." He laughs, taking the handle to my suitcase as we stroll toward the airport parking lot.

"I dozed off when the drink cart came around." I take another sip, letting the sweet substance settle on my tongue for a moment before swallowing. "No drink for you?"

"I finished mine waiting for you. You could've told me the flight was delayed."

"We had to fly around a thunderstorm."

"If I were the pilot, I'd go straight through it, head-first. A bit of turbulence here and there is what flying is all about."

I can't help but make a face. It's like what my mom always said when she taught me how to dive into our community pool when I was four. "Hands up and jump in, headfirst," she would say. "The butterflies in your stomach are what something new is all about."

I look up at my brother. "And that is why you should never be a pilot. I value my life a little more than a precise arrival."

He rolls his eyes. "I'm glad you could make it out here. Wait until you see the view from my new place, and you can hang out at the shop with me," he continues eagerly as we exit the automatic doors, the warm breeze welcoming me to the sunny promise of early June.

Jay and I were close growing up despite the age gap. Even now, with hundreds of miles separating us, we talk on the phone every week. Yet I never would have thought to move in with him had our mom not remarried.

I was her maid of honor in a baby blue strapless dress, everyone cried as the couple spoke their vows, and then there was the wedding reception. Let's just say that most of the guests won't remember that night. The whole ordeal, planned out over the course of an entire year, over in a single night.

Fast-forward a month, Mom and her new husband Andrew were still unpacking in our new home. With four bedrooms, three bathrooms, and a breathtaking view overlooking the rolling green foothills of the Colorado Rockies, my mom couldn't possibly find a way to complain about the whole moving process even if she tried. Not to mention that one of the rooms would act as her personal art studio so she can pursue her passion for painting. The house—way roomier than the two-bedroom, one-bathroom apartment that my mom and I used to rent—is unreasonably big for just the three of us, especially since I'll be off to college in a year.

After finally settling into the new home, Mom and Andrew decided on a honeymoon destination: Europe. There they'll be touring illustrious cathedrals and pres-tigious museums across the continent. I kept telling them they needed a celebratory vacation, but I never expected them to leave for the entire summer, which is why Jay suggested I stay with him in the little lakeside town of Nelson, Idaho, where I have no friends, no job, and no idea of what I'll do to entertain myself. Yet despite the butterflies in my stomach, I'm determined to make it a summer worth remembering.

WHITE. COMPLETELY AND PAINSTAKINGLY WHITE, LIKE the pasty interior of a hospital ward. This is the color of my room for the summer. There's an old wooden dresser and desk, both coated in dust and seemingly untouched since first being placed here. The closet door whines in protest as I slide it open to reveal a small space with a single bar to hang clothes on. I swing my backpack onto the unmade bed and retreat to the top of the staircase.

"Jay?" I holler and he comes into view. "The white one?"

"Yeah, about that." His face contorts as he remembers the current state of the room. "Maybe we can touch it up later this week. I was hoping to do that before you arrived."

I glance over my shoulder at the unadorned room, design ideas flooding my mind. Jay turns toward the kitchen again and I follow, jumping to the wooden floor when I reach the bottom three steps.

"Your sheets are in the wash. Oh, and another thing, there's no bed comforter."

"Wow, you really thought this whole visiting thing through thoroughly, didn't you?"

"You try managing your own business all day, every day." He slaps a couple slices of bread onto two prepared sandwich stacks.

"Is it closed today?"

"Course not," he scoffs. "They're managing without me today."

"How will they ever survive?" I ask him, exaggerating my sarcasm by placing a hand over my heart. "You should probably go check on them, make sure they haven't burned it to the ground yet."

"Do you want this sandwich or not?" He hesitates before passing me the plate. "Maybe you should treat your provider with some respect," he teases, pointing a used knife at me before placing it in the sink.

"Speaking of providing, I'll need a job while I'm here." I don't bother holding back the expectancy in my voice.

"And you think since I'm your brother I'm obligated to hire you?"

"Precisely." I flash him a smile and proceed to take a bite of my sandwich.

Jay leans across the counter, squinting at me and pursing his lips in mock contemplation. "We'll see," he responds.

"Well, while you think on that, I'd like to sleep with a bed comforter tonight, so where do you recommend I go shopping?"

Jay directs me to a home goods store a few blocks away, hands me the keys to his rusted Chevy Cavalier, and offers me his credit card, which I decline. Andrew already made sure I was set for the summer—food, movies, emergencies, you name it. I just didn't expect to use the funds so soon for my own personal episode of Fixer Upper.

"So, you don't mind if I get some paint and miscellaneous things for the room?" I ask as I approach the front door.

"Knock yourself out. I'll be at the shop by the time you get back." Nestled on the edge of the lake across the street, it must take him less than twenty minutes to walk there from his house. "You can stop by later if you want. I'll try to find an application for you to fill out. You'll also have to undergo a series of interviews and a background check before a final decision can be made."

I smile and shake my head before shutting the front door behind me.

The sun is at its zenith, causing my vision to go spotty from the sudden brightness. When my eyes come into focus, I look straight ahead at the lake and its unique figure, the shoreline jutting in and out to create scattered peninsulas. It stretches farther than I can see, disappearing into the ribbon of trees that wrap around it.

Speckled across the cerulean waves are several motorboats, all hauling someone on a wakeboard or water skis.

The sight of it makes my stomach churn.

Arrowbase, the store Jay directed me to, must be the only home goods store within a hundred-mile radius because they offer absolutely everything. Every color in every shape of every item possibly ever manufactured.

Like a Super Target on steroids. The high ceiling seems to stretch on for miles. I grab an empty metal cart and weave my way into the maze of merchandise.

Despite the overwhelming lack of color in my new room, I pick out a discounted white bedspread with a delicate floral pattern sewn into it and wander into the paint section to select a hue, deciding on a lilac grey. After knocking out my two main items, I browse to find a few objects that will give the room added character, knowing that this summer will be the first of many visits to come.

I choose a lamp, string of lights, bulletin board, and a couple of succulents, all with reasonable price tags. I've always been the frugal type, but with the image of the room coming together in my mind combined with the abnormally low prices and money from Andrew, I go ahead and throw in a patterned rug that will contrast well with the dark wooden floors.

"Excuse me," says a girl behind me as she eyes my full shopping cart. She's wearing a dark green collared shirt, khaki pants, and a name tag that reads Jen. She looks to be about my age, maybe older, with pale skin and long blonde hair pulled into a high ponytail. "Do you need help finding anything?" She approaches me with the confidence of someone who thrives off social interaction, even if that interaction is fueled by a responsibility to serve customers.

"Oh, no I was just finishing up," I say, turning away

from a leather chair I'd been picturing behind the rickety desk.

"You know, everything's fifty percent off today and tomorrow for our semi-annual sale, and some of the price tags weren't updated in time."

I can almost feel my eyes bulge out of their sockets. Fifty percent? As if reading my mind, she continues, "Yep, I know. We have this sale twice a year to clear out everything before all the new styles and shipments arrive. I'm not supposed to tell the customers that all of this"—she glides her fingertips across an exhibit of bright pink polka-dotted window shutters—"is out of style." She makes a face. "Then again, I'm not sure if it was ever *in* style."

"Not exactly my preference either."

She walks back to the chair I'd been staring at. "Now this…" She rolls it into the aisle, taking the price tag in her hand. "This should say sixty dollars."

"Too much." I sigh, the image in my head of the bedroom transforming once again. "I'm trying my best not to splurge."

She maneuvers the chair back into its place. "Did you just move here?" There's a subtle pep in her voice, like she's excited about the prospect of someone new in town.

"Kind of. I'm visiting my brother for the summer. Except he doesn't have anything in the guest bedroom to make it homey, which explains my shopping cart." I gesture to the mountain of things I plan to purchase, relieved by the fact that some of them might be cheaper than I thought.

"Well, you could always use a folding chair." She walks farther down the aisle to unfold one and sit down, crossing her legs. "It's not much to look at, but it's comfortable enough and only"—she pauses, twisting around to check the price tag—"nine bucks."

"That'll work." I smile as she slides the chair into my cart.

"I'm Jen, by the way."

"Avery."

"So, do you have any plans while you're here?"

"Not really, just—"

I'm interrupted by a deep voice echoing through the intercom. "Jen, you're needed at Cosmetics; Jen to Cosmetics."

"Sorry, I'd better go. You're all set with the chair and everything?"

"Yeah, thanks."

"We should hang sometime," she asserts without prompting. I admire her boldness, knowing I'd never initiate such an idea with a total stranger. "I could show you around, if you're interested."

"Sure," I respond too quickly, my insides instantly twisting with regret. The prospect of making plans with someone I've only known for two minutes renders me uneasy, regardless of her easygoing nature.

"Great!" She slides her phone out of her back pocket to exchange numbers. "I'll see you around then. Probably near the pier. It's where everyone hangs so I'm sure I'll run into you." She turns to leave but whips back around—her ponytail bouncing merrily—to add in a forced tone, "Thank you for choosing to shop at Arrowbase. I hope you enjoy your experience and have a fabulous day."

I let out an airy chuckle as she shakes her head at the assortment of phrases she's obligated to recite to customers. "See you."

The sun dips closer to the horizon by the time I pull into the driveway, yet more people are outside riding their bikes or sitting by the lake. The surface glistens from the sun's reflection.

Exhaustion from traveling and shopping all day robs me of any energy to unpack my new belongings. Painting the walls and stringing up lights will have to wait for another day, one that follows a full night's rest and a strong iced coffee.

I opt to visit Jay's shop tomorrow and instead take a hot shower and crawl beneath my new comforter, breathing in the fresh scent of clean linen. I remind myself of the months ahead—all the nights I'll be able to stay up late and hang out at Jay's shop. This first one won't make a difference.

CHAPTER TWO

An unfathomable throbbing pain forces me to cradle my head, yet my hand is sluggish to reach it.

I open my eyes to see brown specks floating in front of me. When I inhale, water pours into my lungs, causing my entire body to jolt in agony. I remove my hand from my head —as though through molasses—and try reaching for air, fingers stretching as far as they'll go, desperate to fulfill the foundation of human survival.

Although the murky water limits my visibility, I see a soft iridescent light that can only be the sun's rays piercing through the surface. With the diminutive energy I have remaining, I try swimming upward in the direction of the light, but there's a slow trickle of water making its way down my throat and into my lungs, dragging me down like a tossed anchor at sea.

My chest burns in contrast to the water's frigid tempera-ture, pleading with my body for oxygen. I'm unsure if it's the growing distance to the surface or my wavering level of consciousness, but everything fades to black.

I jolt upright, gasping for air. The throbbing continues, although almost imperceivable. I cradle my head in my hands again, though this time to steady my shaky breaths and regain composure. I strike through a mental image of the number forty-one and replace it with a zero.

Zero days since my last nightmare.

My phone reads ten past five. I groan and roll over, flattening my face against one of the new throw pillows, knowing I'll be unable to fall back asleep. Rather than spend the wee hours of the morning replaying my nightmare as I lie awake in bed, I tiptoe my way downstairs and lace my shoes. The refrigerator's low hum seems to be the only other thing awake at this hour. I step outside and stand on the front porch to scan the area.

The lake is lifeless, asleep alongside its neighbors. To the left, I spot a dirt path winding in and out of a few trees before disappearing into the thick of them. Curiosity pulls me in that direction, and I pick up a quick pace to match the beat of the music playing through my earbuds.

I keep a steady pace for about thirty minutes before questioning whether the path will come to an end or spit me out on a random street at the far end of the lake. I halt, breath heavy and heart pounding. An aching sensation burns through my legs. With the wedding, move, and final exams, I haven't been jogging as much as I'd like, and my body is complaining about my lack of consistency.

The trees grow denser the farther I run, their trunks creeping closer and closer to the path and their branches extending over me to create one endless shadow. As I contemplate the path ahead of me, I imagine it never reaching a distinct end, so I spin a one eighty and retreat in the direction of Jay's house. The path leads me straight without any twists or turns, so I close my eyes for a moment, delighting in the crisp morning air as it brushes against my face.

A second later, a sharp pain races through the palms of my hands as they skid across the graveled dirt, embracing my fall. My heart skips a beat, and my eyes fly open to see that my face is an inch away from scraping the ground. I exhale heavily, blowing up a cloud of dirt in the process, and push myself up with a groan. Once my eyes refocus, I turn around to assess the source of my fall, expecting to see a misplaced rock or broken tree limb.

Instead, all I find is an apple core lying in the middle of the path, smirking haughtily at the damage it caused.

"Really?" I whisper to myself, pocketing my tangled earbuds. My hands—now raw and smeared in blood—throb in pain. Dirt tumbles into the open gashes and my eyes swell with unshed tears. I glance around in hopes of spotting a stream or any indication of water to rinse my hands off, but the silence of the dense forest only reinforces my isolation.

Trying my best to ignore the sting, I wipe the excess dirt off my hands and swat at the dirt on my knees and forearms with my sleeves. I hobble along the path, double checking the ground in front of each step for rocks or sticks to avoid. In my slower pace, I notice a wooden rail fence in the tall grass off to my right. On the other side, where the grass stretches out shorter and tidier, are trees with light yellow and green fruit peeking through the range of brilliant leaves.

Disregarding my desperation to get back to the house, I stumble through the thicket until I reach the fence, unkempt weeds tickling my exposed calves. Unable to use my hands, I carefully place my wrists on the wooden planks for balance and awkwardly hoist myself up and over.

The canopy of trees disperses in front of me, revealing wisps of pink and orange clouds as dawn releases its enthralling colors. The trees are scattered arbitrarily, atypical of an orchard. I would have expected a more linear pattern.

I walk toward a nearby tree that catches my attention. Unlike the others, I see bits of red peeking through the leaves. The fruit, which I can now confirm are apples—something I should've guessed by the lonely apple core on the dirt path—proudly show off their perfection. The branches intertwine to create a labyrinth of shadows beneath me where woodchips crackle under my every step. I look around but don't find a skirt of woodchips under any other tree.

"Why only you?" I glance back to the tree before me, stretching out my still-throbbing fingers to brush the serrated, uneven trunk. The grey-brown wood flakes beneath my touch as I circle the tree, tracing the bark with the edge of my fingertips.

"I guess she's special," a male voice answers from above, making me jump. I stagger away from the base of the tree, almost tripping again over wayward roots protruding from the ground.

"Watch yourself." The voice sounds amused. A pair of legs swing down from the lowest branch and land with a thud on the woodchips.

I scan the person before me: eyebrows that furrow slightly, brown eyes that question my own, and lips that are barely separated, like he's half-expecting me to say something. He's dressed in jeans only, his chest bare, which makes me feel increasingly uncomfortable, like I invaded his terrain. I avert my eyes. Why is he awake this early in the morning anyway, and what is he doing in a tree?

I hesitate, conflicted between the urge to apologize for being in the orchard and the desperation to run away from the boy who almost gave me a heart attack. Before I can make out a full word, he asks, "Are you lost?"

"No," I reply in defense. "I know where I am." I take

a few more steps backwards toward the fence hidden in the tall grass.

"Alright." He hints at a smile, obviously assuming I'm lost. He runs a hand through his light brown hair, tousling the longer strands in the front. Seconds tick away without either of us speaking a word.

"Okay," I finally muster, rotating toward the fence on the balls of my feet. Before taking my next step, I mutter, "Sorry."

I once again ignore the tickling sensation against my legs as I weave through the grass, focusing instead on the task ahead: hopping the fence in a way that looks graceful—as it should be for someone of my age and stature—without the pain in my hands and knees hindering my efforts. I'll at least settle for not falling again. With caution, I climb over the wood using my wrists for support, wobbling even though it's only a few feet off the ground. I can feel the stranger's stare burning into the back of my head as he watches me leave.

Without facing the orchard, I search the ground one last time for something—anything!—that can explain my fall, but there's nothing out of the ordinary to be found. Only the apple core, which continues to sneer up at me. I kick it off the path—a futile attempt at revenge—before jogging back to the house.

<p align="center">~~~</p>

RELIEF WASHES OVER ME WHEN I FIND THE FRONT DOOR still unlocked. I slide inside and make my way to the bathroom at the base of the stairs. After rinsing off the dried blood and excess dirt, I examine the gashes. Just a couple minor scrapes near the bottom of my palms had produced all that blood and throbbing. I rummage through the cabinet to find some bandages, accidentally knocking over a stack of tissue boxes in the process. Before I can finish restacking them, I hear footsteps closing in on me.

"Avery?" Jay mumbles through a mouthful of toothpaste. He's slowly brushing his teeth, looking groggy and confused.

"Sorry, I was just looking for some—"

"Why are you up so early?"

"I was jogging. Couldn't sleep."

He pauses, contemplating this, before asking, "Nightmare?"

I look away, which he accepts as confirmation. Jay never pries when it comes to my terrorizing dreams, although I know it causes him concern, making me wish I'd better masked this occurrence. When he notices me smoothing my fingers over the scrapes, he walks to the kitchen, toothbrush still drooping from his lips, and brings me a box of bandages.

"Thanks."

He steps around me to rinse out his mouth at the sink. "I'm heading to the shop early to take inventory before the morning rush. You better stop in soon if you want that job."

"Should I dress up for the interview?" I tease.

"What? Who said anything about an interview?"

"You did," I remind him. "Yesterday."

"Forget that, just come ready to work." He points his toothbrush at me. Although he tries to hide it, his excitement to share his business with me is hard to miss. It's a good thing too, because without his enthusiasm, the anticipated fast-paced environment and social interactions seem almost too overwhelming to bear.

Upstairs, I dump the remnants of my suitcase onto the bed. The dresser drawers are dusty, so I hang as many clothes as I can with the supply of metal hangers waiting for use. Once all my belongings are neatly tucked away, I notice an envelope on my bed. Decorative cursive letters sweep across the front, elegantly spelling out my first and middle names: Avery Marie. I'd recognize my mom's handwriting anywhere and quickly pick up the surprise envelope from the bedspread where it must have slipped out of my suitcase.

I slit open the top and shake out the contents in giddy anticipation. Out spills a dozen photos. My mom and I have never been apart for more than a few days— she must have printed these to help dull the heartache of separation.

I gather them up and climb onto the bed to look

through them. They're of the wedding, from the rehearsal dinner to the reception. I flip through them, smiling as I recall the occasion. One is of my mom tossing her bouquet of flowers over her shoulder. I was dragged into the crowd of single ladies by my best friend who desperately tried to catch the bouquet. I on the other hand desperately tried to avoid the bouquet by any means possible, not wanting the attention. It ended up being caught by one of my mom's friends who's in her mid-forties, full-figured, and more than a bit tipsy at this point during the celebrations, having accidentally elbowed the lady behind her in the nose as she jumped up for the forest green and cream-colored token of hope.

One is of my younger cousins all holding hands and spinning around on the dance floor. I'm glad the photo was captured since they won't remember it by the time they're my age.

And of course, there's a photo of my mom and Andrew at the altar, both completely smitten and lost in each other's eyes, as if the rest of the world wasn't watching.

Another is of my mom and me in her dressing room before the ceremony, her expression full of awe as she takes in my dolled-up appearance. I kept telling her to stop focusing on me, that it was her special day, but she has a gift of always delighting in her children no matter the circumstances.

The next is of Jay and me, posing and making silly

faces for the camera while I tried not to rip my dress as he gave me a piggyback ride to the dance floor.

The last one I flip to is of me by myself, walking down the aisle as my mom's maid of honor, carrying a bouquet of flowers. I'm thankful the photo can't capture the shaking of my hands or trembling of my knees. I distinctly remember not knowing what to do or how to walk, like I forgot all motor functions. But luckily, I made it to the altar at the correct pace without tripping over the hem of my dress. In the photo I'm glancing down, smiling. I notice a few unnatural streaks near the bottom and turn it over to find a note from my mom, commenting on how it was her new favorite picture of me.

After reminiscing, I set the stack of photos on the desk, making a mental note to pin them to my bulletin board once it's positioned on a wall. I take a cold shower—anything hotter causes my hands to sting again—and throw on shorts and a t-shirt, unsure of any dress code. At last, I grab my sunglasses, wallet, and phone, and set out to find the shop.

CHAPTER THREE

THE SUN BEATS WARM AGAINST MY SKIN LIKE OPENING AN oven door to peek at a fresh batch of chocolate chip cookies. With each step I take, my sandals kick up grainy beige sand. I'm surrounded by beachgoers—sunbathers with their faces buried in books, dog owners playing fetch in the shallow water, and children building sandcastles while ignoring their parents' attempts to apply sunscreen on their backs.

It doesn't take long before the shop appears in the distance, situated just left of the main pier. Although the pier stretches a good distance over the water and it's the unspoken epicenter of the lake's activity, it's nestled far from the bustling streets that sandwich either side of the lake. With no public road access, there's no way to launch boats there, making it the perfect spot to lounge and hang about.

I've visited my brother before, years ago with my mom, but at the time Jay's shop was a dinky hole-in-the-wall joint. This is a major upgrade, not to mention completely isolated from any competition. The nearest shops and restaurants are all downtown, at least a couple miles from here.

The sign above Jay's shop reads JuiSea. Pronounced "juicy," but replaced by the word "sea" even though it's nestled on a lakeside. Completely cheesy. The name—derived from the fact that it's a smoothie shop—was meant as a temporary solution until something better came along, but apparently word spread during the hustle and bustle of setting up shop, so Jay kept it for the small publicity he'd earned at the time. While I see his logic, I pounce on every opportunity to tease him about it.

I stop, place my hands on my hips in sisterly pride, and take it all in.

"Aves!" Jay hollers when he notices. "Come on!" He gestures for me to join him, excitement oozing out of him.

Music projects from speakers lining the roof, creating an upbeat atmosphere. The shop opens from all angles, with two distinct sides. First is the bar, which Jay insists creates a more welcoming environment for customers. If they want to sit and socialize, they're welcome to. If they're just looking for a quick fix, they'll be served in a matter of minutes. The area is lined with bar stools made of wood and manila rope, along with the floor and roof and everything else within the shop's construction.

Opposite the bar, behind what looks to be a storage room in the center of the vicinity, are booths and tables. Ceiling fans circulate the air to keep it from getting too stuffy in the summer heat, and sand is scattered across the floorboards from all the patrons' bare feet.

I hop onto the wooden planks and move around a few customers before taking a seat at one of the barstools. "Waiter." I snap my fingers at Jay.

"Yes, miss?" He plays along. "How may I help you?"

"This is my first time here," I admit sheepishly while scanning a small, laminated menu in front of me, "and I was wondering what you'd recommend." I glance at the black chalkboard behind him where every option is displayed in vibrant colors, the name of each drink written in the shade of chalk that best matches the smoothie itself.

"Well, it depends on what you're in the mood for." He tosses a white rag over his shoulder and leans on the counter between us. "Something sweet, tangy, tart, citrusy…or all of the above?"

"Surprise me."

"I'd recommend going with the Peanut Butter Punch. Strong nutty flavor"—he speaks as if actually talking to a new, contemplative customer and not his little sister—"and loaded with a double serving of Greek yogurt as well as both whey and soy protein powders to help you reach your deadlift goals. You look like you work out."

"Oh, shut up," I scoff, breaking my façade. Ever since I took up jogging as a hobby, I've been boyishly slim with no upper body strength. Jay laughs at me. "Do people really order that?"

"The gym rat approaching the bar is about to," he says without looking up at the middle-aged man he's referring to. I glance to the side to see an incredibly tan bodybuilder saunter up to the counter. The inflation of his muscles looks like it'd be uncomfortable to move at all.

"Joey, my man," Jay exclaims, extending a hand to him.

"Jay." He returns the greeting with a bright-white smile and raspy chuckle, his voice as deep as I would've expected from someone with his physique. "Extra-large PBP."

"You got it," Jay tells him, winking at me as he turns to prepare the drink. "Joey, meet my sister. She's visiting for the summer."

I turn toward him, reaching out to shake his hand. "I'm Avery."

Joey slides off his slim black sunglasses and clasps my hand in his. "Sister?" He leans in closer, pretending to whisper. "He better give you a family discount. If not, I'll get that straightened out for you," he says, cracking his knuckles.

"Don't worry, she'll be getting an employee

discount." Jay switches the blender on, which creates a high-pitched whirring sound. He stops it briefly to add, "Which is basically free in case you were wondering, Aves."

"This punk is putting you to work on your vacation?" Joey shakes his head.

Jay pours the brownish slop into an enormous silicone cup, tapping the sides of the blender to knock out the remnants. He adds a pink paper umbrella that contrasts the green and blue tie dye design on the cup before sliding it across the counter, something I wouldn't have expected for that particular concoction.

"And a frilly pink umbrella for thinking you can scare me."

Joey isn't fazed by the delicate addition. In fact, he picks up the smoothie with his pinky outstretched and takes a graceful first sip. "I'll accept it. Otherwise, it looks like I'm drinking mud poured straight from the Orong River."

Jay wipes his hands on the towel hanging over his shoulder and proceeds to ring him up. "That's what I like to hear. I should hire you to do some advertising."

"You'd have the ladies swarming this joint." He shakes his hips a few times as he walks away, hollering back to me, "Keep an eye on him. If he gets out of hand, you let me know."

"Will do."

"Told you," Jay says to me once Joey is out of earshot.

"Fair enough." My gaze follows Joey as he departs. "Hey, are customers allowed to take the cups with them?"

"The unspoken rule is if you remove one from the shop, leave it nearby where it's visible when we do a perimeter sweep. The reusable material helps the environment, but it's also easy for our customers to take their drinks back to their spots on the beach without worrying about returning them or finding a trash bin."

The feeling of pride for my brother's business continues to swell.

"So." I smack my hands down onto the counter, wincing slightly from the scrapes I'd forgotten about. "What to order." I look to the chalkboard again, overwhelmed by the number of options.

"I already know what you're trying first." He reaches for the stack of clean blenders.

"I don't get to choose?"

"Nope. It's my favorite this week. You're bound to like it, and if you don't, you can't work here."

"Yeah, yeah," I mock him. "Wait, your favorite drink changes on a weekly basis?"

He glances over his shoulder at me. "Absolutely. With the luxury of stocking the shop with whatever ingredients I want and trying out new recipes whenever inspiration sparks, I'm surprised my favorite doesn't change every day."

He pulls out a container of vanilla yogurt from a mini fridge beneath the counter and pours an imprecise dollop into the blender. He walks farther down the bar to grab more ingredients, but I can't make out everything from where I sit, so I return my attention to studying the menu.

"Aha, that's what Jay's Daily Dose must be," I say, nodding to the bottom item on the chalkboard.

"If I've experimented recently and someone is feeling daring enough to try it, then yeah." He fires up the blender.

I look around at the other people gathered there. An older man with a farmer's tan and grey hair twirls a silicone straw around his empty cup. Next to him are two women deep in conversation. One of them must be the man's wife because he looks bored but accustomed to waiting around.

"Alright." Jay's suddenly in front of me again, placing my smoothie on the counter and sliding it toward me in anticipation. "Tell me what you think."

I place my lips on the straw and take my first sip, eyeing the cinnamon and orange zest sprinkled on top. My face scrunches up when the cold substance touches my teeth. Jay raises his eyebrows, waiting for a verbal indication of whether I like it. I take another sip, trying to make out the ingredients.

"Vanilla yogurt," I tell him, even though I'd seen him add that to the blender. "I can see the cinnamon and orange zest on top."

"What else?" he asks, pushing for more.

"Some sort of milk."

"Oat," he confirms and waits for more.

"Strawberries," I add, and he smiles. "I want to say," I pause, taking another sip to contemplate the taste, "I don't know, kiwi?"

"Nope, just strawberries."

"What?"

"Yeah," he confirms, passionate about his latest creation and its simplicity. "It's just ice, oat milk, vanilla yogurt, and strawberries. The aroma from the cinnamon and orange zest overpowers your senses and tricks you into thinking that you're tasting something more complex than it actually is. It's like drinking one of those Cinnazest cheesecakes from Emery's we used to order. Remember those?"

I shake my head in disbelief. "I'm a first-time customer and you tried to trick me. How are you supposed to earn my satisfaction and loyalty?"

"Through enjoyable employment, a steady income, and a summertime supply of smoothies."

I glance around for other employees, but the bar is empty.

"Who else will I be working with?"

"One second." He disappears into the supply room. When he reappears, he's joined by another worker, about my age. "Avery, Raymond. Raymond, Avery." Jay gestures to the both of us.

The lanky boy's dark hair is buzzed on the sides, the

top bleached blonde and long enough to swoop to one side. Beneath a black apron, he wears a pink tank top and teal shorts speckled with tiny images of watermelon slices. He comes out from behind the bar to embrace me in a tight hug.

"I've been waiting forever to meet Jay's baby sister," he exclaims. When he pulls away, I notice thin streaks of charcoal eyeliner along his upper lashes.

"Well, I hope I live up to the expectations," I reply.

"Honey, any sister of Jay's is a sister of mine," he says as he takes the rag from Jay to wipe down the bar. "And God knows family is the last place to hold expectations."

"Alright, get on back here, Aves." Jay tosses me an apron as I down the rest of my drink. I round the edge of the bar and follow him to the back room, which is smaller and warmer than I anticipated.

"This is our dishwashing station." He gestures to the left where a couple of large sinks dictate the space, then turns to the back wall and places his hand on a metal lever. "Back here is where we keep all the ingredients." He pulls on the latch to open a door and I'm hit with a wave of cold air that escapes from the room inside, sending goose bumps down my arms and legs. To my surprise, there's enough space to walk deep inside the unit. He closes the door and turns to the third wall that's lined with shelves. "Blenders, cups, straws..." He trails off.

"Got it," I pipe up as he leads us back to the bar.

There are new faces waiting to be served. Raymond busies himself by pouring different ingredients into blenders and switching them on before moving to take the next order. Jay makes his way to the opposite end of the bar where a young girl kneels on a stool to grab his attention. A second later, he hands her a cup of water. Their customer service is effortless, but the idea of taking a stranger's order makes me nervous for them despite their obvious ease.

"Hey, where's Taia?" Jay asks.

Without skipping a beat or slowing his smoothie-making process, Raymond responds, "She's either a) flirting with a fetching young college student of the male species whilst leaning on his table with her hands placed suspiciously close together to create the illusion that her B-cups look like D-cups and ignoring an older woman at a neighboring booth who's requesting napkins because the dispenser at that table is dysfunctional." He continues without stopping for air, "Or b) texting a fetching young college student of the male species from the stock room whilst ignoring customers and pretending to be doing dishes." He doesn't bother suppressing the sass and annoyance in his voice, which shifts to Jay's face as he marches through the archway toward the booths. Curious, I take a couple steps forward to observe the scene unfold.

Jay stops just inches behind a girl wearing an identical apron to mine and who is in fact leaning over a table next to a guy with shaggy blonde hair and a handsome grin plastered to his face. When Jay clears his throat, the girl almost knocks over the guy's smoothie.

"Ugh," she lets out reflexively, turning to face Jay. "Do you have to do that every time?"

"Until you understand why, yes." He's irritated, and it's not just obvious to me but to everyone else who's now gawking at them. "You have customers waiting," he says with a stern look, which is apparently all it takes because she's quickly in motion.

Jay gathers cups from an empty table before returning, and I quickly redirect my focus to the ceiling fans as if I hadn't been eavesdropping on their confrontation.

"Do you mind helping me grab all these?" He holds up the few he's already collected.

"Sure," I say, rotating on my feet to the nearest deserted table.

"You're new." Taia falls into step beside me, eyeing my work apron. Everything about her has been kissed by the sun: her skin, her hair, which is pulled up into the kind of messy bun that takes about fifty attempts to make look effortless but still cute. "Just a warning, Jay can be completely unreasonable."

I smirk at her attempt to persuade me against my own brother. "I'm Avery."

"Taia." She wipes down the table I cleared. "You just move here or something?"

"I'm visiting my brother for the summer."

Jay comes back into view as if summoned by my words. "Aves," he says, gesturing for me to follow.

"Speak of the devil." I raise my eyebrows at Taia, who—after putting two and two together—grits her teeth slightly.

"Joy," she chimes sarcastically. "Another Warren around here."

Jay talks me through his customer service policies and smoothie-making procedures, showing me where I can find each recipe until I start to memorize them. Referred to as the Blender Bible, Jay keeps a detailed collection of each of his creations including the ingredients, measurements, allergens, and nutritional information, all of which are organized in alphabetical order on laminated pages in a pristine binder. He trains me for the better part of two hours before ordering me to make myself a smoothie and take a break. Having already sampled something fruity, I try my hand at something resembling more of a milkshake. Before switching on the blender, I hear a familiar voice behind me.

"What's the latest, Jay?" Jen asks in her signature-bubbly tone.

Jay engages in the conversation with the same level of passion he showed me about his most recent creation, whipping out the ingredients as they talk. After pouring my drink into a cup, I walk out from behind the bar to where Jen waits for her order of Jay's Daily Dose.

"You were right," I tell her. She had predicted we'd see each other near the pier. Her eyes light up when she recognizes me.

"Hi," she greets me in a sing-song voice. Her hair is in a thick braid, sunglasses perched on top of her head. "I was hoping to run into you. I see you've already discovered JuiSea, a summer-in-Nelson bucket list item if you ask me."

"I would've been dragged here sooner or later," I joke as Jay places Jen's drink on the counter. "Jay's my brother."

She gawks back and forth between us, studying intently. "I didn't notice yesterday, but you two definitely look alike. Same facial structure and coloring. Different eyes though."

Always the eyes. I have my dad's almond-shaped eyes and they're the first thing people notice when comparing me to my mom or brother.

"Anyways, I wanted to tell you about the party we're going to tonight."

"We?" I ask, confused at why my presence is assumed in this plan.

"My friend Bristol and me," she clarifies, "but I'm hoping you'll join us. Tommy's parents are out of town and there's been chatter about needing to celebrate the end of the school year and start of summer. It's just down the road from here and there will be a ton of people we can introduce you to. I figured it'd be a good way for you to make some friends while you're in town. And don't worry, it'll be super laid back and—"

I glance at Jay through the archway as Jen babbles on about the party. He's wiping down more tables but must have been listening because he mouths "go" to me, knowing I'd need a small push.

"—not if I can help it, you know what I mean?" She takes a quick sip of her smoothie, speaking up again before I can respond. "Mmm, I love oat milk in my smoothies. So, what do you say?" she asks, putting me on the spot, one of my least favorite places to be. I feel my palms go sweaty. My definition of a party consists of a few close friends eating way too much junk food and watching movies in our pajamas. I peek over at Jay again, who motions his head to Jen in encouragement.

"Sure, yeah. Thanks." Let the nerves begin.

"Sweet! I'll give you my address and you can meet Bristol and me around seven to get ready."

"Ready? I thought you said it'll be laid back."

"It will be, but that doesn't mean we want to show up looking how we do after laying out in the sun all day. Come on," she takes my arm in her hand, "you'll have fun."

A part of me envies how comfortable she is around me, a total stranger. There's no way of her knowing if I'll have fun or not, but her voice radiates with such confidence that I almost believe her. "Okay."

"Great!" She adds her address to my phone, snapping a selfie for the contact photo. "See you tonight."

After watching her leave, I grip my milkshake and pivot sheepishly to face my brother. He knows I'm not a fan of crowds or vast social gatherings. My glance toward him moments ago was definitely to gain an extra boost of confidence.

"It's just a party, Aves. The fact that no one knows you gives you an advantage because no one expects anything of you. Just go and try to have a bit of fun." His tone is so nonchalant, a stark contrast to the knots forming in my stomach. I stare at him crossly, chewing on the inside of my cheek from the nerves.

"You know, sometimes I wish you were the protective older brother who shelters me from all teenage experimentation and rebellion. But no, I just had to have the brother who's supportive of me saying yes to things I *really* don't want to do, even if there may be alcohol, drugs, and sex involved."

He chuckles. "I know you, though. I don't have to protect you from the things you won't subject yourself to."

It's true. In working with my school counselor, we always talk through what it'd be like for me to take calculated risks and step outside my comfort zone, but I can hardly bring myself to follow through. This definitely falls outside.

I look around. Sunbathers, athletes, people jumping off the pier into the blue abyss—it's crowded in this area, sure, but these crowds don't have the same effect as the ones in closed quarters where mingling is an expectation, an unspoken requirement. At least here I have some semblance of control over my social engagements.

"Besides, I don't think I fall into either of those older brother categories exclusively," Jay says before adding, "You're going."

I can't help but groan.

CHAPTER FOUR

"DEFINITELY A LIGHT SUMMER."

"Really? I was thinking more of a soft summer," Jen refutes Bristol's verdict for my personal coloring palette. It's already been a long few minutes of them discussing the details of my hair, eyes, and skin tones as I sit quietly on the edge of Jen's bed with my eyes darting back and forth between them like a tennis match.

"No, no, look here." Bristol pulls out a beauty magazine from a nearby bookshelf, flipping through the pages in search of a specific article. "Green eyes, fair skin." She shows Jen.

"Right, but her hair isn't as blonde as these people," Jen says, pointing at an image on the page. "It's like a mix between dirty blonde and light brown."

"Two out of three swing light summer," Bristol calls out from Jen's walk-in closet where she's now sliding hangers over one by one, eyeing each item of clothing in quick contemplation.

"Bristol's the expert," Jen tells me, plopping down beside me on her plush bed and showing me the three different summer color palettes in the magazine they referred to.

"Very cool," I tell her. Growing up with an artist as a parent, I'm used to the overly hyped color scheme conversations, but never have I been concerned about how the color of one's makeup and attire heighten the attractiveness of their physical appearance.

Listed under what is apparently my summer color palette are My Best Colors, which consist mostly of blues, tans, pinks, and greens. Other than a deep plum, the hues are generally lighter than those in the soft and cool summer categories. One of My Best Colors is a dull greyish-green, and while I know they aren't going to select anything of that shade, I keep my fingers crossed in my mind.

"Find anything?" Jen asks Bristol.

Bristol emerges from the closet holding a petite dress. I admire the sleeves, albeit short, thinking she'd select something a bit flauntier in style. However, it's the exact shade of plum from the magazine, the type of standout color that shouts, "Hey, look at me!" I should have known that color would present itself—Jen's a light summer too, and her closet is an exact representation of that fact.

"Yes!" Jen exclaims.

"No," I draw out through a forced smile, hoping to not sound rude after their efforts.

"What do you mean, no?" Bristol asks. "It'll look perfect on you."

Before I can find an excuse, they utter in unison, "Just try it on." Four simple words that are almost impossible to refute without sounding entirely stubborn and closed-minded. Besides, it really is a cute dress, something I'd even buy for myself for a special occasion. I just don't want to wear it tonight where my number one priority will be to lay low and avoid drawing unnecessary attention to myself. A dress like that not only compels admiration, it demands it.

We all shift glances between each other and the dress. Slowly I stand up, take the hanger from her, and head to the bathroom to change. Jen bounces with enthusiasm.

I slide the stretchy cotton over my head and torso, the fabric gripping my figure until it reaches my waist where it then ruffles in waves around me. I twist in front of the body length mirror to test how revealing it looks from behind. I place my hands on my hips, turning to face myself head-on again, and sigh.

They were right.

After a moment of collecting my thoughts and trying to calm my nerves, I reopen the door to Jen's bedroom. Both she and Bristol have changed clothes and are in the process of touching up their hair and makeup in front of a little vanity mirror on Jen's desk. Bristol is now wearing a black leather miniskirt and green crop top that complements her shoulder-length auburn hair, which she's left down in its naturally wavy form. Jen is in the process of tying her hair into a high ponytail—reminding me of our first interaction at Arrowbase—and tugging at strands to give it more volume. She's wearing a pale-pink, strapless jumpsuit and white wedges. I glance over to notice Bristol also wearing heels, a pair of strappy black stilettos.

"Please don't tell me I have to wear heels."

They both turn to face me. Bristol smirks in approval while Jen gasps, her eyes lighting up when she sees me.

"Does that mean you'll wear the dress?" Jen asks expectantly.

I let out an airy chuckle and nod.

"Yes!" she cheers, clapping her hands together.

"And no," Bristol adds, resuming her mascara application. "Heels are the last thing you want to wear to a party if you aren't used to them. Your feet will be sore by the time we arrive, you'll start to get irritated, eventually taking them off and forgetting them in a dusty corner where they'll never been seen again."

"Sounds like you're speaking from experience."

"I've learned a lot in the last year." She makes eye contact with me through the mirror's reflection. While my first impression of Jen was bubbly and outgoing, Bristol encompasses more of a quiet, unapologetic confidence—intelligent and charming, yet refusing the spotlight she could so easily inhabit.

"So, Avery," Jen chimes in, "how often do you curl your hair?"

There's something about the way they recommend different styles to me. Rather than judging my lack of effort, they're simply delighted to share their passion with me. I'm already a few steps beyond my comfort zone at this point, so a bit of hair and makeup treatment won't do much to spike my nerves.

"I have a feeling I might tonight."

We all laugh, and they start working away.

ৎৎৎ

WE APPROACH A GREY AND WHITE-TRIMMED HOUSE towering several stories above us. It's guarded by two uncanny lion statues perched on pillars that mark the base of the porch landing. Pop music seeps through the walls as we ascend an extensive staircase to where a mahogany door awaits us, daring me to cross the threshold into the unknown. I'm unsure of just how many people to expect, but the line of cars down the street leaves me suspecting.

My fears are confirmed when we push through the front door into a crowd of people so dense, it stretches into every observable room from our vantage point. The music is amplified, the bass track permeating my body and drowning out all conversation outside my immediate peripheral.

Jen and Bristol are each greeted as we make our way through the teeming foyer. Bristol grabs my hand and pulls me left into the kitchen.

"What's your drink?" she shouts over the deafening music.

"Oh, I—no," I stutter back.

"It'll help with the jitters if you hold something."

I hold up the shimmering gold wallet they let me borrow in place of my raggedy over-the-shoulder book bag.

She smiles and rolls her eyes. "I'll see what I can find."

And with that she spins around, dodging her way through the crowded kitchen. I zigzag in the opposite direction, squeezing past groups of people until I reach Jen, whose attention is fully invested in a conversation with a couple. I take the opportunity to scan my surroundings.

Most people are dancing. A few couples are entan-gled with each other in a massive public display—one couple goes as far as to make out in the middle of the living room. A few stragglers linger on the sidelines keeping up half-hearted conversations and taking sips of their beer every twenty seconds just to have some-thing to do. The congestion stifles the flow of air, resulting in a coalesced smell of colognes and perfumes, each battling to overpower the next, but all defeated by the expansive stench of sweat that's gradually taking over the house.

Bristol returns with a plastic cup in each hand, and another tucked between her arm and bosom. She hands one to Jen who takes a gulp right away, no questions asked. She then hands one to me and I turn stiff.

"Don't worry, it's some orange guava juice or something I found in the fridge," she tells me. "No alcohol."

For a moment, I'm taken aback. I thought consuming alcohol was mandatory at these things. "Thank you," I tell her. She must distinguish the hint of surprise in my voice.

"We don't force anyone to drink."

I bring the cup to my face and take a vigilant whiff before sipping it. It's more of the "or something" Bristol had mentioned than it is the orange guava juice. There's a splash of bitterness, perhaps from an overlooked expiry date, but I'd rather take my chances than have Bristol hunt down another non-alcoholic beverage for me.

The couple Jen had been talking to starts to dance, their arms wrapped around each other's neck and waist. Now it's just the three of us standing in a triangle.

"Let's see who you could meet," Jen ponders, eyeing the groups of people closest to us.

As she and Bristol discuss which friends to introduce me to and which guys might fit my type, I observe the room again, trying to avoid accidental eye contact until I stumble across a set of eyes staring in my direction. I continue to look around, thinking he might be checking out one of my newfound friends, but when I glance back, his eyes lock with mine, eyes belonging to a smug face by the way he lifts his chin and narrows his gaze on me. He stands across the room, an array of dancers dipping in and out of our line of sight, not that it fazes him. I decide it's time to reengage with Jen and Bristol in hopes that he'll find a different imposter to gawk at.

A hand touches my shoulder from behind, making me jump and whip around. Before I have a chance to react, Raymond wraps me in a hug as he did at JuiSea. He's sporting a crisp floral button-down that's tucked into shorts, which are held up on his slender waist by thin suspenders.

"I didn't expect to see Jay's baby sister here!" he exclaims.

"Wait, you're Jay's sister?" Bristol asks.

"I forgot to tell you that," Jen responds.

"Girl, your brother's hot," Bristol says in a matter-of-fact tone.

"She's right," Raymond agrees, moving past me to hug the girls. "He is."

A laugh escapes me. "Okay," I say, not knowing how to respond to such a statement coming from two of the only three people I know here. Although Jen might share a similar opinion.

The music pulsing through the sound system

changes, at which point Raymond pipes up, "I love this song! Dance with me." He takes my free hand and starts dragging me to a precious spot of unoccupied space in the center of the room.

"No, please," I plead with him, trying to resist his pull. "You really don't want to dance with me. I'm awful—"

"Nonsense," he swats the air in front of him as if literally brushing my comment out of the way.

"—and I really don't like crowds."

"Come on." He turns to look at me. "You need to loosen up a bit."

I let out an exasperated sigh and place my cup down on the nearest table. Holding out my wrists as if to be handcuffed, I allow him to drag me to the center of the floor without resisting. Vibrations from the music ooze through the floorboards and course through my body. The blaring noise I can handle—living with Jay as a teenager made sure of that. It's the shoulder-to-shoulder contact that stresses me out.

Raymond grips both of my hands and starts moving in an unrhythmic fashion, stepping forward and back and side to side at random intervals. He shakes my arms. "This. What is this?"

"What is wh—"

"This tension. Why are you so nervous? No one is watching us. You can let loose! Throw caution to the wind! Act ridiculous!" He makes a show as if to prove his point. "No one cares."

Unbeknownst to him, someone is watching me, someone with an arrogant smirk and unwavering stare. Maybe that's the underlying reason I feel tense, even though as I look across the room now, I can't spot him.

"Spin," Raymond instructs me without a second's warning before thrusting me away in a spiral formation. I feel Jen's clunky necklace bounce on my collar bone. Wisps of hair—intentionally left down from my half-up hairdo to frame my face—scatter across my face. Raymond tugs me back toward him, and I oblige, spinning again.

"You need a distraction," Raymond insists.

"Okay, hit me."

"How do you like working at JuiSea?"

"I like it."

"That's it?" He rolls his eyes. "Tell me more, give me the deets of your first day," he says, pushing me into a dip. Nobody else is twirling or dipping, but Raymond doesn't seem to notice or care for that matter.

"Well." I think back to the shop. "It'll be nice spending time with my brother."

"And me," he intercedes.

"And you," I agree. I think of Taia and how it won't be as nice having to spend time with her. "I was wondering, is there any reason why Taia doesn't like my brother?"

He lets out a loud, one-syllabled belly laugh, causing nearby heads to turn. One girl even jumps despite the music being much louder than Raymond's sudden outburst.

"Girl, she *loooooved* your brother," he says, drawing it out. The rhythm of the music quickens, but Raymond continues to hold my hands and move about freely. "She'd come to JuiSea every day just to flirt with him. It was repulsive, although I do give her props for trying. Most people just admire him from afar."

I'm slowly starting to realize my brother's popularity, something I was never aware of before now.

"She applied for the job to spend more time with him because let's be honest, her extended visits as a customer weren't accomplishing her agenda."

"I'm surprised he hired her," I scoff, making a mental note to inform Jay of one of his more senseless decisions.

"I'm not! While she was a customer, Jay had to treat her as such, always smiling and friendly and helpful and charismatic—"

"I get it," I cut him off with a smile, amused by the effect my brother has on Raymond.

"But when she started working for him, he was able to lay down the law, get all stern with her if she ever slacked off, all that jazz. It was truly a delight to witness." He looks elsewhere as if reminiscing about a fond memory. "Still is. But my favorite part is what annoys her the most."

"Which is?"

"When her friends stop by to visit, they still receive

the friendly customer service from Jay, the treatment Taia so desperately sought after." He laughs. I must admit it's funny, partially due to Raymond's recalling of it all. "All joking aside, she really draws in the younger male crowd so who could blame him for keeping her around?"

Maybe not so senseless after all.

The song transitions again, and I ask Raymond if we can take a break from dancing. He weaves us around a group of people to rejoin the girls, arriving mid-conversation.

"—been almost a year already?"

"Right? It hasn't felt that long."

"What's been a year?" I ask.

"Oh hey, welcome back!" Jen exclaims, the alcohol starting to take effect.

"We were just saying that Dalton Valtos hasn't been to one of these parties in about a year," Bristol shouts over the music.

"Which one is he?"

They point across the room to where a guy stands with his hands in the front pockets of his jeans, accentuating muscles that are visible despite his long-sleeve shirt. A few rebellious locks of hair fall onto his forehead.

The guy from the orchard.

At that moment, Dalton takes notice of the four of us staring blatantly in his direction and we quickly look away. While the others resume chatting, I slowly peek again, wondering if he recognized me. I doubt it. Still, a newfound courage seizes me, tempting me to dare his memory.

He catches my stare and glances over his shoulder to check that it's in fact him I'm looking at. His eyebrows cave inward, questioning, but then he flashes me a half smile. Maybe he does recognize me.

In this moment, the last remaining nerves melt away as I embrace the feeling of inclusion with my new friends and the thrill of receiving a stranger's smile from across the room. Remembering Jay's comment about how not knowing anyone gives me an advantage, I decide I don't have to be the same Avery I was back home here, the girl afraid of branching out and taking risks. I can heed Raymond's advice and throw caution to the wind.

"What is this?" I ask Jen as I take her cup from her and chug half of it in two gulps. The intensity of the liquor burns my throat as I guzzle it down. My friends holler in surprise, and I surprise myself by laughing at my sudden act of rebellion.

"Let's get this girl a drink!" They all cheer, excited to finally see me relax into myself.

෴

TIME CEASES TO EXIST. WE ALL WILLINGLY SURRENDER to the effects of our brews. There's more dancing—with the addition of dreadful singing—and to my delight, plenty of laughter. At some point all the lights and music switch off, causing a couple people to scream from the sudden darkness. But when electronic music surges through the speakers again accompanied by a rainbow strobe light, the entire house erupts in excitement.

The girls dance with boys whose names I can't make out above the noise, and I dance with Raymond when he isn't also dancing with another boy. Raymond gestures for me to spin, but as I turn, one of my feet gets caught on the other and I almost fall over. We lose ourselves in a fit of giggles, which doesn't help when I'm already trying not to topple over. When I regain composure, I rest my head on Raymond's bony shoulder to keep from stumbling again, and we sway to the music despite the techno vibe and everyone jumping around us like a rave.

Fatigue creeps in, my eyelids struggling to stay open. "I think I need to pee," I say without reservation, my voice sounding funny.

"You must really be a lightweight," Jen comments. "Your voice is even *slurrier* than mine."

"Bathroom?" I inquire in a childlike voice. Bristol points.

I shove my way through the crowd, having given up on avoiding skin-to-skin contact with strangers. The music sounds muffled, my feet feel like concrete, and just before I reach the doorway, an arm crosses in front of me to block my path.

"Where you off to so soon?" a voice drifts into my ears. It takes me a few seconds to realize that the voice came from the same body whose arm halted me. I look over. His face is familiar. I've seen that smug look before.

"Let's dance," he decides, and then places his hands on my arms.

"I can't right now," I say, trying to continue my quest to the bathroom.

"Come on," he insists, gripping tighter and restricting me from stepping past him. "Dance with me, baby."

"What?" I ask as a reflex, thinking I misheard him.

"Oh, so you'll dance with that queer but not me?" He juts his chin in the direction of Raymond. I wish I knew how to respond—how to defend myself, my friend— but I remain frozen in place, unable to form the words. I feel the guy's hands move from my arms to my waist, snaking their way down my body. He flashes me a toothy grin. I try pulling away, but he grabs a stronger hold of me.

"Let go of me!" The words escape my lips, but I remain in my stupor, feeling lethargic and helpless. A few heads turn.

"Maybe I will, after you dance with me."

My limbs are too heavy to resist his painful grasp. I look around. Everyone blurs together. Even Smug-Face looks distorted. Everything is fading. I can't think. All I can feel are calloused hands perusing my body in gradual, selfish aggression.

And then they're gone.

Someone side-steps in front of me and I'm hit with a wave of cedarwood and citrus. My eyes try adjusting to the closeness of the figure.

"Leave her be, Isaac," the mass in front of me speaks, his voice aggravated.

The guy who'd been forcibly groping me—Isaac, apparently—laughs haughtily, tilting his head backwards and looking around to his friends as if to ask, "Can you believe this guy?"

"Who's going to stop me, Dalton? You?"

Dalton doesn't budge, using his body as a buffer between Isaac and me. I feel as though I might pass out. I muster up all my remaining energy to refrain from resting my forehead against his back just inches in front of me.

"If it comes to it."

Isaac reaches out to shove Dalton out of his way. I'm knocked backwards, clobbering into someone before hitting the hardwood floor. I see a fist in the air and hear a crack when it makes contact. A few screams cut through the air from neighboring spectators while the room around me sways.

And then there are arms around me, hoisting me onto my feet. I manage to push them away, but the aggression from the hands that clung to me moments before is replaced by hesitancy. When I look up, I see

Dalton's face and realize he's trying to help. He looks me square in the eyes with a concerned expression as if trying to detect any source of pain.

"Are you alright?" he asks urgently.

Any words I would have uttered catch in my throat, so I nod.

"Follow me." He places one of my hands on his shoulder and gently grips the other. We maneuver through the crowd to the front door, my legs barely keeping up. I peek behind me and see Isaac push himself off the floor, his face fuming and smeared in bright crimson.

"You alright, Nolan?" A guy with a husky voice bends down to help him.

"Get off me!" Isaac bellows, pushing his friend away. In my foggy state, I can't comprehend if the aggressor's name is Isaac or Nolan.

I notice my friends at the far end of the room looking toward the commotion. I want them to see me, to know where I'm being led, but I'm out the front door and descending the flight of stairs before my fatigued body can change course, and I wholly surrender.

CHAPTER FIVE

WE STUMBLE DOWN A DARK, ABANDONED STREET. WELL, I stumble. He walks slowly beside me, occasionally shooting me sidelong glances to check on my stability. I notice him pull ahead of me by a few steps.

"Would you slow down?" My voice sounds whiny. I want to cringe, but I don't have the energy. "And I still have to pee."

He rotates to face me with an amused look, trying to conceal a smile. "You stopped walking."

I look down to see my feet planted firmly on the cement. A deep, guttural laugh that I've never heard before leaks from my lips. "Oh." I chug forward again. "You know, I know you."

"Oh yeah?" he asks as if playing along with a child's imagination.

"Yeah, you were that Tarzan guy swinging from the

mightiest tree branches like *whoooosh*," I gesture, the motion swaying me off balance. Thankfully, Tarzan is there to steady me.

"I hardly think that's an accurate representation," he tells me after I'm walking somewhat straight again, but he now keeps a hand on my back to catch me if necessary. "It was one branch, and I dropped to the ground."

"But you were half naked," I giggle, pointing a flimsy finger at him. "Seems to me like you're the Tarzan version of Clark Kent."

"You're making no sense right now." His words sting, my heart feeling more vulnerable than normal, but at least he chuckles.

"You know, like you go undercover as Tarzan to rescue damsels in distress. Like me," I add cheerfully and then pause, feeling an uneasy gurgling in my stomach. "Oh no."

"What is it?"

"I feel not good." I bend over, staring blankly at the black wall of cement.

I feel his fingers brush my loose strands of hair behind my ears. "It's not much farther," he tells me. "Can you keep walking?"

"Yeah," I say, although I think it's a lie. I pull myself upright and see black spots in my vision. "I can...keep... wa—" I attempt to say before collapsing into strong arms.

෪෪෪

I'VE ALWAYS WONDERED WHAT IT'D BE LIKE TO TOUCH THE clouds, to hold one in my hands. But not just any cloud, a robust cumulus cloud. Would it feel cool and soft, or would it be like touching air, seemingly nonexistent? I ponder this as white cotton candy clouds leisurely roll by. It's a lazy afternoon and they, too, don't have any place to be.

I sit up in the canoe, which rests gracefully on the still waters of a rocky alcove. Quaking aspens and Douglas-firs line the shore's edge, providing shade from the prevailing sun. Birds sing from high in the treetops as if just for me.

The water is clear, exposing colorful stones at the bottom and small fish that dart haphazardly in all directions. My eyes scan the surface, making their way toward the horizon, but they come across a dark object floating in the water. I take the oars and row toward it with curiosity, each stroke creating small ripples that cause the object to bob slightly. As the canoe approaches, I see that it isn't an object.

It's a body.

A man, fully clothed and face down in the water. Goosebumps race over my body like pinpricks.

"Hello?" I manage to croak through quivering lips.

No movement.

"Hello!" I try louder, terror seizing my voice.

My whole body is shaking now, but I know what needs to happen. I reach my hand toward the man in the water. I need to pull him out. I need to perform CPR.

I need to save him!

A dragonfly attempts to land on my nose. "Go away!" I

shout, violently swatting at it. This man needs my help, but as I reach toward the water again, the tickling sensation on the bridge of my nose grows stronger, as does the panic inside me as I succumb to the realization that it's too late to save him.

My eyes snap open to find a fluffy mass of golden hair and a black button nose not two inches from mine. The excited figure resumes licking my nose.

So that's what it was.

I reach up to give the friendly goldendoodle a quick pet, but the pressure in my head is so unbearable that I tuck in my knees and push my hands under my pillow, ready to resume unconsciousness. Before I doze off again, my mind replays moments from the night before, and my drowsiness evaporates in an instant as I push myself upright. The sudden movement amplifies the pounding in my head tenfold and causes the dog to bark and bounce up and down.

"Shhhhh," I try cooing, not wanting the owner or whoever might be lurking nearby to come in here. I check the tag dangling from its collar.

"Hey, Sally." I caress her curly hair. All her energy is channeled through her tail, which wags uncontrollably, making her entire rear end sway back and forth.

Sunlight pours through the windows that line the high-vaulted ceiling, making my stomach twist nervously at the thought of how long I've been gone. The windows are all above eye level, restricting my ability to scope out my location.

There's a stack of folded clothes next to me on the bed: grey sweatpants and a navy-blue t-shirt. I notice my flats on the floor beside me and a small nightstand housing Jen's gold wallet and clunky necklace, which are laid out with precision. There's also a tall glass of blue liquid resting on a coaster. My parched throat and growling stomach plead for a sip—not to mention my desperation to rinse out the foul taste in my mouth—but I restrain myself, not knowing what it is or who it belongs to.

I slide out of the bed and walk to the center of the uncharacteristically large room, Sally trotting eagerly behind me. It reminds me of a warehouse, and my stomach tightens at the thought.

Off to one side is a bed and dresser. No closet, but there's a stand-alone clothes hanger fashioned from scrap wood. I take note of the men's clothing that hangs from it.

Along the lengthier wall is a living space—TV, glass coffee table, and a blue fabric couch with a stack of folded-up blankets and pillow perched on top. Everything from remote controls to the window curtains overhead seem meticulously placed.

The back of the room resembles some sort of workshop. There's a large toolbox, circular saw, and other machinery I don't recognize.

There are three doors along the room's perimeter. The one farthest from me, near the back of the room, is open to reveal a bathroom. I start there.

In the mirror's reflection, a disheveled-looking girl with staticky hair and smeared makeup stares back at me in horror. Her dress is wrinkled and there are heavy bags under her eyes. The look of her frightens me.

What happened to me?

I try smoothing out my hair and washing away the streaks of makeup smeared around my eyes when something triggers my gag reflex. A repulsive odor fights to sneak past a Clorox safeguard.

And then it hits me.

The revolting taste in my mouth, the overpowering aroma of cleaning supplies, the drink on the lampstand. I most definitely got sick last night, and someone cleaned up after me. Probably the same someone who slept on the couch.

Blips from last night drift in and out of my mind as I strain to piece them into a coherent memory. When I do, I'm flooded with embarrassment. As well as stupid thoughts like hoping I didn't snore in front of him. I have no recollection of anything I said or how sick I was, but I remember Dalton. I remember his perfect timing at the party and his hand on my back as we strolled down the empty street.

My memory expands beyond Dalton. What about Jen and Bristol? Do they know I'm safe? Are they worried about me?

Jay.

I quietly run back to the bed to grab my stuff, Sally

still in tow. I open the wallet to where I'd stashed my phone. Dead battery.

Of the two remaining doors, I try the middle one first, but the closer I get, the more I can make out muffled voices on the other side. There's a woman, her voice soft, and a man's response. I back away and head toward my final option, praying it'll provide an easy getaway.

Before reaching it, a picture frame on a nearby dresser catches my eye. It's of Dalton with a girl, both laughing with their arms around each other's shoulders. The girl has long wavy hair and perfect teeth—she's beautiful. Another wave of embarrassment leaches into my core as I realize I just slept in a bed that belongs to someone's boyfriend. Does she know? I wonder how she'll react when Dalton tells her about last night. *If* he tells her about last night. Two days in town and I'm already well on my way to establishing some enemies.

A scratching noise pulls me from my troubled thoughts. Sally lays at the base of the middle door, mauling at it with her paws.

"Sally," I whisper urgently, not wanting her to attract the voices on the other side. She turns to me with attentive eyes, then lays down, resting her head over her paw to stare at me from across the room. Very well-behaved, and completely adorable, though her scratching makes it even more pressing for me to find an exit. I take the final doorknob in my hand and twist it slowly.

Sunlight seeps through the crack and I can't recall a time I've felt more liberated. I sidestep the door and take off in a sprint down a dirt path in the woods.

CHAPTER SIX

"TELL ME AGAIN," JAY DEMANDS, HIS VOICE SUGGESTING he had been worrying long before I walked through the door. It's now ten in the morning.

"I was with Jen, Bristol, and Raymond the entire night until I had to use the bathroom," I tell him, dreading what followed next. "Some guy was bothering me, so this other guy stepped in and removed me from the situation. I was tired and didn't feel well, so I crashed at his place because it was just down the road." *I think*, I add to myself. "Nothing happened. I'm fine." Even as I explain it, I know how stupid and senseless it sounds.

My first explanation I kept vague, saying that I hung out with the girls all night and when I got tired, I crashed at someone's house. Although apparently Jen and Bristol were worried about me too and already called the shop this morning to ask if I'd made it home safely, at which point Jay rushed home to find an empty bedroom.

"Why didn't you go back with the girls?" He paces back and forth in the living room while I sit solemnly on the couch.

"I don't know." I shrug. "I wasn't thinking clearly."

"But you weren't drinking?" I avoid making eye contact, which stops Jay in his tracks. "Come on, Avery, you said you wouldn't be drinking."

"I didn't say that. You assumed I wouldn't because I —I," I stutter, desperate for a worthy explanation. "I'm sorry," I tell him, although I've lost track of how many times it's been said by now.

"You've only been here a couple days and you've already managed to give me a heart attack." He runs his hands over his face.

"You were the one who—"

"I know I was the one who told you to go. I just thought you'd make wiser decisions." He sighs heavily. The disappointment in his voice matches the misery in the pit of my stomach. "Okay, go shower or whatever it is you need to do. I'll meet you at the shop."

I take the stairs two at a time, desperate to get out of this dress. "This is why I could never have kids," I hear Jay mumble on his way out the door.

I've never known if it's because of the age gap or growing up without a father, but Jay's learned how to step into that role when a situation demands it. Lucky for me, I know he won't repeat a word of this to our mom, not after the countless times he snuck out to party and drink at my age. I suppose this one stress-inducing incident as my temporary guardian is just a taste of his own medicine.

I think back to the dirt path that guided me home, the same one I'd run on the previous morning. A couple favorable turns led me straight to Jay's front lawn. But deep in the forest as I passed the wooden fence and woodchip-skirted tree beyond it, I hoped Dalton wasn't perched on a branch watching me leave.

<center>~~~</center>

THE FOLLOWING WEEK PASSES UNEVENTFULLY, AT LEAST compared to my inadvertently eventful start to my stay. Days are spent working at the shop and meandering the town with Jen and Bristol, and nights are spent watching movies with Jay while we eat buttered popcorn and pretzel M&M's. It's become somewhat of a routine for us.

I try not to think about what happened the night of the party, mostly because whenever I do, my stomach twists into knots and my mind spirals into all the possibilities that might have occurred in my unconscious state. I try to remind myself that nothing serious happened, that a lot of teenagers drink at parties, that it's only my distorted memory and unfamiliarity with the situation that's messing with me—regardless of if that's true. Isaac may have laid a hand on me, but I was pulled away before it escalated. I may have slept at a stranger's house, but I woke up safe and found my way home after.

I also may have been violently sick in front of a cute boy who sacrificially cleaned up after me. Who has a girlfriend but let me sleep in his bed. Who rescued me and walked next to me with a hand on my back for support in the dead of night.

I guess I'm still trying to process that part.

It doesn't help that he started appearing near the shop in the days to follow, which explains why I'm now standing in the storage room over a steaming faucet wearing a damp t-shirt and washing a never-ending pile of dishes with prune-like fingers.

Raymond walks in carrying a couple more blenders and cups, placing them next to my station.

"What's the update?" I ask him. He's become my lookout whenever Dalton nears the premises, helping me to avoid any accidental eye contact or awkward interactions.

"Still here, Boss Junior."

"Don't call me that," I laugh, starting on one of the blenders he brought me. Raymond had been very persistent the morning after the party, prying for the details of my disappearance. I tried keeping it vague like I'd attempted with Jay, but as soon as Dalton came around the first time, Raymond knew I was hiding something. Lucky for him, I couldn't resist his tenacious curiosity and told him everything I could remember.

"And get this." Raymond leans backward over the steel surface enough to meet my gaze under his wave of bleached hair. "He ordered something."

I groan. The few times Dalton has come around this week, he walks close enough to peer into the bar, but never orders anything. Who knows how long he'll stay this time? I'm running out of options to stay busy back here.

"This proves that he's here for you," Raymond continues. "So, you should stop acting so furtive and go talk to him."

"How does him ordering a smoothie prove that he's here for me?" I shoot him a doubtful look.

"Let's see." He brings a hand up to stroke his chin. "I haven't seen him around JuiSea in months, and within two days of you showing up in town he magically reappears, which also happens to be less than twenty-four hours after you snuck out of his bed chambers."

"I wouldn't call it—" I try cutting him off. Bed chambers sounds so much worse than what happened that night, but he continues without hearing me out.

"And then I spot him not-so-secretly peering over here two more times within the week. You're right though." He throws his hands up in a shrug. "He probably just wanted the smoothie."

Thinking of that night makes me want to curl up in the

fetal position to escape my humiliation. I'm grateful for Dalton's help, but I wish he'd just put it behind him like I'm trying to do. Besides, how did he know where to find me?

Not wanting to admit Raymond's right and drag on the discussion of Dalton's motives, I redirect in a mock-serious tone. "What smoothie did he order?"

Raymond snaps into character, replying in a grave voice. "He ordered the Boysenberry Blitz, ma'am."

"Hmm." I lean over the sink, my forearms supporting my weight against the curved steel. "At least he has good taste."

"What are you two doing?" Jay stands at the entrance to the storage room carrying a rag and multiple used blenders.

"Dishes," I respond, hurrying to resume where I left off.

"Talking," Raymond admits. I suppose his good rapport with Jay grants him a bit of lenience, but I still have to stifle a laugh at his blatant honesty.

"You," he nods toward me. "Hurry up and finish those. And Raymond, there's a whole cluster of people waiting to order."

"On it, Boss Senior."

Jay narrows his eyes in confusion, not under-standing the new title. "Don't call me that." He sets the blenders down and grabs a container of silicone straws on his way out, Raymond trailing behind him.

After a moment, Raymond pops his head around the

corner and speaks in a loud whisper. "He's cute. Just talk to him."

"Why don't you talk to him if you think he's so cute?"

"That's not a bad idea." He has a determined look in his eye.

"No, don't be friendly." I change my mind. "I don't want him hanging around here."

"Honey, he's probably straight if he's pining after you, so if I turn on the charm, he's bound to leave sooner."

And with that, he disappears around the doorway again. I look down at the mountain of blenders in the sink, my eyes taking notice of the dark boysenberry remnants in one of them.

CHAPTER SEVEN

"How's my baby girl doing?" My mom's voice sings through the phone. I lay across the end of my bed facing the ceiling, the walls of the room still bare and blindingly white.

"Good." I can't help smiling at her soothing voice.

"Oh, come on, I want to hear everything," she presses. "Have you made any new friends? How's working at the shop? Isn't the new location beautiful?"

"Yeah, it really is beautiful. It's exactly how I pictured it from the thousands of times you described it to me."

"Oh, hush." She laughs. I can tell she's enjoying her getaway by the lightness in her voice. "Oh, Andrew just walked in. Andrew, Avery's on the phone," she tells him.

"What's good, Avery?" Their voices recede now that I'm on speaker phone. "How's the lakeside summer vacation treating you?"

"It's good. I've made a few friends. One of them works at the shop, too," I tell them. "But enough about me, tell me about your trip."

"Oh Avery, it's just wonderful here!" They proceed to tell me about all their endeavors starting with the flight—what meals were served onboard and my mom's pleasant bewilderment at the complimentary wine. She describes to me the castles, cobblestones, cuisines, you name it. Despite them being awake in the middle of the night to catch an early flight from Budapest to Rome, they show no signs of fatigue, only exhilaration and anticipation of their next destination.

Meanwhile the front door opens, announcing Jay's arrival. I wander downstairs to meet him, thanking my mom for the pictures she snuck into my suitcase.

"Oh sweetie, you're welcome," she says, her voice nurturing. "I hoped it would make the time apart just a smidge more bearable. I even brought copies of them here with me. I think I looked at them five times on the flight over."

"Six," Andrew calls out from somewhere in the background.

"Well, it was really thoughtful of you," I tell her. "Jay's home now so I'll let you talk to him."

We say our goodbyes and I hand the phone off to Jay. I then queue up a movie and settle in for our nightly routine.

THE CANOE ROCKS VIOLENTLY, NEARLY CAPSIZING AS I REACH toward the man's body. With adrenaline surging through me, I'm able to grab a fistful of his shirt and heave him toward the boat.

The man's head snaps up just a couple inches from mine, his eyes crazed and bloodshot red and his teeth exposed in a loathing snarl. My breath catches in my throat, and I'm frozen in place. He grips my wrists with such ferocity that the veins in his arms and neck bulge. The man lets out a blood-curdling cry, clenches my throat, and wrenches me overboard.

Water rushes up my nose and down my throat. He continues to choke me, his fingers squeezing tighter and tighter until I can't breathe. He thrusts me underwater, resistant to my feeble hands and kicking legs trying to pry him off me. My chest burns, and my vision goes spotty.

This can't be how it ends. All I wanted was to help.

Pain and panic swell within me as the world around me begins to fade. All I can make out past the water's surface are the man's eyes, clear as day. I've seen them before—they're all too familiar to me.

Like gazing into a mirror.

I awake with a start, frantically searching my surroundings. It always takes a few seconds to realize it was another nightmare, and although frequent, I never get the sense that I'm dreaming when I'm in them.

I rise from my pillow, now damp with perspiration, and try focusing on the slanted sunlight spilling through the curtains, but it's not enough to calm me down. It's almost six o'clock, so I grab my shoes and sweatshirt and head for the door.

The dirt path is shaded, silent. The perfect space for me to unwind. Until my feet come to a sudden stop at the wooden fence that is. Maybe curiosity got the better of me. Maybe I want to prove to myself or to Dalton that I'm not as helpless as I might seem.

The tree is easy enough to spot. The skirt of wood-chips, the red splotches hidden within its greenery, but something's different this time. I walk toward the fence to get a better look.

There's a plank of wood swaying from side to side, suspended in the air by two thick ropes that run up to the lowest branch.

A swing.

When my eyes reach the branch, they catch a glimpse of movement. There, sitting with his back against the base of the tree, is Dalton. He holds a book in one hand and tosses an apple in the other.

So, this is the guy who took care of me, I think. The guy who defended me at the party, assisted me back to his place, cleaned up my vomit, and offered up his bed. To a complete stranger, no less.

The guy who respected me in my state of vulnerability, unlike the motives of so many others.

He sits motionless on the branch, the hand that had been tossing the apple now still, his interest captivated by the piece of literature. Without warning, his face turns from his book to where I stand in the unkempt grass. I avert my eyes, but there's no way to cover up my watching him. During all my years of algebra and American history, you'd think they'd throw in a course on social decorum. Not that there would have been a unit on How to Act When You're Caught Observing Someone Reading in a Tree at Dawn.

I glance back at him. Despite the distance, I notice a smile creep onto his face. He lifts a hand to wave, wiggling the fingers that aren't gripping the apple. I suppose this unexpected encounter now gives him full permission to peruse JuiSea's surroundings since I'm the one spying this time.

I shoot him a sort of smile and give a rigid, clumsy nod, thankful that we're too far apart to exchange any words.

I take a few hesitant steps in the direction of Jay's house. Dalton takes a casual bite of his apple and resumes reading, apparently thinking nothing of this incident.

Knowing myself, though, it'll stay on my mind for hours.

CHAPTER EIGHT

THE SUN ASCENDS TO ITS ACME. A STEADY STREAM OF customers keeps us busy, walk-ins waiting at the bar and booths filled to the brim. While I normally stay behind the bar, we need all hands on deck, meaning I'm now rushing back and forth between the bar and tables, taking orders of four to six smoothies at a time and producing them simultaneously.

"Alright, time to recharge," Jay says when there's a lull in customers. "Ray, make a round."

"On it," Raymond replies, grabbing a plastic crate to collect the empty cups scattered along the beach.

"Taia, you can start on dishes, take a break from serving." She heads to the back room.

"What can I do?" I ask, following him under the archway from the seated area to the bar. He turns to face me.

"Relax." He motions to suggest I should slow down.

He leans sideways against a wall. "Seriously, you've been here every morning when we open and stay late into the afternoons. You don't have to work this much, you know."

"I know." I move to one of the mini fridges beneath the bar, crouching down to count what needs restocking. "I like it though, keeps me busy." I eased into the position a lot smoother than I expected, probably due to Jay's support and Raymond's laidback nature.

He crosses his arms. "Well, I won't argue with that. You're a natural."

"Whatever you are, be a good one," I tell him, counting the number of blueberry containers on the top shelf.

"Abraham Lincoln."

I turn my focus to him. "How'd you know?"

He looks at me thoughtfully. "It was one of Dad's favorites."

A moment passes with neither of us saying a word. It's not often we discuss our father, so I feel ill-prepared at the mention of him.

"Oh," I finally respond, returning my attention to the missing blueberries. Jay busies himself by gathering up the empty cups along the bar and bringing them back to Taia. I recount the fruit containers with a stronger concentration, noting to myself how many of each I need to grab from the walk-in freezer to replenish the bar.

"Three blue, one razz, four strawberry," I mumble to

myself, shutting the door and rising from my squatted stance. "Three blue, one razz—"

"Why are you avoiding me?"

I jump, and gasp, and basically flail my arms as I grasp my chest. It doesn't take much to catch me by surprise. When I look up, Dalton is standing directly in front of me, his hands gripping the edge of the counter.

"Sorry, I didn't mean to startle you," he says, taking in my perplexed posture. Up close and having full control over my mind and body this time—well, after recovering from my initial fright at least—I can make out his exact features. The slight curliness in the front of his hair. The suggestion of dimples if he were to smile. His features had become hazy in my mind after the party, but now I can see everything from his soft, brown eyes to a minute scar above the end of his left eyebrow. I swallow, regaining composure.

"You didn't," I tell him. "And I'm not." I start to walk the length of the bar, determined to restock the fridge to appear busy, but I can't remember how many containers of each fruit I need. I decide I'll just grab a couple of each and call it good.

He follows me along the outside of the bar. "You know you're a terrible liar?"

"What gave it away?"

"The gasp had me suspicious, but the jump sealed the deal," he responds.

"Okay, so I scare easy." I shrug, looking around. Most customers have left by now, and with Raymond making his rounds, he wasn't able to warn me of Dalton's proximity. Then again, with Taia doing dishes, I wouldn't have been able to hide out for long.

"And you've been avoiding me," he states again, knowing full-well that he's right.

It's an interesting relationship we share, an overnight I hardly remember and several glimpses across an empty orchard. We know next to nothing about each other, but after everything he did for me, I'm starting to regret my avoidance, no matter how embarrassed I feel about that night.

"Maybe a bit," I admit, smiling sheepishly. "Is that why you're here? To point out that I've been avoiding you?"

"No, I'm actually a huge fan of the Fruit Fairy." He points to an item listed under the kid's menu on the chalk board behind me, one that blends into a vibrant pink concoction with confetti sprinkles scattered across the top.

"That's interesting," I tell him. "I guess I pegged you as more of the boysenberry type." I turn my back toward him and shut my eyes, realizing what I just gave away. I grab a rag and start wiping down the counter in hopes of dodging what comes next.

"You and Raymond have been talking about me."

I hesitate. "It's important for me to know what our customers like so I can satisfy them," I improvise.

Why'd you have to use the word satisfy? I think.

"What about you?" he asks.

I turn to meet his gaze, my eyebrows caving inward in confusion.

"What do you like?"

Something about the way he asks makes me think he isn't talking about smoothies anymore. I can't help it, my lips twitch upward. And then I remember the picture frame in his room, the girl in the photo. The way he acts seems like he's single, but you can never be too sure.

Out of the corner of my eye, I spot Raymond returning with a crateful of empty tie-dye silicone cups and mentally prepare myself for another interrogation, knowing he'll pry for as many details as possible. Another customer approaches the opposite end of the bar.

"What I like," I respond, "is keeping my job, which means I should probably go help the lady at the end there. Unless you want to order something."

"Believe it or not, I don't always come here for the smoothies."

I pause, not entirely sure how to respond, so I give a curt nod. "Right." Not knowing his intentions has me treading high waters. I remind myself of his behavior the night of the party, that if he had ill intentions, I would know by now.

"This isn't you avoiding me again, is it?" he asks when I'm halfway down the bar.

"Not this time," I assure him, although I'm not yet certain if that's true.

"Good. I'm hoping this was enough of an icebreaker to move past that." He smiles. He looks sincere enough, giving me the confidence to tease him.

"We'll see about that."

He drums against the bar a couple times. "Goodbye, Avery Marie." And with that, he turns to leave.

I stand there stunned for a moment, not being able to recall a time when I'd told him my name. Or my middle name. And yet.

Jay returns from the back room as I'm preparing the lady's Mango Mania and stands beside me to restock a stack of clean blenders.

"Finally," he says while letting out a breath.

"Finally, what?"

"Took you long enough to talk to him."

"What are you—" I start to ask, unsure of how much Jay knows.

"I'm not oblivious. I saw him coming around here the past week, and I know it wasn't for the drinks." He winks at me before attending the booths.

"Who's coming here?" Raymond asks me, placing the crate on the back counter.

I sigh. "Dalton stopped by, and we talked."

"Ooh, girl, finally coming out of that shell of yours," he teases me. "I'm surprised you didn't fake a ruptured appendix or something heinous to get out of it."

I slap him with my rag. "Hey, I don't see what the big deal is."

"Oh, it's not a big deal. You talking to him is about as

simple as it gets. The big deal," he says with growing emphasis, "is you avoiding him for the past week for no reason."

"I had my reasons," I refute.

"You had a rough night, maybe got a little sick, and he helped you out. We've all been there. No need to fret over it." He describes it so nonchalantly, making me feel worse for my reaction to that night rather than the night itself.

I rest my elbows on the counter with my hands cradling my head. It looks like Dalton may be around more than I thought. If I'm to fully move past that night, it's time I draw on my other connections.

CHAPTER NINE

BRISTOL AND I SIT AT A TABLE IN THE WONKA ROOM—a self-serve frozen yogurt shop downtown—waiting for Jen. We're surrounded by chrome-colored tables and neon chairs as a stream of rainbow lights rains upon us.

"Got any plans next weekend?" she asks me between bites of her cake batter frozen yogurt topped with strawberries and sour gummy worms.

"Mostly work," I tell her. "I might catch a movie if that storm rolls in." I take another bite, twisting the spoon upside-down in my mouth before pulling it out. Flavors of cheesecake and cherries waltz on my tongue. "What about you?"

"My dad will be home from his business trip by then, and he's been harping on about me getting an internship next semester. It's gotten to the point where I'd rather stay cooped up in my room all day filling out applications than suffer another conversation about it."

"Won't it be your first semester at college though? Aren't you supposed to get an internship right before you graduate or something?"

"My thoughts exactly," she agrees, her annoyance evident by the curtness in her voice. "But he says the first semester is always the easiest and that I should do one now while I have more time on my hands."

"Probably couldn't hurt."

"No, no," she protests. "It's my first semester at college, my first time away from my parents and out on my own discovering the world. New people, new places." The eagerness in her voice is undeniable. "I want to experience as much of it as I can before I have to spend the rest of my life working." And the eagerness dies again. "Besides, I'm double majoring in Criminal Justice and Psychology. I hardly think any semester will be easy."

Bells jingle above the entrance as Jen walks in wearing a yellow floral sundress with her hair curled to perfection.

"Hi Levi," she greets the cashier in her sing-song voice.

He looks up and flashes her a bright smile. "Hey Jenny."

Their eyes linger on each other a second longer than normal. Jen sits down next to me and the area is immediately saturated with whatever perfume she must have bathed in before coming here.

"You look fancy," I tell her. "Another party tonight?"

"Twelve o'clock," Bristol responds in a flat tone, scraping the last of her frozen yogurt from the paper bowl.

I look ahead to see Levi chatting with some customers. He's handsome, with umber skin and the type of charisma that makes each person feel like he truly cares about them.

"Uh huh." I smirk at Jen. "Mr. Contagious Smile?"

She lets out a blissful sigh. "I'm going to get some fro-yo," she says, her voice full of glee. As she gets up again, my eyes shift to Bristol, eager for more information about Jen's obvious infatuation.

"It's a recent development," she tells me, twisting around to toss her bowl in a trash bin behind her. "And the reason why she was running late after work. She refuses to be seen in her work attire if she knows her CRI will be here."

"Her CRI?" I inquire.

"Current Romantic Interest."

I let out a laugh. "There have been that many that you felt the need to abbreviate it?"

Bristol laughs too. "Perhaps."

Jen approaches Levi to pay for her frozen yogurt, handing him her rewards punch card, which he snips two holes in rather than the standard one per purchase.

"Chocolate with cookie dough again, Jenny." Levi tsks and shakes his head. "You should mix it up a little, try something new." I can't tell if Jen's that much of a regular or if Levi just happened to memorize her previous order, but my guess would be the latter.

"There are just so many options, I never know what to get," she responds in a tone so flirtatious that both Bristol and I have to suppress our laughter.

"Can't blame you," Levi says, ever cheerful. "Maybe next time I can choose for you. It'll be a surprise."

"What's the satisfaction rate for that?"

"Don't know, you'd be my first client. But I'd say one hundred percent satisfaction guaranteed or your money back."

She pauses, pretending to mull over the offer even though she's undoubtedly overjoyed inside. "Guess I'll be seeing you tomorrow," she says, and walks back to our table with a pep in her step. She sits down and eyes us suspiciously. "What are you two laughing at?"

We can't hold it in any longer.

"Can you be any more obvious?"

"What? I just love frozen yogurt." To prove her point, she eats a heaping spoonful of her chocolatey doughy goodness.

With both of them finally here, my time of stalling is up. I need to ask about Dalton and hopefully move past what's holding me back from engaging with him, even though in doing so I'll have to elaborate on where I disappeared to the night of the party. I'd used my New Girl card to shrug off questions about who or where, pretending that I didn't know.

"There's somebody I keep running into," I start,

carving away at my dessert to seem nonchalant, "and I was wondering what you guys know about him."

"Okay, who is it?" Bristol crosses her arms.

"Um, his name is Dalton?"

"Orchard Boy," Jen comments. So, they know that much about him. "What do you want to know?"

"Why do you want to know?" Bristol tweaks Jen's question.

I shrug. "I've just seen him around JuiSea a lot." But I know I won't be able to maintain my vague story for long, whether it's Raymond who informs them or me who lets it slip. It may as well be me. "And he was the guy who helped me the other night after the party." There's a bit of shyness that creeps into my voice.

Their eyes widen in delightful surprise.

"What? Really?"

"Seriously?"

Relief extinguishes my nerves. From the short time I've known them, I've learned they love talking about boys and will probably know exactly what will put my mind at ease.

"Why is that hard to believe?"

Bristol answers, "Remember when we said it was the first party he's been to in almost a year? Well, he hasn't exactly been the most social person lately."

That makes two of us, I think. But that doesn't explain him coming by the shop almost every day to socialize, or the photo I saw in his room, if he is in fact the recluse they make him out to be.

"Why is that? Doesn't he have a girlfriend?"

"Where'd you hear that?" Jen asks.

"Just a picture I saw in his room," I explain. "It was of him and some girl. They seemed really happy together."

Jen and Bristol exchange a knowing look. When Bristol speaks, I detect a sense of gravity in her voice. "Must have been his sister." She pauses. "Amy." I look back and forth between them, knowing there's more that I'm missing. The bells at the entrance jingle again as more customers stroll in. The colored lights overhead shift from blue to purple on our table, making a round through its multicolored spectrum.

"Anyhow, I can't believe Dalton broke Isaac's nose!" Jen circles back to the party, her remark taking me by surprise. "Good for him. That must have felt invigorating."

"I didn't know he broke it." There's a strange dissonance between guilt and relief in my stomach. "We probably could have slipped out before anyone got hurt."

"Don't feel bad," Jen says. "Isaac's a chauvinistic jerk"—she stabs a chunk of cookie dough in her bowl as she enunciates each word—"who bullies the LGBTQ+ community and treats women like they're his own freaking possessions." She glances up to make sure Levi hadn't seen her moment of violent infuriation.

"This is all very helpful," I joke. "I'll gain years of

social insight from you two and then skip to the part where I decide who I want to spend my time with."

Bristol sits back in her chair and gracefully places her palms up. "That is why we are here, my friend."

The conversation drifts away from Dalton as Jen and Bristol reminisce moments from that night. It helps to remember the good times with friends rather than the punch, the puke, and every other instance that fills me with either embarrassment or regret. I'm able to snag a few more details about Dalton here and there, but they move on to share stories from parties in their pasts, inviting me into their lives before our paths merged.

When we leave an hour later, Levi asks Jen if she'll be back tomorrow to try his own creation, reaffirming his eagerness to see her again. From the admiration in their eyes to the life in their smiles, I can't help but wonder what it'd be like to experience the giddiness I witness between them.

CHAPTER TEN

THE STYROFOAM CUP LANDS WITH A PLOP ON THE counter in front of me. Dalton approaches the bar with a chuckle and shake of his head. In general, we only use the Styrofoam cups for little kids, but I wanted to give him the full effect.

"Please tell me this is what I think it is," he says, sliding onto one of the wooden barstools.

I grab the tin canister of sprinkles and dust some across the top of his drink to add a little pizzazz, topping it off with a bright yellow straw. "One Fruit Fairy." I slide it in front of him. "Your favorite."

Without hesitation, he sips and nods in approval. "I'm not sure why it's on the kid's menu, I would actually order this." Another sip, and then he hands me his credit card. I'd told him previously—albeit awkwardly —that the drinks are on me as a way of thanking him for the other night, but he insists on paying for them. I give him a steep discount as a compromise.

"Have you tried it?"

I give him a derisive look as I swipe his card. He holds out his drink to me and I roll my eyes, which prompts him to hold it out farther. I concede and take the tiniest sip before handing it back to him. My taste-buds are confused by the conglomeration of flavors, all of which result in a taste too sweet for my liking. No wonder the kids love it.

"You're ridiculous," I tell him.

Dalton swings by the shop every day now, making our time together a regular occurrence. I fix him a drink, he sips it slowly, and we talk in between me serving other customers. Gradually, I've become more relaxed around him, apparently to the point where we drink from the same straw now.

I clear my station, taking my dirty dishes to the back and returning with more supplies to stock the bar. It's hot out, the temperature each day hovering in the high eighties. It's only late morning and people are already swarming the lakeside with lawn chairs and coolers, frisbees and floaties. Hardly a person passes without leaving a scented trail of suntan lotion. And as always, Jay's music entertains the entire scene from his rooftop speakers.

"Do you have a signature drink on the menu yet?" Dalton asks me.

"May I remind you that I've only been working here a total of two weeks."

"Yeah, but I hear you have connections with the owner. I'm sure he wouldn't mind."

"If you knew anything about my brother, you'd know that he's very particular about his recipes." I pull out the Blender Bible to show Dalton, flipping through to show off its laminated pages and top-notch organization.

"Oh wow. That's really something—"

"Whatcha got there?" Jay strolls behind the bar. Upon seeing the binder splayed out in front of Dalton, he quickly snatches it away. "Avery, this isn't just any Bible," he scolds, trying to sound lighthearted but there's an underlying layer of stress in his tone. "You can't just go around preaching this gospel to anyone." He notices the Fruit Fairy sitting in front of Dalton in its small disposable cup. "Did you order that?"

"Yes," I answer for him, another sign of my increasing comfort. "It's his favorite."

"No." He shoots me a mischievous look, sending a fluttery feeling through my stomach. Little by little I'm realizing the handsomeness of his features, especially when he banters with me. "I didn't order it," he continues. "And it's not my favorite. But I'm not going to lie, it's definitely up there. I was just telling Avery that it should be on the main menu."

"Funny," Jay points to him, "You're not the first

person to suggest that." He disappears into the storage room.

"Did you hear about the lunar eclipse happening tonight?" Dalton asks.

"No, but it sounds cool."

"Yeah, it's supposed to be incredible. Um—" He hesitates, and then takes another sip. "Well, there's a group meeting up near Shepherd's Point later tonight to watch it. I thought maybe you'd want to check it out?"

"A group?" I question, unsure if he's referring to a quaint gathering or the equivalent of the shoulder-brushing, boundary-flouting crowd from the party.

"I heard about it from a few of the guys, but honestly I'm not sure who's all going to be there," he admits, sensing the suspicion in my voice.

"That's fine." I quickly cover up my reservations, although doubts about what he's asking me race through my head. Is he suggesting I show up on my own or inviting me to go with him? If it's the latter, does that make it a date? And if so, how many others are showing up to this rendezvous anyway?

I realize the abnormally long time it's taking me to answer such a simple question. A social gathering like this, especially during summer break, shouldn't prompt a whirlwind of questions.

"Uh," I waver. "Where's Shepherd's Point?" Stalling has become a coping mechanism I've become all too acquainted with over the years.

"It's just up the shore a couple miles. I guess you're supposed to get away from all the lights in town for the best view."

No more questions necessary. My mind is made up.

"It's on the water?"

"Yeah, why?"

"Just curious," I lie. In reality, I need to know. And now that I do, I'll lie again to prevent him from asking further questions I don't want to share the answers to.

"So, do you want to go?" he slowly inquires again, confused by my disposition. "It might be fun." He shrugs. "It should be pretty laid back."

That's what I was told last time and look where that got me, I think.

"It sounds neat, but I already have plans tonight." I bite my lip. "I'm sorry."

"Don't be, it's fine."

I hate lying to him, but it sounds like the last place I'd want to be. Being near the water is fine. Heck, my job borders one of the largest bodies of water in the state. It's being near the water with people who will likely be consuming copious amounts of liquor. There are too many uncontrollable factors.

I try not to think about it.

"Thanks for invite though."

"Invite?" Raymond enters the bar, snagging an apron to start his shift. "Morning D-Swag, A-Bae," he says to us as he approaches. Every day's a new nickname, but thankfully he's kept the winks and obvious stares in my direction when Dalton's around to a minimum.

"Shepherd's Point," Dalton answers him. "You going?" He must assume Raymond's already in the know. Although Dalton just graduated and Raymond has another two years to go, I've learned that Nelson High School is small enough where everybody knows everybody.

"Abso-frickin-lutely. Is Avery going?" He swivels his attention to me.

"Can't. I have plans."

"What could you possibly have going on that surmounts a night under the stars with your favorite people, witnessing a spectacular galactic phenomenon that'll only happen once in your entire lifetime?"

"These happen every year, pal," Dalton interjects.

"Hush, I'm trying to sway her."

"It's not going to work." I chuckle, hoping they can't detect the hint of panic I feel.

"Fine. What do you have going on? You can bring whoever you have plans with."

I'm running out of options. Why is there a lull in customers right now?

"Hey, Jay?" I beckon toward the back room, trusting that he'll understand the concealed urgency in my voice. He knows me almost as well as I know myself.

"Yep?" He emerges from the storage room.

I turn my back to Dalton and Raymond.

"We're still on for tonight, right?" My eyes are firm, pressing into his. My eyebrows arch in earnest. My entire stance pleads with him to go along with it.

His eyes shift between the guys and me. He squints, unsure of my reasoning, but doesn't miss a beat. "Movie, right?"

"Yeah," I confirm, and add a silent "thank you" after.

"You can't watch the movie some other night? It's a blood moon we're talking about!" Raymond exclaims.

Jay must understand the other details of the invite because he gives me a knowing look.

"Nope. Today's the last day it's available to stream. Hey, Avery, incoming," he says, jutting his chin in the direction of a forthcoming customer. I know he's sending me as an escape.

In the corner of my eye, I see Dalton pick up his petite Styrofoam cup and down the rest of his drink. "I should probably head out anyways," he says. He's never left this abruptly, and suddenly I regret declining his invitation. "I'll catch you guys later."

Once Jay and Raymond move on to their next tasks, Dalton adds just for me, "See you tomorrow."

"Have fun tonight," I tell him, hoping he perceives the sincerity in my voice.

"It'll probably be lame." He shrugs, and then smiles, revealing the dimples in his cheeks.

I keep glancing toward the customer, waiting for a

sign that they're ready to order and feeling trapped between my responsibility to serve and my desire to draw out this thin, unraveling thread of conversation with Dalton.

Until tomorrow.

CHAPTER ELEVEN

THERE'S A KNOCK HALFWAY THROUGH OUR MOVIE. JAY sets the bag of pretzel M&Ms on the coffee table and makes his way to the front door. I reach over to snatch the remote control and pause the movie until he returns. Familiar voices float through the house. I close my eyes, not wanting to rehash my conversation at the shop.

When Jay rejoins me on the couch, he grabs the bag of candy and waits for me to resume the movie as if nothing's happened. I stare at the coffee table solemnly, chewing on the inside of my cheek.

"Jen and Bristol?"

"Yep. I told them you weren't feeling great," he says, popping a blue M&M into his mouth. "You gonna press play?"

"I'm sorry."

"For what?"

"You're lying for me."

"I didn't lie. Look at you," he says pointblank. "I don't think you're feeling too great right now, Aves."

I'm wearing my favorite pair of baggy sweatpants and sweatshirt, curled up under a fuzzy blanket eating a monstrous bowl of buttered popcorn while watching a movie with my brother. It seems like a decent night in if it weren't for the part where I sit here sulking to myself the entire time. There's a constant battle of self-pity and anger fighting for precedence in my mind. Pity that I'm missing out on a lunar eclipse with my new friends, especially when I was invited by a boy I think I like. And anger that I'm the one who put myself in this predicament, who declined the invitation in the first place. And to top it off, I'm on edge by the fact that it's not too late for me to show up at Shepherd's Point. And yet I sit here pouting. Jay's right —physically I possess no ailment, but mentally I'm a mess.

Jay exhales loudly as if he was following along with my train of thought. "Avery, I couldn't care less about lying if I have the tiniest belief that I'm protecting you by doing so." My eyes remain fixed on the table in front of me. "If being near the water causes you that much anxiety, then don't go. Okay?"

I nod. It's the exact opposite of the work I've been putting in with my school counselor. She encourages exposure therapy and coping mechanisms to manage my anxiety rather than constantly running from it. Jay is locked in on protecting me from the panic attacks altogether.

"Do you want to finish the movie?" he asks.

I do, but I'm plagued by competing thoughts and emotions, my brain too stunned to press play on the remote control.

"Would you rather talk about it?"

No. I grab the remote and hit play. I give Jay a small, appreciative smile. He grabs my shoulder for a moment in an attempt to comfort me.

Awhile later, after the credits roll and we both retreat to our rooms, I slide open my window and relocate the fold-up chair Jen recommended so that it sits in front of the window, creating a step ladder for me to crawl onto the roof.

The air outside is refreshing. Not cold, but cool enough for me to tug at the sleeves of my sweatshirt and hug my knees to my chest. My back rests against the side of the house, just next to the open window permitting my escape. Friendly conversations speckled with fits of laughter drift up to me from the lake. But mostly I listen to the crickets and their rhythmic midnight opus while my eyes connect the dots between low-lying stars, creating unexplored shapes between them. Most of my view is veiled in darkness aside from some moths fluttering in the spotlights of nearby streetlamps. The sky overhead is dense with clouds, a blank slate that masks the moon's visibility.

The first time I declined an invitation I was seven

years old. It was Maisy Clarke's birthday, and she invited all the girls in our first-grade class to her house. I remember the excitement I felt when she handed me the invitation at recess, with its bright-colored balloons and block letters on the front that read "You're Invited" in all caps. The sense of inclusion instantly became my favorite feeling in the entire world. It may have looked different back then, but the desire to be accepted never really leaves a person.

I tore open the envelope, which was sealed with an inflatable beach ball sticker, and pretended to read the details scribbled inside. In my excitement, I was only able to see the fancy piece of paper for the feeling it created inside me. I was too elated to care about when or where the party was happening. I was invited, and that was all that mattered.

When my mom picked me up from school later that day, I raced over to her and showed her my personal invitation, asking if I could go.

"Of course you can go, sweetie," she told me, taking the invitation from my hands to read the information inside. "It says here that there will be games and cake, and that everyone should bring a bathing suit because they have a pool in their backyard."

Dread washed over me, cleansing all traces of excitement. It had been almost a full year since I last swam, and every time I thought about it, I was flooded with horrific, unwelcome memories, the kind you wish you could erase indefinitely for all the terror they carry with them.

"A pool?" I asked my mom.

"You don't have to swim, dear," she tried soothing me.

But I didn't just want to not swim. I didn't want to be around the pool. I didn't want to watch my friends play in the pool while I sat there haunted by my past.

"I don't want to go," I told her decidedly.

"Honey, you could still go and—"

"I don't want to go," I repeated, my voice raising in pitch as I fought back tears. I had been so thrilled, and now that feeling had completely disintegrated.

"Okay, you don't have to go," she told me, unable to disguise the sadness that seeped into her own voice. She reached down to grab my hand as we began our walk home.

The following day I informed Maisy Clarke that I wouldn't be attending her birthday party. No mention of the pool, no explanation as to why I wouldn't be going, just a simple, curt rejection of her convivial invitation. Little did I know then that Maisy and her best friend, Lilian Reynolds, would stop talking to me for the rest of the school year because they thought I didn't like her.

In the following week, I listened as the other girls in class talked about what presents they'd bring and what swimsuits they'd wear. The only source of relief came from my brother. He had recently earned his shiny new driver's license and decided to take me for a drive on the Saturday of the party. The entire time I kept asking him where we were going, and he kept telling me it was a surprise.

He steered our mom's rundown Volkswagen into a parking spot outside of a coffeeshop called Emery's. We strolled up to the counter where an enormous glass display of cheesecakes awaited us. There were at least two dozen flavors to choose from, some drizzled in chocolate and caramel, others speckled with graham cracker and cookie crumbles, and a few smothered in berry purees. My eyes felt like they were going to explode from the wonder that laid before me.

Jay smiled down at me. "So, Aves, what'll it be?"

We sat across from each other and shared two slices of cheesecake while playing Chutes and Ladders, one of the many board games that were stacked on a bookshelf near the back of the coffeeshop. Looking back now, I probably enjoyed that afternoon with my brother more than I would have enjoyed the party anyway, but the sting of exclusion never quite vanished.

Years later, my middle school group of friends arranged for us to visit Water World over the summer. One of the boys who'd be going was Aiden McAllister, otherwise known as My First Crush. While most boys at our middle school obsessed over comic books and video games, Aiden would read thick fantasy novels and spend his afternoons practicing archery or fencing.

He was known for his nerdy attributes, and that's exactly what drew me to him.

I'd secretly liked Aiden for a few months by the time the idea of visiting Water World was in the works. I didn't want to go and look like a wimp for opting out of rides or not wading in the wave pool. I didn't want Aiden to think of me as boring or scared, even if it was true. I decided it'd be better to not go at all, so I came up with some pathetic excuse to back out of the plan last minute.

After that weekend, a couple girls in the group told me all about how Aiden and Darcy sat together on every ride and wouldn't stop talking to each other all day. Within a month, they were dating, and I felt the first puncture of heartbreak in addition to the wounds of missing out.

There were other incidents too, times I purposefully excluded myself from social gatherings due to my growing apprehension of water. Going through the motions—the rejections and excuses—became easier over time, but the pain of each instance accumulated. It wasn't just the feeling of being an outsider anymore. It was everything—the fear, the memories, the self-hatred.

That's not to say that I don't know how to swim. Every so often when the temperature plummeted and it became increasingly difficult to keep the apartment heated, my mom and I would bundle up in our winter gear and meander down to the hot tub in our apartment complex. Sure, there wasn't enough space to swim laps in that five-by-five-foot container, but there was just enough space in the very middle of it for me to tread water without touching the bottom.

So I practiced.

Each time we went to that hot tub, I made sure I still knew how to swim because you never know when you'll be thrown into a calamitous situation, and I like to be prepared. Never did I swim in the pool though. Something about the way it looked—the blueness and depth—made the memories a bit harder to shake.

I sit on the roof in my cradled position, thinking of all the times I've put myself in this exact situation. A tear escapes from the corner of my eye. I sniffle and wipe it away with my sweatshirt-covered hand. When I look up again, I see it.

The clouds have parted just enough to reveal the lunar eclipse. I now understand why Raymond referred to it as a blood moon. The crimson color glows magnificently, the lake mirroring its image in a shimmering red reflection. I only wish there was someone sitting next to me to share this moment with. If it wasn't for Shepherd's Point, I could have had that. If they met up anywhere else, I might have joined them.

Images of my friends accompany me. I picture Jen and Bristol lying side-by-side on a bed of soft sand, gazing up at the enchanting sight. I imagine Raymond howling at the moon without a care in the world, pretending it's the only moment in his life where he'll witness a lunar eclipse despite their common occurrence.

I wonder what Dalton makes of it, what he's doing right now and what feeling the moon elicits inside of him. Is he perched on a rock, lying on his back in the sand with his hands behind his head, or standing in awe of the moon's radiance? Did the first sight of it fill him with the same amazement I felt when the clouds separated? Does he know we're gazing at the same beauty and wonder this very moment?

There's something comforting in that fact. That although I'm not there to experience it with him in person, we're witnessing the same thing. Unable to speak about it, but both influenced by the phenomenon taking place. Insignificantly small in this galaxy but connected all the same.

CHAPTER TWELVE

"HE DIDN'T SHOW," RAYMOND DECLARES AS HE AMBLES behind the bar to start his shift.

I'm in the process of serving someone their drink, dunking a silicone straw into their green concoction and wishing them a nice day. Raymond's statement is lost on me in his abrupt entrance and my multitasking.

"What?" I ask him at the tail-end of a yawn. I'd been stuck in the moon's trance until late into the night, unsure of what time I crawled back through the window and under my comforter.

"He didn't show," he restates, articulating each word in a knowing tone, like he's right about something we discussed earlier, yet I can't remember the conversation. He stares at me, eyes expectant, waiting for me to fit the puzzle pieces together.

"Dalton," he finally professes. "Dalton didn't show up to Shepherd's Point last night and that, my dear friend, confirms his intentions in showing up here day after day. Although we already knew why he was coming," he rambles on as if carrying on a dialogue with himself. "At least I knew why, even if you kept denying it. Really, Avery, just accept the fact that he likes you and be grateful for it. Some of us aren't that fortunate."

I am grateful. Grateful that Jay had to run to the bank and isn't nearby to overhear Raymond draw conclusions about my love life. At first, Raymond's forwardness came as somewhat of a shock to me, but I've come to enjoy—and even look forward to—these morning shifts when it's just the three of us. He's reliable when customer traffic is heavy, entertaining when it's not. And even though we haven't known each other long, our quality time at the shop has made him comfortable enough to start referring to my mom as Denise—despite having never met her—and asking for regular updates on her and Andrew's European escapade.

A few hours later, the sun reaches its peak, encircled by a ring of inflated cumulus clouds. The lakeside exhibits its everyday crowdedness. Jay returns from the bank and another coworker, Crystal, arrives for her afternoon shift, sporting her everyday athleticwear and pulling her coarse black hair into a bright bandana. I suspect her entourage of seven younger siblings will be arriving shortly to visit her.

I remove my apron, grab a plastic crate, and step

onto the sand to collect abandoned cups along the shoreline. Customers generally leave them in noticeable locations. People hanging out at the sand volleyball courts will all set them on the nearest bench so we can spot them from a distance, and today I see some there.

I start my journey over to the sand courts, flicking up hot sand with the heels of my sandals. Jay's music gradually recedes into the background, now competing with a paddling of cackling ducks and motorboats zooming by. Small waves created by the boats crash onto the shore.

Four empty cups sit ownerless on the bench. After placing them in the crate, I turn around to trudge back through the sand, collecting a few more along the way. I'm about halfway down the beach when someone comes running up behind me.

"Hey," Dalton hollers as he catches up to me, making me jump. "Whoa there." He places his hand on my shoulder in an attempt to steady me. I take a deep breath, willing my heartrate to return to normal.

"You can't do that," I urge him, shaking my head at my own reaction.

"You might just be the jumpiest person I know." He's wearing swimming trunks. No shoes, no shirt.

"Well?" I say, shrugging in acceptance. I continue to zig-zag my way across the beach to collect empty cups. Dalton continues to walk with me, taking a few steps ahead of me whenever we reach one so he can grab it and set it in the crate before I have the chance. It feels wrong having him assist me at my job, but the silent collaboration makes me feel just as warm on the inside as the sun on my skin.

"Were you able to catch part of the eclipse?" he asks me.

"I saw all of it," I admit. "I climbed onto my roof after the movie."

"Good. The whole time I was watching it, I was hoping you were too." I bite the inside of my cheek, trying to conceal my giddiness. Not only were we viewing the same spectacle at the same time, but we were both thinking about each other too.

"You saw it?" I ask, thinking back a couple hours to when Raymond said Dalton didn't join the viewing party. Dalton already caught me give away that Raymond and I talk about him once, so confessing it a second time won't come as a surprise. "I thought you didn't go."

"I didn't," he looks down, smiling to himself. "I did, however, watch it from the orchard. It was more peaceful. No crowd, no fuss."

Maybe I'm not the only one who dislikes crowds.

We step into the shop, and I place the crate on the back counter. "So, what'll it be today?" I ask as I retie an apron around my waist.

"Oh, uh." He hesitates. "I should get back to the sand courts."

"I must've missed you when I was over there."

He taps his fingers against the bar. "I went to grab

something out of my bag when I saw you coming." He reaches into his pocket to pull out a folded-up piece of notebook paper with an embarrassed look on his face.

"What is it?"

"It's a—" He pauses, letting out a long exhale that ends in a chuckle. He now taps the piece of paper against the countertop rather than his fingers. "It's really stupid. I had this whole idea of coming up to you and asking you to make a recipe for me since you sometimes dabble around and make your own."

"Okay," I say slowly, confused by his fidgety behavior. "Do you still want me to make it or…?"

"No. Well, yes." His cheeks flush. "It's just that, well, it's not exactly a recipe for a smoothie, per se."

"What's it a recipe for, then?" I ask, puzzled.

He stares at me, lips pursed in contemplation. He sighs and chuckles to himself again. "You know what, never mind. I should get going. If you could just forget this ever—"

Before I can think twice, I seize the piece of paper from his loose grip. He immediately reaches out to snatch it back, but I'm already leaning against the back counter out of range. His face is one of instant dread.

"Please," he almost begs.

"You were going to give it to me anyways, right? You said so yourself."

"Yeah, and then I thought better of it." A nervous smile is plastered on his face, his hand still extended toward me in hopes that I'll hand over the secretive note.

I squint at him, and then begin to unfold the piece of paper, curiosity fueling my impish behavior.

"Oh, God no, stop, please," he pleads, still wearing that regretful smile. "Fine! Fine, you can read it. Just, please don't read it while I'm here." He quickly changes tactics to halt my progress. "I've already made a fool of myself, and I don't like where this is going."

The paper is folded in half with only one flip to go until the mystery is revealed, but I restrain myself.

"I've got to say, Dalton, this is the most entertained I've been in a while, watching you squirm like this." He doesn't respond, only stares at me with imploring eyes. I hold up my hands in surrender. "Okay, okay, I'll stop."

"Can I have it back?"

"Nice try. Have fun playing volleyball," I say with a teasing smile, a verbal nudge for him to leave so I can indulge in the note that I now hold with high anticipation.

"Mmm." He looks around and back to me, perhaps contemplating breaking the rule that says no customers are allowed behind the bar. He knows there isn't anything he can do except leave at this point. Nodding, he turns to walk away. When he reaches the end of the bar, he says, "If there's even just the slightest chance you don't think it's stupid and you want to give it a shot, I'll see you at three."

I bite my lip. Why do I suddenly have plans with Dalton after work?

He rubs his fingers against his forehead as if working out tension there. "Oh, Warren," he says as he disappears from sight.

I smile at him addressing me by my last name and unfold the final crease.

The Perfect Picnic
Total Time: 2 hours

Ingredients:
2 openminded participants
2 peanut butter and jelly sandwiches (boysen-berry preserves, obviously)
2 hand-picked apples
1 package of Double Stuf Oreos
A dash of daringness
A pinch of positivity

Preparation:
If you're ready at three, leave the rest up to me.

My mouth hangs open. I'm not reading a recipe for a picnic.

I'm reading a recipe for a date.

CHAPTER THIRTEEN

A GURGLING STREAM WINDS ALONG THE EDGE OF OUR path, the water flowing opposite of the direction we're headed. We've been hiking the trail for twenty minutes now, making small talk as we weave our way through the forest.

"What I still don't understand," I inquire, "is how you knew my middle name and that I'd be at JuiSea." He's walking behind me, so I shoot him an over-the-shoulder glance. He's wearing a fresh t-shirt and the same shorts from earlier, with a backpack that I can only assume contains the rest of our ingredients.

"The night of the party," he starts. "When we left, I checked your wallet to—"

"You what?" I interject, perhaps a bit too accusatory, although I never noticed anything missing from that night.

"Not to steal anything!" He laughs, ever amused by

my reactions. "I was looking for an address, hoping to get you home. Except I didn't think my truck had enough fuel to make the thousand-mile journey to Colorado."

"It would have been interesting waking up in a stranger's truck halfway across the country," I muse. "Still, when did you check my wallet?"

"I wouldn't be surprised if you don't remember our interactions from that night. You were in pretty rough shape when I found you."

I continue to walk in silence, not wanting to relapse into the pit of embarrassment it took me several days to crawl out of. The sound of rushing water grows louder, and the dirt becomes damp and slippery beneath the soles of my shoes. We walk a few more paces before he speaks again.

"Do you remember the part where you wanted to change clothes?" He almost laughs at the thought of it.

Oh, no. I swiftly try to sort through the hazy memories I have locked away in the furthest chamber of my mind, the ones I no longer wish to remember. But now I need to sweep away the cobwebs and recall this moment that Dalton claims happened. All I can remember is that I woke up in the same dress that I wore to the party.

"You didn't, obviously. But you were very adamant about wearing something comfortable to bed." That I can believe. I'm a strong advocate of comfy clothing whenever possible. "You were furious at me when I told you that you didn't need to change, but I figured it'd get you to stop whining and go to bed so I grabbed you a spare t-shirt and pair of sweatpants."

The stack of clothes on the bed. It all makes sense now. Those were for me to sleep in.

"You were passed out on the bed before I could even make the ten steps over there."

"Sounds about right," I admit sheepishly.

"You're quite the whiner when you're uncomfortable. Hasn't anyone ever told you to step outside your comfort zone?"

I know he's teasing, but he's oblivious to the tightrope he's walking on. The only ones who truly know the parameters of my comfort zone never bother to push me outside of them—except for my school counselor of course. They know about the trauma. They've seen glimpses of what would happen if I challenge those boundaries. And although I sometimes wonder what it'd be like to conquer my fear, I have to remind myself that actually overcoming it is about as likely as being selected for the first man mission to Mars.

I hold my hands to my head in humiliation. "It's a lot worse hearing about what happened that night from you than how I pictured it in my head."

"Would it help if I told you that I pulled the covers over you? At least I gave you that comfort, right?"

No, it doesn't help knowing that not only did I whine to you, but you tucked me into bed like a child.

Okay, maybe it does kindle a warm feeling inside of me.

Before I know it, the trees disperse to reveal a rushing waterfall that crashes into a frothing pool below. Flat rock walls covered in small patches of moss curve around three quarters of the water's perimeter, causing the roaring sound of the crashing waterfall to echo off the pool's natural barricade. A few tree limbs intermingle with cracks in the walls, while others stretch far across the water, creating the illusion that this pocket of paradise is just for us. The moss so bright and green, the water so clear and blue. All of it is so picturesque I would almost classify it as breathtaking.

Almost.

If it wasn't for the image that flashes through my mind of a man getting ready to jump off the rock wall. The image vanishes almost as quickly as it forms, but only after sneering at me, taunting me.

Dalton watches me as I take it all in.

"It's beautiful," I tell him. A candid response, even if it requires restraint of other emotions.

He smiles. "Come on," he says, walking across the pebble beach.

"Wait, this isn't it?"

"It is, but I like to look at things from a different perspective."

I follow him around the water's edge, across a slight wooden bridge where a small stream trickles away from the pool, and up the embankment until we're standing on large boulders near the top of the waterfall.

"This," he breathes in awe. "This is it." He slings the backpack off his shoulders and walks toward the edge of the cliff. My stomach clenches, my breath catching in my throat. Before I can say anything, he sits down and unzips the pack to retrieve our picnic supplies.

"You coming?" His feet dangle off the sloped edge. One wrong move and he could slide off its slick surface.

I stand motionless, frantically searching for the right words to say, too frightened to move forward yet terrified of him moving back. The pit in my stomach stirs up the caldron of self-rage I've slowly built up over the past eleven years.

"Um, I—I, uh," I stutter, and try taking a deep breath to calm my nerves. "I'm afraid of heights." Another lie. I hoped we had moved past them, but the situation calls for it. If I tell him the truth, what I truly fear, he'll ask questions, probe, maybe even tell me to shake it off. What's worse, it would unlock the closet of nightmares I've worked so hard to keep hidden from onlooking speculation.

"Oh." He sounds surprised, not expecting this impediment to his plan. "It's not too high, maybe twenty, twenty-five feet?" He leans forward to get a better look. I brace myself from the wooziness.

"No, I know, but uh—" I stammer. "Maybe we could sit back here?"

"Yeah," he obliges, gathering up the items he'd started to unpack. I can't watch as he stands and takes the few steps to rejoin me, not while he's that close to the edge, lest I let the panic overtake me.

I find a smooth surface to sit on while he unpacks the PB&J sandwiches, apples, and Double Stuf Oreos, as promised. After taking my first bite, I remember the guarantee of boysenberry preserves as well, which he faithfully upheld.

"So," he starts, swallowing a bite of his own sticky sandwich, "how long are you here for?"

"Well, your recipe said two hours, so I'd assume another hour or so before we head back."

He rolls his eyes at me. "You know what I mean."

"Two months," I answer him and take another bite. He nods in thought. "What about you? Are you leaving for college soon?"

"I'm not going to college."

This doesn't come as a huge surprise to me. I've known plenty of people who skip the whole college part of society's expected life cycle. My mom didn't go and neither did Jay.

"What are you going to do instead?"

"Stick around for the harvest, help out my parents." He holds up his apple as he mentions this, having already gobbled down his sandwich.

It never occurred to me that the orchard belongs to his parents. I just assumed it was operated by a large corporation rather than a family-owned business. But this would explain why he hangs out in the apple tree. I picture him plucking these two apples from deep within its branches.

"Here I thought you were trespassing all these mornings."

"Nope, that would be you," he turns my accusation around on me.

"What can I say? I'm a daredevil." I reach for my apple, its bright red skin polished and pristine. Dalton watches me carefully, making me self-conscious to take the first bite and hoping the juices don't drip all over me.

"You're just lucky I didn't warn the authorities," he tells me, still eyeing my every move with suspicious curiosity.

"Yeah, I would've been terrified had you gone running to your mom for my incriminating behavior."

"Hey, you don't know my mom. She can be intim-idating."

I bring the apple to my lips. Here goes nothing. I sink my teeth into it, pulling apart a chunk of its pulp with a loud crunch. Dalton keeps his eyes on me, making mine wander to anywhere but his as I chew, but it's too weird without calling it to attention.

"What?" I ask after swallowing.

"Nothing."

"Why are you staring at me so intently?"

He looks away with a devilish smile but doesn't answer me, just continues to nibble around the core of his apple. After inspecting to make sure it's fully gnawed, he chucks the core far into the trees.

"Wait a second," I speculate, thinking back to a time where a devious apple core caused me to fall and scrape my hands. "It was you!"

He looks startled. "What was me?"

"The apple core on the dirt path next to the orchard," I tell him, my voice saturated with blame even though he has no clue as to why I'm worked up about an apple core. "Your little baseball act put me in danger that day." I hold up one of my palms in front of him.

He squints and reaches forward to steady it in his hands. His fingers move across the length of my palm, his touch delicate and smooth. "These right here?" He looks up, locking eyes with me.

"Yes," I say, suddenly short of breath.

"And you're saying," his soft voice harmonizes with the gentleness of his touch, "that an apple core did this to you." There it is. A hint of sarcasm.

I yank my hand back to study it. I guess I hadn't noticed that the gashes are mostly faded by now. Not very impressive.

"*Your* apple core," I point out, trying to convey the appropriate amount of responsibility he had in the matter. "I tripped on it," I add, a bit mortified by that fact.

"Duly noted. I'll try to land them over the path next time." He moves on to the stash of Oreos, paving the way for me to do the same. But first, I take another bite of my apple. Dalton instantly looks my way, hiding a smirk.

"Okay, what? You're making me feel like I'm in a zoo. Apples are hard enough to eat without you studying me."

"I'm just curious about the way people eat apples," he confesses. "Like it reveals something about their personality."

"Well then, what's your verdict? Other than the fact that I don't like people staring at me while I eat them."

"It's hard to tell." He shifts his weight forward. "It makes most people look more arrogant. And if they really chomp on them, it could mean they're imprudent and opinionated, maybe have a bit of a temperament issue." He states this like it's a scientific fact, as if a prestigious university released concrete findings on the correlation between eating mannerisms and the personalities of apple consumers.

"You on the other hand," he continues, "you shy away, trying to make yourself small and unnoticeable."

"And what does that say about my personality?" I ask, and then take a large, aggressive bite without reservation, slurping a bit of the juice in hopes of throwing off his judgement.

He chuckles. "I think—" he starts and then takes a moment to contemplate. "I think you can be indecisive and lack self-confidence. You probably overthink a lot of things. But you're humble, and you always look for the best in people," he concludes determinedly, and then pops an entire Oreo into his mouth.

I nod, impressed. "Not bad."

"Okay." He shifts on the rock again to face me square on. "Your turn."

"No," I scoff. "I don't know the first thing about apple-ology."

"Just try. Whatever comes to mind." He brings his hands together, tapping his fingertips in anticipation.

Whatever comes to mind? Everything I think of is subjective to our previous encounters. From the moment he scared me in the orchard, half-smiled at me across the party, supported me when I couldn't walk on my own. All the times I hid in the storage room while he strolled past the shop, unaware of his intentions in doing so. The way he awkwardly presented his hand-written recipe and proceeded to beg me not to read it. His smile and the powerful ripple effect it has on me. The way his hair tousles when he brushes his hands through it. Those charming dimples. The almost imperceptible scar above his left eyebrow. The happiness I feel in knowing that he stops by the shop every day just to chat with me, and that he wasn't afraid to admit it the first time we talked across the bar. He seems caring, and my type of funny, and I know I'd be devastated if he ever stopped coming to JuiSea.

But this is an apple we're talking about. And the way he devoured it is somehow supposed to inform me of some undisclosed personality trait.

"Well," I start, trying to sort through the tangled thoughts in my head. "You *don't* shy away when you eat apples, so by your definition I guess that means you're decisive and know what you want?" He remains quiet, drawing out as much of my interpretation as possible. "You know who you are and don't seek reassurance from other people, which I commend. And although you're an arrogant apple eater, I believe you also search for the good in others, even when it's undeserving."

"And you said you didn't know about apple-ology," he teases.

"Guess I'm a fast learner." And to prove it, I nibble off the last edible chunk of apple and toss the core as far as I can muster, which is only a few trees away. He chuckles at my attempt, nonetheless.

I reach for an Oreo, twisting it open to eat the half without cream filling first.

"Don't even get me started on what that says about you."

I smirk at him, and then lick the cream filling on the other half.

⁓⁓⁓

WE SIT AT THE TOP OF THE WATERFALL, CARELESS OF TIME and the world beyond our al fresco outing. Wrens and chickadees chirp and flit between tree branches as leaves tremble in the light breeze. I kick off my sandals to soak in the final sunbeams as more clouds start to creep in, legs stretched out in front of me, ankles crossed. We've been sitting in silence, mesmerized by the rushing water.

Without prompting, Dalton inhales deeply and declares, "It's time." He pushes himself off the ground. In a moment as tranquil as this, I expected both of us to draw it out more. I didn't anticipate Dalton's eagerness to leave so abruptly.

But then he takes his shirt off.

I must admit, there's a slight delay where my brain can't process what's happening other than the fact that he's taken his shirt off. He then kicks off his flip flops and returns to the edge of the wall where he had originally sat down.

"Wh—what are you doing?" I falter.

"Going for a swim," he replies nonchalantly.

"How do you know it's deep enough? There could be rocks at the bottom," I sputter frantically. "You could hit your head." I close my eyes and yearn for the image in my mind to disappear.

"I've done this a thousand times. It's a lot deeper than it looks." He tries to soothe me, but it has zero effect on my increasing concern. He glances over the waterfall, making my stomach clench. "And it looks higher up than it is. Just look the other way and I'll holler at you from the water so you know I'm okay. How's that?"

Unless you hit your head, I reiterate the very possible outcome to myself.

"It's alright," he assures me once more, then turns toward the edge. I bury my head in my knees, which I had drawn close to my chest in the midst of the uncertainty.

It's okay it's okay it's okay, I repeat in my head, a self-soothing mantra to combat my trepidation.

Without warning, I hear the splash, its echo rico-cheting off the surrounding walls. My heart plummets in my chest. I wait for a response, anything to signal his safety, but I can't make out anything over the roaring waterfall. Seconds tick by, which feel like an eternity.

"It feels so good!" Dalton finally shouts from below, accompanied by laughter and a sigh. At least one of us is having fun. My fists clench in frustration at myself.

I carefully scoot closer to the edge, enough to peer down and see him floating in the pool with his eyes closed. He opens them to find me staring over the edge from a cautious distance, and smiles.

"You know, you could always walk down here and join me," he suggests.

Even if I was planning on going in, walking is not the way to go. With each step, the anxiety would multiply, making it virtually impossible to take the next.

"I'm not wearing a swimsuit," I tell him, hoping that he'll drop the idea altogether, but he ignores my justification.

"I have to admit, I'd be thoroughly impressed if you faced your fear of heights and jumped over the ledge, right here, right now," he tells me while treading water.

You and me both. But it isn't the height that's holding me back. I groan.

"You can do it, Avery. I can swim down to the bottom to show you how deep it is. Your feet won't even touch. And I'll be right here the entire time. It's over before you know it."

My palms are sweaty, my mouth is dry, and I'm running out of excuses. I could just tell him the truth, the real reason why I can't jump, but then all the lies and explanations would have been for nothing. He just jumped and he's fine. Happy even. And now I have the chance to impress him, which I so desperately want to do.

My face feels hot, yet chills run down my spine. I remind myself that I know how to swim, or at least tread water, and Dalton just proved that it's safe to jump. A part of me—the part of me that has dictated every decision for the past eleven years—is screaming that this is a bad idea, to shut down the notion once and for all.

However, despite the jitters and the nerves, the overwhelming fear and impending doom, there's a new part of me—no matter how small—that dares me to try. I'm not sure if this unforeseen daringness has sprung up from the deep, vindictive pit of self-shame or if it originates from a new place of hope that things could be different. That my life could be different. I could be different. That there's redemption to be found after eleven years of being controlled by my past. The opportunity in front of me displays few differences from the one that crippled me so many years ago. All the pain, the heartache, the nightmares, the fun times I missed out on—all of it could be redeemed in this very moment. After always sheltering myself from these situations, how was I to predict a shift in mindset at a moment like this?

Dalton resumes floating, letting the small ripples from the waterfall bob him up and down ever so slightly.

My breath quickens. I'm taking too long to decide, but I can hardly think straight. Is he waiting for me? What will happen if I jump? Or if I don't, for that matter. It feels like the weight of my future is riding on this one decision to dive into the darkness of my past.

Fed up with myself, I do something I never would've imagined in a million years, especially amid encroaching anxiety. I decide it's time I try, and I won't let myself change my mind now.

Slowly, and quite shakily, I rise from my cradled position. There's no chance I'm slipping off my shirt and shorts feeling this lightheaded. I'm already a couple feet from the ledge and don't want to risk falling in the process.

Dalton opens his eyes and beams. "Yeah! Here we go!" he cheers, unaware of the terror in my head and tension in my body as I inch my way forward.

Words my mom once spoke to me come to mind.

Not the parent I expect to think of at this moment, but her words are comforting, nonetheless.

"Hands up and jump in, headfirst. The butterflies in your stomach are what something new is all about," she told four-year-old me. Back then I had her encouragement to coax me and her proximity to protect me.

Here I have Dalton. While not the same, I trust him.

Although I keep my arms tucked in and the butterfly sensation feels more like a stampede of wildebeests, my mom's encouragement impels my final step as I leap over the edge.

CHAPTER FOURTEEN

IT'S SHOCKING THE NUMBER OF THOUGHTS YOUR MIND can generate while you're mid-air, between the moment your feet kiss security goodbye and the second you make contact with your worst nightmare. Enough to experience regret. To feel the yank on your stomach as you free fall. To envision your greatest fear become tangible right before your eyes. The span of one second filled with a myriad of unspoken memories.

Panic rushes over me faster than the water as I plunge into the tarn. Water shoots up my nose from the impact, but I keep my eyes shut, unaware of my depth or how close I am to the rock wall. I reach out my hands, grasping for air.

It's just another nightmare, I tell myself. But I've never been able to recognize a dream when I'm in them. This time, it's real.

My fingers break through the surface as I kick my

way up, trying to tread but unable to stop thinking of my head—am I bleeding?—although I hadn't felt anything.

I think of his head. He was hurt.

A coughing fit seizes me as my lungs fight against the unwelcome water. Still, I dart my head around to find him. He needs my help. I'm not going to let him drown, not this time. All I can see though is a blur of color, my head spinning too fast to calculate the swirl of images around me. There are shouts of victory nearby, but they sound muffled, indistinguishable.

My arms and legs flounder just enough to keep my head afloat. My heartrate, breathing, whizzing eyes—they all quicken to the point of giving out. It's all too much. I don't know what's happening. That's when the tears come.

Is this how it ends? Karma's payback? If so, I'm well-deserving.

The muffled voice continues to shout, yet I can't make out what words are being said. And then my hand makes contact with something in the water, followed by my foot. I look over, expecting to see the towering rock wall. Instead, I see what resembles a face, except tears and black splotches in my vision hinder my view of him.

His arms are quickly around me, tugging at me, pulling me through the water. My limbs continue to thrash until his hands grab my own and drape them around his neck.

"Hang onto me." His words are scarcely audible, despite being just inches away.

I close my eyes and hold on tight, burying my head in the crook of his neck and trying to steal breaths of air when the punishing water isn't overlapping my face.

I see my dad's face, his green eyes staring back at me in disappointment. Maybe that's how the term "piercing eyes" came to be, from the sharp pain they can inflict on someone's heart.

"Dad," I whimper softly, gurgling the water that finds its way into my mouth.

Dalton's arms cradle my legs and back as he carries me out of the water and sets me down gently on the pebble shore. I may be on land, but the sobs only intensify, accompanied by the occasional coughing fit. Dalton doesn't remove his hand supporting my back.

My entire body trembles uncontrollably, from the chattering of my teeth to the shaking of my hands, which are close enough to conceal my face that they bounce off my lips. My sopping wet clothes stick to my skin like the strands of hair that fall across my face. I don't bother fixing them.

My vision slowly returns, as does my hearing, but I can't wrangle my mind loose from the death grip of anxiety. I tell myself to stop, to pull myself together, that I'm overreacting and embarrassing myself, but it only makes the splutters and sobs worse.

Make it stop make it stop make it stop.

I sense Dalton's impulse to help, but he's not sure

how. Still, he keeps his hand on my back. I lean into him, giving him the okay to wrap his arms around me in a secure embrace. He sits with me until the sobs rescind into silence.

∼∼∼

TEN MINUTES? A HALF HOUR? I'LL NEVER KNOW HOW long it took before the visceral sobs reduced to feeble cries, and the well of tears eventually dried up. Dalton remains silent the entire time, a sturdy refuge in my inconsolable moment of weakness.

When all that remains are a few dispersed sniffles and the chattering of teeth, he pulls away. Reflexively, I wipe my eyes. Despite having had a total breakdown in front of him, there's something uniquely different about seeing the tears on someone's face.

I turn to face him, managing a weak smile, and then rest my head against my knees. All that crying makes my head ache with heaviness.

Dalton, whose expression remains a combination of concern and confusion, turns toward the water with his forearms resting on his knees. He stares at the ground in front of him. When he speaks, he keeps his voice soft and slow. "You're not afraid of heights, are you?" he asks.

I shake my head, hoping he sees in his peripheral.

The sun has vanished, the late afternoon sky now completely shielded by clouds.

"I don't want you to feel rushed," he tells me, his voice still gentle, "but whenever you're ready, I'll take you home."

I feel completely drained, thoughts no longer fighting for precedence in my mind. I just feel empty, void of all energy and emotion and the voice in my head that orchestrates each of my negative thought spirals.

I take a deep breath and exhale fully, mustering up the strength to speak. "I'm ready." My voice, barely a whisper, sounds hoarse and frail. I clear my throat.

"I'll grab our stuff. Are you okay to wait here?"

I nod.

He jogs to the top of the waterfall, returning with his backpack, shirt, and our shoes. He sets my sandals on the ground in front of me to slip on, and then holds out his dry t-shirt to me.

I swallow, feeling unworthy of his kindness, but reach up to take it anyway, trying my best to give him another small smile as a sign of my appreciation. My arms and legs are covered in goosebumps from sitting in my wet clothes for so long. I pull my shirt over my head and slip into his dry one, which envelops me in the recognizable scent of cedarwood and citrus. He extends his hands to me, helping me to my feet. My legs feel numb, and I know it'll take extra exertion to make the journey home.

"If it helps, I know mouth-to-mouth," he mentions as we begin walking. "I'm just saying, I'll keep you safe."

I rub my hands over my face, unsure of how to respond.

"Bad timing?" he asks me.

I nod again and try to contain the dorky grin that wants to escape. I applaud him for getting me to smile given the circumstances.

I think back to strolling the vacant street at night, how his hand had supported me then too. This time he lets me walk on my own despite my wobbly legs, trailing close behind in the event I need support.

Of all the possible outcomes for how our picnic could have ended, this one hadn't remotely crossed my mind. Yet despite the giant wrench in Dalton's plan and the agony that will surely accompany me home, there's something heartening about it all.

CHAPTER FIFTEEN

Hot water rushes over me as I sit on the shower floor, the tiles leaving textured creases in my skin as steam rises to fill the bathroom like a sauna. Every breath I inhale is vapor. Although almost scorching, the water helps to relax the tension in my neck and shoulders.

I'm bombarded with images from that dreadful day. How is it possible for one day of my childhood to contain both my favorite memories and worst nightmares? How can one day incapsulate them both?

It was the last day of school and I'd officially graduated from kindergarten to first grade, a day worthy of celebration in my six-year-old eyes. School let out early and whenever I was granted a half day, my dad would take the afternoon off for some father-daughter bonding. We had a little tradition where he'd strap our two-seater canoe to the roof of his car and drive us far into the mountains to an area teeming with twisting rivers that linked together countless lakes.

I was wearing my favorite sundress, purple with white polka dots. Plump cumulus clouds lined the western horizon, the sun so bright that my dad placed his favorite Grand Teton National Park ballcap on my head to shield my eyes. Although it was far too big for me and slumped down over half of my face, it made me feel important.

We made our way down the winding streams, my dad rowing as he sang made-up songs about stories I'd request. If I'd wished to hear about a princess in a magical pink castle, he'd improvise lyrics about the most beautiful princess and enchanted castle I could ever imagine. He pointed out fish in the water and told me the names of every bird species we saw, though he focused mainly on the ducks because those were my favorite. I'd try imitating their quacks as we fed them scraps of bread.

On that particular day, we came across a new canal, one framed by quaking aspens on either side of the gentle current. We glided down the unexplored path and pulled into a rocky alcove. The shore was stacked with towering boulders that resembled a tiny mountain.

My dad decided to go for a dip to cool off. Whenever he did this, he would swim underneath the canoe to scare me. I always thought he was going to flip the boat over, although he never did, and I had no reason to believe that he ever would. He would just swim underneath me and pop his head out on the other side, startling me into a fit of giggles, which would make him laugh in return.

I remember the look of surprise on his face after he came up for air. He couldn't believe how deep the water was in relation to the small width of the stream.

"At least twelve feet," he told me. "Deeper than the deep end at the pool."

"Whoa," I muse, unable to comprehend that sort of depth at such a young age. But then again, I was only three and a half feet tall at the time.

He was looking toward the shore, his eyes wandering up the stack of boulders, outlining a clear path to the top.

"Do you think Daddy can jump off the top of that rock there?"

My eyes followed to where his finger pointed. When I saw how high up it was, my eyes bulged.

"Nope!"

"You don't think I could do it, Aves?"

"Nuh uh," I shook my head, certain that I was right. It had to be at least a hundred feet in the air, or so I thought. Looking back, it probably measured about fifteen feet above the water.

"Okay, let's bet on it. If I get to the top and chicken out, you owe me ice cream," my dad said, treading the iridescent water. "But if I jump in, then I owe *you* ice cream. How does that sound?"

It didn't occur to me that he reversed the bet to be opposite of my prediction. I didn't think he'd jump because, well, the rock was a hundred feet high. He flipped the bet in my favor knowing he wouldn't back down. All I knew was that we were going to get ice cream afterward, so I started cheering.

He swam to the shore and climbed the miniature mountain that was calling his name. Meanwhile, I was contemplating which flavor of ice cream I was going to get and what toppings to mix into it.

When he reached the top, he shouted, "Are you ready?"

"Yeah!" I shouted back to him.

He prepared his stance, knees bent, one foot positioned slightly behind the other. He leapt off the top of the boulder, propelling himself forward into the crystal water below. I turned my head away from the splash and held onto the boat as the waves rocked it back and forth.

When I peered over the edge of the boat again to find him, he was nowhere to be seen. I bit my lip, searching the water with squinted eyes. There was a sudden splash as he popped his head out of the water behind me, yelling "Boo!" in a playful manner. I jumped, and maybe even shrieked, but I remember giggling again all the same. It happened every time.

"I guess I owe you ice cream, bud." His hands gripped the edge of the canoe.

"I bet you can't do it again."

"Oh yeah?" He smiled and raised his eyebrows at me. He was always smiling from what I can remember. "And if I do?"

I bit my lip in concentration, thinking of what could enhance my ice cream prize. My eyes lit up. "If you do, we have to go to that place where they make the swirly rainbow cones!" My mouth salivated just thinking about it.

"Swirly rainbow cones, huh?" He chuckled. "Alright, here I go."

He swam to shore again, climbed the stack of boulders, and positioned himself to leap over the edge. He looked down at me sitting cross-legged in the bottom of the canoe, where I always sat when my dad was swimming. It helped me feel steady in the wobbly vessel.

His eyes met mine. "This one's for you, kid."

So many nights when I couldn't sleep, I'd think of these five words, see my dad's beaming face, hear his carefree laugh, and feel the stab of guilt, knowing he did it for me.

He took one final step to close the gap between where he stood and where he'd freefall. There must have been loose dirt or gravel or something beneath him, because when he tried setting his foot down, it slid over the curvature of the rock. I heard a crack and a second later the sharp slapping noise where his unstable body greeted the water below. He'd landed on his back, much closer to shore than his last jump where he'd launched himself away from the boulders.

I waited for him to surface, preparing myself for the moment when he'd pop out of the water and scare me. The seconds ticked away, adding to the anticipation. I twisted around, shifting onto my knees and peering into the water behind me, but he didn't appear. I turned back to the epicenter of his wake where ripples of water extended toward the canoe. My eyes stayed glued on that spot. My dad could hold his breath a long time, but after another minute of silence, my eyes began to glance around again, searching the water in all directions.

There was no sign of movement in our hidden alcove.

"Dad?" I called quietly, unsure of where he went. Another minute passed. And then another. My teeth began to chatter as they always do when I get nervous.

"Daddy?" I asked again, my voice even softer as tears welled in my eyes. I sniffled. He wouldn't just leave me out here. He owed me ice cream. Presented in a colorful swirly rainbow cone.

"Daddy!" I called out as loud as my little voice could muster. It echoed through the surrounding forest. Tears poured out as I sat alone in our two-seater canoe. At the time, the pain I felt stemmed from a feeling of abandonment rather than complete and total loss. It didn't occur to me that I would never see my dad again.

The sun eventually slipped behind the trees, and I

still sat there, bawling helplessly, unsure of what had happened or what to do next. Just a scared six-year-old girl, alone, deep within a maze of winding waterways.

Hours had passed since nightfall. The surrounding forest was pitch black. I cradled my knees to my chest, having pulled my dress over my legs to keep them warm. I couldn't see how far I was from the shore, but I could distinctly hear every bird's coo and creature's padded steps in the darkness, paralyzing me with fear.

Off in the distance I heard the blare of a siren, screeching through the air one second and silent the next. I turned my head toward the sudden noise. A bright spotlight shone from its direction. There was the low hum of a motor, and then the brief siren went off again. The sounds moved closer, as did the spotlight.

And then I heard her.

"Avery!" My mom's voice pierced the night, flooding me with a sense of relief, although her tone was far from it. I wasn't alone anymore. My mom had come to save the day, to find me and figure out where my dad went so she could bring him back to us.

"Paul!" she continued to shout. "Avery!"

"Mom," I croaked, my throat sore from crying. I swallowed, and then called out again, this time a loud wail, "Mom!"

"Avery!" Her voice was earnest now, filled with the ravenous determination only a mother can have. "She's that way, hurry! Avery, keep calling to me, baby!"

"Mom!" I cried. "Mom!"

The speedboat pulled up next to the canoe. There were four other people on the vessel with my mom: two policemen, one firefighter, and the skipper.

My mom's arms were over the edge and pulling me up before I could move. She embraced me in a hug, tears pouring down her face.

"Avery," she cried. "Oh Avery. Where's Daddy?"

"I don't know." My voice cracked.

"Where did you last see him?" one of the policemen interjected, his voice deep and stern.

"Let me!" my mom snapped. I'd never seen my mom snap at anyone before, but she had been on the brink of a heart attack for the last several hours. "Where did you last see Dad, sweetie? Where is he?" she asked me, trying to sound soothing but unable to mask the panic in her voice.

The other police officer was at the back of the boat, speaking into her walkie-talkie. "We found the girl. Still no sign of the husband."

"He, um," I started, talking in between sniffles. My mom wiped away the tears on my cheeks. "He jumped in the water, and then—and then I don't know where he went."

"He jumped out of the canoe, sweetie?"

I shook my head. "No. Up there." I pointed toward the boulders, although they were hard to make out in the dark of night when the spotlight wasn't shining in that direction.

Another boat approached the one we stood in.

Police officers and firefighters were moving about both vessels now. One of them handed my mom a large towel, which she wrapped around me to keep me warm. The second boat pulled up to the shore and a couple men hopped out. Lights shone on the towering rock structure and into the water below.

My mom moved her hands up and down my arms to generate heat. She was acting reassuring but distracted by terror, her eyes bloodshot red as she watched the men on shore start wading into the water.

"We have a 10-54," one of them stated, and proceeded to describe the distance between the shore and where he stood in the water, among other details I tuned out.

My mom, however, was quick to respond. "What's a 10-54?" she asked the remaining officer in our boat.

"Ma'am, I'm going to have to ask you to bring your daughter to the back of the boat."

"What's a 10-54!" she shouted at him, her voice echoing through the eerie forest. I clung to her, terrified of what was unfolding before us.

"Ma'am, please," he gestured toward the rear of the vessel.

"No, you tell me what a 10-54 is!"

Another officer appeared—he must have climbed onto this boat from a third one I hadn't noticed pulled up—and placed his hands on my mom's arms, ready to forcefully remove her from the bow.

She jerked his hands away. "Paul!" she shouted

toward the firefighters in the water. "Paul, where are you? Paul!" The police officer tried again, this time my mom giving in as he pulled us to the rear of the boat and helped us into the third boat.

From there the night occurred in snippets, the trauma making it difficult to recall all the details. We were extracted from the scene, picked up by one of my mom's friends, and taken back to the house where we were reunited with Jay.

The following days were a blur of lasagna and sympathy cards brought to us by neighbors and members of our church, extended family flying in and filling each room of the house we once could afford to live in, my mom answering questions about how my dad would have wanted his funeral so his siblings could take care of the details.

I remember my Aunt Tracy taking me out for ice cream so my mom could grieve in private. What my Aunt Tracy didn't know was that my dad was supposed to be the one taking me. I ordered my ice cream in a bowl that day.

Jay locked himself in his room that summer. It was the least I'd ever talked to him, and perhaps when I needed him most.

Shortly after my dad's passing, an officer came to our house carrying a Ziploc bag of the items my dad had in the canoe that day. The bag contained his wallet, keys, and phone.

There were fifty-six missed calls from that night.

I should have known that his phone was in the canoe. I should have found it and called for help. My mom, the police, anyone. The moment my dad disappeared, I should have done something. Maybe he'd still be here today if I had.

The police report identified the cause of death as drowning, but when he slipped, he hit his head, knocking him unconscious before falling into the water. Following the Rule of Threes I learned later in my middle school health class, someone can survive without oxygen for three minutes. That's one hundred and eighty seconds I could have gotten out of the boat and found him. I may have only weighed fifty pounds, but I could have at least held his head above water and yelled for help. Maybe if he could have breathed, he would have eventually come to consciousness.

I could have done something.

It's eaten away at me for eleven years, and the reason why I now sit lost in thought on the shower floor. It's not just the flashbacks or fear of drowning that occupy my mind whenever I'm in a similar situation. It's the responsibility, knowing that I was his only hope. I'm the reason why my mom had to raise us alone, deprived of the love of her life by her side, and why my brother lost both his father and best friend at age fifteen.

My heart aches for them the most, which I didn't think was possible, given how much it aches for my dad and myself. I know my dad had a rich life, filled to the brim with love and laughter. Not that it makes it okay that he departed this world so soon, but at least I know he left with no regrets. Me on the other hand, I don't deserve to feel sorry for myself. All the anger and guilt and anxiety—well, it's my fault to begin with.

My afternoon with Dalton ended in mental exhaustion, so I decide it'd be best to wrap up my shower and call it an early night, hoping to sleep off the negative energy. I scrub my entire body with an exfoliator to remove any grime or stench the pool of water might have latched onto me.

After changing into pajamas, I head downstairs carrying my wet clothes from earlier along with the rest of my laundry. The storm has already begun outside, raindrops tapping on the rooftop. When I step onto the main floor and turn toward the laundry machines, Jay calls out to me from the kitchen. I gasp, not realizing he was home.

"I'm going to have to start charging you for utilities," he says, leaning onto the kitchen counter over a bowl of cereal. "You sure like your showers."

Normally I'd try to come up with some witty remark, but I can't seem to find the words. My face remains emotionless, staring blankly at him while he crunches on his cereal.

Always the wiser, he sets his spoon down and asks, "What happened?"

"I don't want to talk about it."

He looks at me with creased eyebrows and pursed

lips, but gives in after a moment, taking another bite of cereal. "Okay."

I turn to the washing machine, throwing in my clothes perhaps a bit too aggressively.

"It looks like the rain's supposed to continue throughout tomorrow. We won't need as much staff," Jay speaks as he rinses his bowl in the sink. "Take the day off. Call Jen, or Bristol. Do something fun." It feels more like an order than an offer.

Jen works on Sundays, and Bristol is likely spending her day applying for internships now that her dad's back in town. Besides, fun for them includes lying out by the lake and soaking up sun, which won't be an option anyway.

Regardless, I respond with a quick "thanks" and toss the final piece of clothing into the machine: a male t-shirt that's two sizes too big for me yet fits just right.

∼∼∼

"AVERY?" A MAN'S VOICE WHIMPERS NEARBY.

I turn my head to look around, the slightest movement causing the canoe to wobble. It's pitch-black out, the only light emanating from a lantern resting on the seat at the end of the boat. Thunder rumbles high above me, menacing and ominous.

"Avery," the voice repeats, weakened by strife.

I glance down. A white-knuckled hand grips the edge of the boat. I peer outside of the canoe and into the obscure water, dark as night. My dad's pale face floats on the surface next to where I sit.

"Save. Me." It strains him to speak, barely able to make out each syllable.

I try grabbing ahold of him, desperate to pull him onboard, but my arms won't obey. Nor my hands or any of my fingers. My muscles refuse to cooperate. I'm completely immobile.

"Ave—" His eyes, frail and lifeless, are locked on mine.

"I can't," I whimper, feeling defeated. "I can't move. I can't save you."

His eyes turn rancorous, his face suddenly alive with the acrimony of hatred. He screams, a blood-curdling sound that sends chills up my spine.

"How could you!" he yells at me. The river starts to boil, surging pockets of scalding water exploding all around him and causing him to gargle as he continues to scream at me. "I gave you everything! How can you let this happen! How can you just sit there and watch me die!"

Tears stream down my face, but my muscles still refuse to move. Thunder cracks overhead as the storm clouds unleash their torrent upon us.

"I'm sorry," I cry, inaudible over his raging screams. "Dad, I'm so sorry." My voice cracks. His hand lets loose of the canoe, and the swell of the river pulls him under.

I wake to a sharp thunderclap outside my window as the shrill wind whistles through the cracks in the house. Somewhere in the middle of the storm, I swear I can hear a man screaming.

CHAPTER SIXTEEN

THE TWO-NOTE CHIME OF THE DOORBELL RESONATES from downstairs. I pause my music, set down my paint brush, and sidestep around the mound of plastic-covered furniture I'd slid to the center of my bedroom earlier that morning.

The front door swings open to expose Dalton standing on the front porch, rocking back and forth on his feet with his hands shoved into the front pockets of his jeans.

"You." I know it's a weird thing to say to greet somebody at your door, but it just sort of slipped out.

"You," he echoes and stops rocking on his feet. "I tried knocking first, but I didn't think you could hear it over the dance party going on upstairs."

My cheeks flush. I'd been listening to a boy band I was avidly obsessed with during my middle school years. He must have heard the music blaring through my open window.

Other small factors of this unanticipated encounter suddenly stand out to me: my hair tied up in a messy bun (an actual messy bun, not the cute kind of messy bun), the subtle perspiration on my forehead from painting (okay, and maybe dancing) in my room, and how all my natural social cues around this guy seem to be out of whack since yesterday's incident. Note to self: always check a window and mirror before answering the front door.

"What are you doing here?" I question.

"Your brother sent me."

"My brother?" I ask, thoroughly confused.

"I swung by JuiSea to—you know." He tapers off, obviously unsure of the correct etiquette in referencing yesterday's episode. "But your brother mentioned you weren't working today and that I could find you in the house in this direction with the Cavalier parked in the driveway."

"That's...weird." I can't picture Jay sending a male teenager to come find me in a house I had to myself for the day.

"Anyways." His eyes wander to my shoulders and arms like he's checking to see if I'm physically alright despite it being mental turmoil he's following up on. "Are you okay?"

"Yeah." Short. No room for questioning. At least not while we're standing in the open doorway. I'd thought about it lying in bed last night, how he deserves some answers after being there for me, but I still want a say in when and where those answers are given to him.

"Okay," he says, accepting my taciturn behavior. "Enjoy your dance party."

"It's not a dance party," I quickly deny. I can't let him walk away with that image in his head. "It's a paint party."

"You paint?"

"No." I chuckle. No matter how great my mom's canvases turn out, I did not inherit the artistic gene. "Only walls. Anything requiring more than one color I leave to the professionals."

"You're painting your room?" I nod. "Mind if I see?"

≈≈≈

THE RADIO PLAYS ON SOME SORT OF POP ROCK STATION, projecting quieter than before, but enough to fill the empty space between our conversations. Upon entering my room and inspecting my work, Dalton picked up a small paintbrush and touched up on an area near the baseboard where a few white speckles peeked through the first coat of paint. I never thought I'd be jealous of how steady someone can stroke a paintbrush against a flat surface. And this includes knowing my mom, although her painting technique is a bit more haphazard in style.

At that point, the room was half-white, half-lilac

grey. Now he and I each have a paint roller in hand as we take on the two remaining walls. I'm standing on my folding chair to reach where the wall meets the ceiling. The gaps in our conversation stretch on for minutes at a time. It surprises me how comfortable I feel around him without the urge to fill the silence. Just as I think this, he speaks up.

"Two Truths and a Lie."

"What?"

He looks up at me. "Please tell me you know the game Two Truths and a Lie."

I do know it. All my high school teachers would make their classes play it on the first day of a new semester as a way of getting to know one another. It didn't matter that all the students already knew each other, and over time the game became boring and monotonous, at least for those of us who aren't creative enough to switch up our three statements each semester.

"Well, sure, but isn't it just some classroom icebreaker that teachers use to pass the time on the first day back from break?"

"No," he draws the word out and tilts his head back as if my question inflicted physical pain. "How dare teachers give this game a bad rap. It's criminal, really."

"You must be really good to have this great a passion for it. Or you had more creative teachers than I did."

"Oh, come on. You can't hate this game. It's like hating people."

"That's a stretch. How do you even jump to that conclusion?"

"It's a game of sharing details about your life and it offers people an opportunity to care about something you wouldn't otherwise bring up if you weren't asked to think about two truths that make up your identity and one lie that often speaks louder than the truths about the kind of person you are or aspire to become."

"I'm assuming you already have your truths and lie in mind, then."

"Nope," he states. "I never recycle the same statements, that's cheating."

Huh, I guess I do cheat in school.

"Come on, Warren. Let's redeem the depraved reputation your teachers bestowed upon you."

"Fine," I say, stepping down to slide the chair farther down the wall. "But you go first."

"Fair enough." He squats down to apply more paint onto his roller, staring at the pile of furniture in concentration. Thunder growls in the distance, warning us of the impending storm. After a minute, he picks up his brush and resumes painting.

"Okay," he says determinedly. "When I was five, I used to dream of being a space pilot who'd go on these top-secret missions to battle aliens that planned to take over the world."

I immediately realize how much more interesting and elaborate his statements will be compared to my own. I'll have to think a lot harder to come up with ones that can compete.

"I used to have this sleeping disorder growing up and I had to be home schooled for a few years because of it."

He pauses, as if thinking of what his final statement should be, although I know that anyone with his level of enthusiasm for the game wouldn't just rattle off two statements without a third already in mind. He's playing strategically. I can imagine him sitting in a classroom a few desks in front of me, trying hard to fake the other students even though no one else really cares. The rest of us are just waiting for the bell to ring so we can be dismissed. Although now, playing the game outside of a windowless, brick-walled, stained carpet classroom with someone I'm actually interested in getting to know more, I have to admit his love and strategy for the game is somewhat endearing, albeit nerdy.

"And I hate money."

His final statement—so short and to the point—catches me off guard. Not to mention that it's completely absurd. Who hates money? I get that some people may not be as consumed by money as others, but I doubt that anyone can straight-up hate money altogether.

"Interesting," I comment.

His first statement is believable. Every five-year-old dreams of becoming something highly improbable. I remember I dreamt of becoming a unicorn whisperer around the same age.

His second statement doesn't sway me one way or the other. It's possible that he had a sleeping disorder, but he could have just as easily made that up on the spot.

His lie has to be the last one.

"You don't hate money," I state confidently. "I'm not even sure if that's humanly possible. No matter how unmaterialistic someone may be, money buys necessities, it helps us to survive."

He doesn't respond right away, causing me to stop painting and to turn to look at him. There's a sly smile on his face as he meets my gaze.

"Hate to break it to you, but that is not the correct answer."

"Okay, so you didn't have a sleeping disorder?"

"No, that's true too." I should have known. Seeing him awake in the orchard before dawn does provoke suspicion. "I never wanted to be a space pilot who fought alien villains."

"Really? I was certain that was true." I picture a young, dimple-faced Dalton in an intergalactic war suit and quickly shake away the image. "Besides, your money statement was so concise I just thought you were bad at coming up with lies."

"Concise, yes, but the truth is usually simple when you think about it."

I guess I never think about the truth, then. My mind

is always a complicated mess with lots of moving parts that make it impossible to summarize anything so concisely.

"No one hates money," I tell him, holding my ground on this belief.

"I don't hate wealth. Or bank accounts and credit cards and being debt-free. I just hate physical money. The thought of how many hands it circulates through..." He shudders and moves to the wall I'm painting, helping me cover the last remaining section of white. My eyes follow him, eyebrows scrunched in disbelief.

"So what you're telling me is you're a germaphobe? Also, that's practically cheating! So you don't like physical money, but that doesn't mean you hate all types of money." My voice grows in volume as I accuse him. "It's a half-lie, and it's against the rules."

He looks at me in shock, and then lets out a laugh, obviously entertained by me getting worked up about a game I had previously rolled my eyes at.

"It's not cheating," he defends his strategy. "I really hate dealing with physical money." He lathers more paint onto his roller. I've completely stopped working, my focus on the game now hindering my ability to multitask.

"And I'm not a germaphobe," he adds, defending what his statement might reveal about his personality. "Just when it comes to money."

"You could have said cash," I grumble.

"You still would've guessed the sleeping disorder if I had."

We stare each other down, me indignant with slightly squinted eyes and a wrinkled forehead from furrowing my eyebrows in frustration, him with that same amused grin he wears every time I have a big reaction to anything.

"Your turn," he says after a moment and begins painting again.

The tumultuous weather is gaining traction, the wind now howling through the nearby trees and ruffling the plastic that covers my furniture as it blows through the open window. I sit on my bed in concentration, the plastic protesting loudly beneath me every time I shift my weight. I allow Dalton to single-handedly finish the final wall I'd been working on. He's considerably better at it and seems to enjoy the work. He's almost finished filling in the corner where the two walls meet when I speak up.

"Well, for starters, I won a limbo contest at a neighborhood barbeque when I was nine," I say proudly. He doesn't turn around, only nods his head. Another minute passes as I brainstorm.

"Last summer I broke my collar bone falling off my bike." And another minute. "And..."

The last one has to be a truth. I rummage through my brain, searching for details of my life I can use that might be misleading, thinking all the way back to my early childhood. I don't know if it's because of yesterday's undesirable turn of events or simply because I try to avoid thinking that far back, but everything that comes to mind has to do with my dad and that day. Whether it's the two-bedroom apartment I later called home, wearing some of Jay's hand-me-down shirts when my mom couldn't afford to buy me new clothes, the tight-knit relationship I developed with my mom, the protection I'd always received from my brother. Everything that has become my life and shaped who I am, it all leads back to that one picturesque afternoon on the water. My inability to save him on that fateful day has compounded into so many more repercussions and consequences than the loss of a life.

Dalton's words repeat in my mind: *The truth is usually simple when you think about it.* It never occurred to me that everything I know and feel about that day, about my dad, about my life and the lives of my mom and brother, can boil down to one simple, yet truthful statement.

The words are out of my mouth before I can think about what I'm saying, whispered before I can catch them escaping through the crevice between my lips.

"I killed my dad."

CHAPTER SEVENTEEN

DALTON EXHALES HEAVILY, HIS FINGERS INTERLOCKED behind his head as he stares out the window trying to wrap his mind around the story of that day. I've only ever described it to two other people outside of my family before, a close friend of five years and my school counselor. Admittedly, there's a small sense of accomplishment that it didn't end in waterworks. I don't think either one of us could bear another breakdown. At least not on back-to-back days.

"You don't have to say anything," I tell him, assuming he's at a loss for words. I get up from the edge of my bed, restless from the anticipation of whatever's going on in his head.

He turns to me, dropping his hands to his side. There's so much concern in his eyes as they shift back and forth between mine. I feel sorry that he has to endure the weight of my story, the heaviness of my past.

"I—" He pauses, swallowing. "I am so sorry."

"Or apologize," I add. "I didn't tell you so you'd feel sorry for me or treat me any different because that's not what I want. I—I actually don't know why I told you," I confess, although I'm somewhat relieved that it's finally out in the open. No more lies, no more lunar eclipse rejections or picnic panic attacks. Hopefully.

"I'm glad you told me." He takes a cautious step toward me, hands in his pockets again, head tilted down. He takes a deep breath, exhaling gravely, and whispers, "I don't know what to say." His face remains downcast, but his eyes glance up to take in my expression. I try my best to look alright, if only for his sake. He seems to be really taking this to heart, as if it happened last year rather than last decade.

"Then don't say anything," I whisper back.

A gust of wind sweeps through the room, scattering a few loose strands of hair that catch on my eyelashes. The bedroom door slams shut from the force, the sudden thrash rattling through the walls and floorboards. I inhale sharply, tensing at the deafening noise. Dalton on the other hand remains steady, taking another step forward and eliminating the gap that separates us.

He reaches up and carefully pulls aside the loose strands of hair on my face. His soft brown eyes move from my eyelashes to where he tucked my hair behind my ear, over my cheek and down my jawline until they stop at my lips. His hand stays behind my ear, warm against the skin of my neck.

"Avery Marie," he whispers, standing less than a foot away.

I swallow, trying hard not to disrupt the delicacy of the moment. I can feel my heart pounding in my chest, hands stagnant at my sides, gaze shifting down to his ribs, afraid to make eye contact. I wonder if this is how Jen feels around Levi, or how my girlfriends back home feel with their significant others. The seconds leading up to these awaited moments, speaking in hushed tones as if anything louder would unravel the connection we're both feeling.

He slides his thumb gently over my collarbone. "Which side did you break?" he asks.

"Why are you so sure that wasn't the lie? You're underestimating my limbo skills."

He smiles and moves closer, resting his forehead against mine. I close my eyes. We stay this way for a while, me focusing on keeping my breath slow and steady, him obviously hesitating or having second thoughts. Maybe I'm not the only one with nerves right now.

"How's it coming in here?" Jay swings the bedroom door ajar, stopping it only a couple inches from the wall to ensure it doesn't touch any wet paint. Dalton and I both take a large step in opposite directions. My face is instantly hot, and I'm sure it's bright red to show for it.

Growing up, we had an open-door policy, not that anything would have happened anyway, not with the thin walls and cramped space that is. Still, we didn't even change clothes in our own bedrooms, always in the bathroom where we could lock the door. Jay, knowing that I'd be at home painting when Dalton stopped by, must have taken that as a green light to intrude without warning. He doesn't look at us right away, just stands in the doorway scanning the walls to inspect our paint job. We wait in awkward silence.

"It looks good," he tells us. Only afterward does he land his gaze on Dalton, staring at him with his arms crossed and his broad shoulders pulled back in a protective stance.

"We just finished the first coat," I say, hoping to draw his attention away from the fact that Dalton and I had been practically entangled when he barged in unannounced.

"You'll need to wait a few hours before applying the second coat," he says to me, although he keeps his eyes on Dalton.

Dalton, whose hands have found their way back into his pockets—must be a nervous habit—shifts his weight and then clears his throat. "I think I'll head out." He steps around me to where my brother stands in the doorframe. Jay moves aside to let him pass.

"Hey, Dalton?" I call to him as he reaches the top of the staircase. He spins around to face me. "Thank you. For helping me." I hope those five little words convey what I truly mean. That not only am I grateful for his steady hand with a paintbrush, but also for listening to my story. For his comforting embrace on the gravel beach yesterday and for being honest with me just a moment ago when he didn't know what to say. Those actions hold greater meaning than spoon feeding me what everyone else says upon finding out about my dad, as if people are handed a script to read when acknowledging my past, a list of acceptable phrases and approved dos and don'ts.

Dalton gives a knowing nod and retreats from view.

I look at Jay, who's staring at me with one eyebrow raised.

"What?" It sounds more aggressive than curious. I really don't want to discuss what happened thirty seconds ago, especially with my brother.

"Nothing." He raises both eyebrows this time and leaves the room.

Through the crack in my closet door, I see Dalton's t-shirt folded neatly over my empty laundry basket. I breathe a sigh of relief that I forgot to return it to him. That would have prompted a whole other level of unnecessary intimidation had Jay seen Dalton leave with an extra shirt in hand.

CHAPTER EIGHTEEN

THE WONKA ROOM SMELLS OF SUGAR AND SWEAT AS WE hide in the back-corner booth.

"Aren't they supposed to have these pointless little rallies over the weekend, like after they play their last game or something?" Jen asks, irritated by the band of young soccer players stomping around in their cleats. There are about fifteen girls in total, probably in the third or fourth grade, all accompanied by at least one parent as well as two team coaches, who are busy unpacking a box of participation trophies onto a nearby table.

"I mean, I can hardly see him." She almost whines, staring longingly into the space between Bristol's head and mine. I look over my shoulder to where Levi stands behind the counter talking to a few of the girls about their frozen yogurt, using phrases like "Good choice!"

and "That's my favorite too!" It's obvious the girls are fawning over him.

Most of the kids and parents have already taken their seats at their makeshift dining room table. They slid over almost every chrome-colored table and neon chair in the vicinity to create one giant table, the table legs creating high-pitched screeching noises as they scraped against the floor. Although a few dads stand around chatting with one another, the view from our booth to the cash register isn't entirely blocked. But when I turn back, Jen's lower lip is jutted out in a pout.

"So much for your prime viewing location," Bristol snorts, commenting on Jen's strategic table selection. She claims that the corner booth puts just enough distance between us and Levi that he won't assume anything of our repetitive visits—in reality, it puts as much distance as possible between us and Levi, which I find extremely obvious, like she's overcompensating for her increasingly stalkerish behavior—while also offering up prime observation of the cash register, or rather the person operating the cash register. She can face Bristol and me while secretly watching Levi in between us the entire time. Like I said, stalkerish.

Jen sighs, watching as Levi chats with the young Megan Rapinoes.

"Jealous of a bunch of third graders?" Bristol observes.

"No," Jen defends herself. "Actually, it's kind of hot. I can totally picture him as the father of my children."

"Ew," Bristol retorts.

"Oh, please, like you've never thought about some guy as the future dad to your kids."

"I don't want kids," Bristol tells her plainly. Jen looks at me.

"I don't want kids," I second, pausing before adding, "Yet."

"Well, me neither. But someday." Her eyes drift to the cash register again.

The group of soccer players converse loudly, each voice competing in decibels to drown out neighboring conversations. I take another bite of my chocolate frozen yogurt drizzled in warm peanut butter sauce. Jen has been switching it up too, no longer sticking with her chocolate and cookie dough combination. Rather, she's moved on to more exotic flavors, if only to stimulate conversation between her and Levi at the counter. First it was black cherry tart, then oatmeal cookie batter, and even a pistachio flavor. Today she dunks her spoon into her black bean brownie frozen yogurt, a flavor advocated by a group of local vegans.

"Maybe he'll be at the sand courts on Saturday," Bristol tells Jen in an attempt to cheer her up after her Levi Time was interrupted by the chaotic soccer squad.

"Maybe," she repeats. "He might be working that day."

"Of course you know his schedule." I smile. Although I find it incredibly creepy how much information Jen can scavenge about a person, there's something undeniably sweet about how smitten she is with Levi.

"I don't know his schedule, thank you very much," she defends herself again. "I only know that a couple weeks ago, I saw him here on a Saturday afternoon at twelve-twenty and if that's a regular shift for him, then he won't be playing this year."

Jen's eyes stay focused behind us as she slowly consumes the frozen yogurt from her spoon. Bristol and I glance sideways at each other, trying to suppress our laughter.

"Ugh, I'm never telling you guys anything about my love life ever again if you're going to act all weird about it."

"Oh, I'm sorry," says Bristol. "I didn't realize we were the ones acting weird about it."

Jen stabs her spoon into her bowl, glaring at us with flaring nostrils.

"Aw, don't take it out on the poor vegan dessert," I tell her.

"Yeah, what did the little black beans ever do to you?" Bristol agrees.

"I swear," Jen, now annoyed, starts. "I'm never coming back here with y—" Her eyes catch sight of movement behind me and her entire expression morphs from frustration to pure bliss as she let out a frilly, lighthearted laugh. "You two are just so funny!" She laughs again, louder this time. A few of the soccer moms turn to look at us. Jen's eyes follow along the wall opposite of where we're sitting. I assume Levi is walking toward the back to replenish the self-serve dispensers. He must disappear behind the wall because in an instant, Jen snaps back to her snarling, exasperated self, eating her frustration.

"Take a breath, Jen. He likes you," Bristol consoles her. "Besides, you might not have to drag us here anymore if he joined a team this summer. Then you can have your rendezvous at the courts."

"God, I hope so." She mixes her yogurt. "I'm running out of flavors to choose from, and I've been avoiding cotton candy and piña colada." She twists her mouth in disgust.

This is the third time in the last week I've heard about a sand volleyball league, the first two times coming from groups of teenagers sitting in the booths at JuiSea.

"What is this about joining a team?" I inquire.

"Sand volleyball," Jen answers. "Teams compete over the four Saturdays in July, and then the playoffs are a couple weeks after that during the Harvest Festival."

I think back to when I was collecting empty cups along the beach and Dalton startled me from behind. He'd mentioned something about the sand courts. I wonder if that means he'll be competing in the league too, and I'm keen on finding out.

Look who's the stalker now, I think.

"I'll ask Jay if I can have that afternoon off," I tell them.

"You better come," Bristol insists. "Your man will be tearing up the courts."

My stomach does a somersault at hearing Dalton referred to as "my man." It's been over a week since he helped me paint my room and left without a clear reso lution to our forehead-to-forehead moment. Since then, our time together has dwindled back down to his daily visits to JuiSea where we maintain casual conversation and share secret smiles while Jay and Raymond aren't paying attention. It's become somewhat of a game for us, really. Our own game, not some overused first day of class ritual.

"And can you please wear a bathing suit?" Bristol asks me. "It's supposed to be in the nineties this weekend and you're going to develop some seriously weird tan lines if you continue to wear tank tops and t-shirts every day."

I push my sleeve up to reveal a faint farmer's tan and chuckle. "I think that ship has sailed."

"It's never too late to work on a tan," she responds.

"Easy for you to say," Jen chimes in. "You never have to worry about getting sunburned like the rest of us." She has a point. Bristol can be outside for less than five minutes and she'll have new tan lines to show for it. Always bronzed, never burned.

Since bathing suits are first and foremost associated with water and swimming, I don't own one. At least, I didn't pack one with me when I came to visit, and the only one I have stored away at home probably doesn't fit me anymore anyway. I've had no reason to own one, not since we moved out of our apartment complex and lost access to the hot tub there.

Then again, apparently I'm the type of person who makes reckless decisions and jumps off cliffs into unfamiliar bodies of water knowing full-well that it's the exact scenario of my worst nightmare. I guess I should have a bathing suit for those occasions.

I notice Jen's attention is lost again between the gap in our heads. The chatter coming from the soccer team shifts into an eruption of cheers whenever a girl's name is called to collect her trophy. The noise rings through the room, reverberating off the walls and floors with nothing to absorb the impact. Some of the young girls must misunderstand what it means to applaud for a teammate, instead their shrill screams penetrating the entire room. Good thing the frozen yogurt is served in paper bowls, otherwise there'd be broken glass everywhere.

"Have you had your daily fix of ogling, so we can get out of here? I can hardly hear myself think." Bristol rubs her temples in annoyance from all the clamor. I feel like I might have a headache coming on myself.

Jen gives a small sigh in Levi's direction before releasing us from our misery. We slide out of our booth and make our way under the colorful lights and through the cloud of sweat toward the front door. One of the girls has remnants of her frozen yogurt drying on her cheeks. Another one belches, causing her teammates around her to whine "Ew" and one girl to laugh and say, "Nice one."

"I take back what I said earlier about ever wanting kids," Jen says, clearly repulsed by the young athletes. "They're disgusting."

We walk past the counter where Levi is replenishing the toppings bar. "See you," I tell him. He glances up to wish us a good day, giving Jen a wide smile, which she returns.

"Bye Jenny," he says, ever cheerful.

She waits until we're on the other side of the door to say, "Okay, only if they're his kids too." Bristol and I laugh, rolling our eyes at Jen's helpless infatuation.

CHAPTER NINETEEN

THE FRONT DOOR OPENS TO A WALL OF SAVORY AROMA, the smells of rosemary and lemon wafting through the house. I slip off my shoes and walk toward the sound of slicing baguettes and slamming oven doors. When I round the corner, I see Jay in one of his JuiSea aprons fanning the air above the stove. It's not much smoke, just enough to conclude that it's his first time preparing this particular meal.

"What are you doing?" I ask, confused at the sight of my brother using kitchen appliances.

"Making us dinner," he responds nonchalantly, as if it's a regular occurrence.

"You don't cook, remember?"

"Pfff." He wraps a dish towel around one of his hands to remove a pan of chicken from the oven. "Hot, hot, hot."

I walk over to a drawer and pull out a pair of oven mitts that our mom gave him for Christmas a couple years back, holding them up in front of Jay's face. He responds by holding up the dish towel in front of mine.

"I can cook," he says. "Besides, I've got to take better care of my sister."

My eyebrows scrunch in confusion. Never have I received this kind of care from my brother. Protective? Sure. Always there for me? Absolutely. But worried about my alimental intake?

And then it hits me.

"You talked to Mom today."

"She just wants to make sure you're getting your vitamins and minerals and whatever. What even is riboflavin anyways?"

"Five thousand miles apart and she's still harping on me to eat my vegetables." I drop a plastic Arrowbase bag to the floor and slide onto one of the counter stools. "I can take care of myself."

"Fine, I'm doing it for me then. We've been eating nothing but sandwiches and cereal for the past two weeks, Aves."

"Don't forget about the boxed mac and cheese," I add. He makes a face at me.

"Exactly my point." He pierces a piece of chicken, checking to make sure it's cooked all the way through.

"I don't know about you, but I cook elaborate five-course meals on my days off," I tell him with poise.

"And you never think to save some for me? What a lousy sister I have, even after giving her a job and place to stay."

"Maybe if I had more days off, I could do more cooking around here."

He spins around to point at me. "Deal."

"Saturday?"

I know he'll give me the day off, but he gives it added thought anyway, probably curious as to why I want that specific day off. "Sand volleyball?"

"Yeah, Jen and Bristol want me to come watch with them."

"Sure," he says, easygoing. "Tell Dalton I say hi." There's a level of mockery in his voice, a playfulness I wish to avoid.

"Uh, I will if he's there." I try shrugging it off.

"If he's there." Jay chuckles to himself. "Okay."

He moves the pan of chicken to the counter between us, along with a dish of charred green beans and slices of baguette.

"Voila!" he exclaims with his hands in the air, proud of the outcome. I'm just relieved the house didn't burn down in my absence. Is there an app I can install on my phone that'll alert me whenever the stove or oven is turned on? At least then I could rush home to monitor things whenever Jay's feeling unusually nurturing.

"Bon appetite," he says in an aggressive French accent, gesturing for me to dig in. I pinch some green beans between my finger and thumb and move them onto my plate, then do the same with a few strips of chicken, burning myself in the process. Jay comes around to sit in the other stool, grabbing his food in the same fashion. We use utensils to eat, just not to serve our plates.

"What's in the bag?" he asks while taking a bite of his rosemary lemon chicken. "Hey, this isn't bad."

I glance down at the folded-over bag at my feet, already forgetting about my recent purchase. Inside are just two of the dozens of bathing suits I was pressured to try on after confessing to Jen and Bristol that I didn't bring one with me. One is a mauve one-piece with a string that zig-zags up the center of my chest, and the other a light blue bikini with removable straps. Bristol was pushing for the bikini since the removable straps will help eradicate my existing tan lines. Jen settled the dispute by reminding me of the employee discount she'd give me and suggesting I buy both as long as I promise to alternate between the two. In their minds, they could always use another bathing suit. Seeing as I didn't own any an hour ago, they thought buying two was a smart decision. Any other person would have probably agreed with them.

Staring at my reflection in the full-length mirror of the changing stall, wearing one of the countless flashy bathing suits Jen had flung over the door for me to try on, I felt something unfamiliar. It wasn't a new feeling per se, but it did give me pause as I stopped to acknowledge what it was exactly. The sense of inclusion, of belonging in a group. I'd felt it before, of course, with friends back home, in extracurriculars at school, and even here in Nelson with my new friends, but I never imagined I'd feel it regarding anything related to water. Everything that I thought I was to forever miss out on —boating with friends or wading in wave pools— included swimsuit shopping with my girlfriends, contemplating the style, look, and feel of each one while laughing at the ones that looked utterly ridiculous.

But there I was at that moment, and there was something uniquely special about them not knowing why it was significant to me. There was no caution or hesitation as they demanded me to try more styles on, no filtering when they talked about how I'd look at the lake, just the flinging of bikinis over changing stall doors and blunt observations when I twirled in front of them.

Presently though, with Jay as my company, what would have been a fond memory with my girlfriends now has the potential to be tainted by confusion, questions, and the remembrance of childhood trauma.

"Just some new clothes," I answer him.

"Cool. What'd you get?"

How is it that I have the one brother who's interested in his sister's clothing purchases?

"Oh, just a couple things Jen and Bristol picked out." I take another bite, trying to act as if they're insignificant, which really, they are. Heck, they won't ever be used for the one thing they're intended for. "You know how they can be about style. Always wanting to look trendy and spread their love of fashion."

"I didn't know that, actually," he says, forcing down some green beans. "But it sounds intense, like they're giving you a makeover. Let's see it."

"What?"

"Let's see what they picked out for you," he repeats.

I break off a piece of baguette and reach for the butter, using the hands-on action to stall. Jay won't understand why I'd spent money on the bathing suits. He'll assume I'm only trying to fit in, that I care too much about what other people think of me or that I lack self-confidence. Maybe he'll think that my friends are pressuring me to swim, in which case he might want to take matters into his own hands.

"I'm sure it'll look fine," Jay tells me, still assuming it's some normal article of everyday clothing. "What's the big secret?" He pauses, his fork midair and his face suddenly uneasy. "Please don't tell me it's lingerie."

"No, what?" I deny, my voice becoming more defensive as my hourglass runs out of sand.

He exhales the breath he must have been holding and resumes eating. "What is it, then?" he asks through a mouthful of food, laughing at the suspense of it all.

I've accidentally built it up far greater than it is, the exact opposite of what I intended. Oh, how I wish I'd bought something else along with the bathing suits, jean shorts or a new pair of running shoes I could show him while keeping the suits hidden beneath.

Reluctantly, I bend down from the chair, clutching the counter for support, and pull the bag into my lap. I reveal part of the one-piece and stare at him, as if daring him to comment on it.

"Nice. Is it—" He stops when he realizes what it is. He takes another bite of food, creases appearing on his forehead as he ponders why I'd purchase something to be worn in or around the one thing that terrifies me. He turns to me again, the bag of concealed bathing suits once again out of sight. "Why?"

"It's, like, ninety degrees every day. Why not?" I shoot back.

He shrugs, shaking his head. "Just seems odd to me, that's all."

"Why, because I don't swim? Just because I own a bathing suit doesn't automatically mean I have to go swimming. I can lay out and tan with my girlfriends if I want to. It doesn't mean anything, Jay."

He looks at me with his eyebrows raised in shock. I can tell he's considering how to proceed with caution. There's hardly a time in my life when I've lashed out at my brother, and I'm not entirely sure why I feel the urge to do so now.

"That's fine. It's unlike you, but so is this." He gestures to me, my attitude amplifying as the conversation gains traction. "I thought you steered away from wearing bathing suits because you thought people would expect you to go in the water if you ever wore one, that they'd make you go in. Now all of a sudden you don't think that?"

"Why does it matter? Why do you even care if I wear a bathing suit or not when I'm hanging out with my friends? We're girls, we like to tan."

"And I'm saying that's fine! But you've always said that you wouldn't do that because it's just asking for peer pressure. I don't know if someone made a comment about you or if you feel the need to blend in because you're new here or whatever. All I'm saying is that I don't get it. That's all." His eyes are wide, portraying a sort of frenzy as he tries to get his point across.

My hand grips my utensils tightly, heat rising in my chest from the annoyance I feel toward my brother. "Whatever," I mumble.

He sets his fork down aggressively, the metal clanking loudly against the plate. "What is your deal right now? Seriously." He turns so that his entire body faces me head on. "I've been nothing but supportive of you over the years. I've stepped in when you needed a friend, whenever you missed out on things because of your anxiety, whenever you needed a father figure. Forget the fact that I was only a teenager in need of one myself. May I remind you that you weren't the one who drowned, Avery?"

My heart clenches at his words. I remember the day all too vividly. I might not have drowned that day, but I may as well have. As a bystander, I can't help but think about any pain my dad might have felt, what it was like to be in his shoes rather than the harmless interior of the canoe.

"This fear of water you've let accumulate over the years could have been avoided. You could have overcome it years ago, but I never pushed you. Never." He pounds his fist against the counter. "I was always there for you without question or reservation your entire life, even though it hurt me to watch you agonize over everything and confine yourself all these years. And now you're throwing this attitude at me because you bought a bathing suit? All I did was express my confusion, that's it. So don't take your self-pity out on me."

Silence, yet the articulation of his words resonates in the air around us. He resumes eating, hastily shoving the rest of his dinner down his throat, the enthusiasm he once had over his home-cooked meal vanished. I on the other hand can't take another bite, not with the lump in my throat. I try to swallow.

"You gonna eat?" Jay asks, his voice depleted.

I slide off the stool and walk to the trash bin. Jay snatches my plate from my hands before I can dump the remaining food in the trash.

"Don't be stupid." He sets it beside his own, picking at food from both.

Rage burns inside me. I need to get out of the same room as him. I grab the Arrowbase bag and head toward the stairs.

"You're welcome," Jay calls out to me in exasperation.

"Oh right, thanks for dinner," I tell him, trying to keep the level of frustration in my tone to a minimum. "Then again, I should just thank Mom the next time I talk to her." I sprint up the flight of stairs, taking two at a time, and let the door slam behind me.

CHAPTER TWENTY

THE NEXT MORNING, I GRUDGINGLY SLIDE OUT OF BED, get ready for work, and trudge my way along the shoreline. Normally the sights and sounds of summertime shenanigans contribute to an uplifting mood. Today however, I wish I could drown them all out. They only further aggravate me after waking up still upset about last night. I pass groups of upbeat beachgoers soaking in the late morning rays as I drag myself to the last place I want to be right now: in Jay's presence.

"Yow, you too?" Raymond asks as soon as I'm within earshot. I haven't even said anything, yet he can decrypt my irritable mood. "What happened at the Warren household? Yeesh." He shudders.

"Nothing worth mentioning," I tell him, the intonation of my voice reflecting my level of impatience.

"You know, despite whatever disagreement you two

had, you're still scary alike. Even the way you handle the aftermath of an argument is the same."

"Fascinating."

"Here." He slides a used blender across the counter to me as I tie the strings of my apron into a bow on my lower back. "Drink this."

"What is it?"

"Your pick-me-up. You look terrible. And scarily mean, which I didn't think was possible. Now take that to the back and drink up."

I peer at the remnants in the blender, the strong cocoa aroma wafting up from the recent order. JuiSea is advertised as a smoothie shop, however there are always ingredients lying around to whip up a competitive milkshake.

"I wasn't dumped or anything. I don't need to drown my sorrows in chocolate."

"Fine, I'll take it then." He reaches toward the handle of the blender, but I snatch it up in my hands.

"No, I want it," I say, shooting him a possessive look.

He rolls his eyes at me. "Women."

I walk to the back room with my mood-booster where Taia's washing dishes. I tilt the blender upside-down to gulp the rest of Raymond's milkshake straight out of the container. The door to the walk-in freezer opens and Jay steps out just as I'm slurping up the chocolatey goodness.

"When you're done contaminating my property you can take over the dishes," he tells me, not bothering to make eye contact. Taia swivels around to take in the two of us, a conspicuous smile creeping across her face. She's obviously entertained, and probably relieved that she's not the cause of Jay's impatience today.

"Taia, go cover the floor," he further directs. It's odd being placed behind-the-scenes while Taia runs around serving customers. Jay usually has these roles reversed seeing as Taia rarely breaks away from tables with attractive prospects. Both she and I stand still, probably due to the shock of inverted responsibilities. "Now."

Taia quickly shuffles out of the room with Jay in tow. Although I don't mind doing the dishes, it still feels like punishment.

〰〰〰

ONE HOUR AND TEN PRUNED FINGERS LATER, JAY LEAVES for his lunch break, relieving me of my dish duties to serve at the bar. As I depart my den of time out, I see Jen and Bristol chatting at the end of the bar toward the pier, two tie-dyed silicone cups collecting condensation on the counter in front of them. I make my way over.

"She survived!" Jen announces when she sees me coming.

"Barely." I hold up my hands to show them the shriveled-up result of my sibling torture.

"Raymond filled us in on what happened," Bristol tells me. "How are you holding up?"

"Raymond filled you in?" I question. I didn't exactly

tell him anything, and I'd be dumbfounded to discover if Jay had. "What did he tell you?"

"Oh, just that you and your brother got into some huge fight and that the two of you are acting like children."

"Wow, thanks for that, Raymond." I look over my shoulder at him. He looks over from his blender station and shrugs innocently.

"So, what happened?" Bristol asks me, taking a sip of her purple smoothie speckled with chia seeds.

I shake my head. "I don't want to talk about it."

"Raymond also predicted you'd say that," Jen says. "Whatever, boys can be stupid, especially when they're your brother."

"I kind of hoped that it'd wear off by his age," I retort.

"Hey Raymond? Why do boys act stupid?" Jen calls out to him from across the bar.

He lets out an exasperated groan. "I don't know, sister. But if you find a pretty one who doesn't, let me know." The woman he's serving watches the exchange with an appalled look, as if she wants to perform an exorcism on him. Raymond notices her condemnation and shoves the smoothie rather rancorously toward her chest. She hesitates, the look of horror still plastered on her face.

"It's not contagious, lady," he tells her. She takes it from him and swiftly leaves the premises.

"Rude," I mutter.

"I'm used to it," Raymond responds, making his way over to us. "The price I pay for being fabulous." He flicks his longer strands of blonde hair that waterfall over the buzzed sides of his head.

The four of us chat, occasionally interrupted by the alternation of Raymond and me serving customers. It's Raymond's turn next, but when I see Dalton approaching and feel the flutter in my stomach, I slip away from my friends who all give me sly smiles.

"Hi."

"Hi."

He sits on a bar stool, and we stare at each other, infatuated. Without Jay or other customers around— my present friends excluded—we don't have to act sneaky with our helpless grins. I can fully admire his adorable dimples and appreciate the way he looks at me with that charming curiosity.

"So," I break the silence, "do you want to choose today?" I grab a blender from the back counter.

"It's always better when you decide," he tells me. I shrug. "Although if I could request something that'll give me extra energy, that'd be great."

"Why, were you in your tree at 4 a.m.?"

"No, I'm meeting up with the guys soon for some volleyball." With the sand volleyball league only a couple days away, I wonder why he still hasn't mentioned it to me. I try not to linger on the thought for too long before making his drink, deciding to go with the Orange You Glad It Has Banana smoothie for the energy boost. Besides, I want this one as well.

"Hang on, have you seen me in the orchard that early?"

"So, you *are* there that early," I conclude. "I've been wondering when your morning ritual begins, but I'm hardly awake that early to find out for myself."

I plop the final ingredients into the blender and seal the rubber lid on top. There's an intermission in our conversation as the machine whirs. After drizzling honey around the interior of his cup, I pour in the smoothie and dump the remaining bit into a second cup for me.

"I sort of feel bad that you're always serving me. I should make something for you in return, like home-made cookies."

"Now there's an idea," I say agreeably. "Or I can just set up a tip jar whenever you come around. The last time I accepted food from you, you proceeded to study me like a lab rat."

He laughs, almost choking on his drink. After swallowing, he claims, "Hey, rats are great. They're smart and sociable and cuddly."

"I'm not all those things." He looks at me in contemplation, trying to determine which characteristic I rule out for myself. "But if you really feel bad about it, you can try to make it up to me."

"How so?" he asks with a wry smile.

My heart skips a beat as I think back to our unfinished business in my bedroom. That hadn't been what I had in mind, but I wouldn't mind some alone time with him. I glance to my left to find Raymond, Bristol, and Jen all watching from the opposite end of the bar, talking in hushed tones. When I catch them staring, Jen pretends she wasn't looking—I hope she's smoother at this in The Wonka Room than she is here—and Bristol stands on the footrests of her stool to reach over the counter and yank Raymond's t-shirt so he's facing the other direction.

"Maybe you can start by hanging out with me somewhere where we aren't being watched by three sets of eyes."

Dalton follows my gaze down the bar to my small ensemble of friends. Despite Bristol's attempt to avert Raymond's attention, he stares, unflinching, with no shame in snooping. Dalton raises a hand to him. "Yeah, we should do that. When are you free?"

"I have Saturday off," I tell him, hoping to steer the conversation toward the sand volleyball league. I know I could just mention it, but it feels strange that he hasn't brought it up already, especially if his skills on the court are as staggering as my friends claim.

"I have something on Saturday," he responds, "but I could do the day after?" I take another sip of my drink, the flutter I felt moments ago now deflated. "Does that work for you?"

"Yeah, sure." I nod, and then realize my tone doesn't match the appropriate level of enthusiasm I should have for the situation. "That'll work," I say with more pep this time.

We continue talking while he works on his drink. After he departs to meet up with his friends, I rejoin our audience of three, slowly walking up to them and biting the inside of my cheek as I think about why Dalton would leave the sand volleyball league unmentioned.

"Uh oh," Jen says once she sees me.

"What happened, flirty cakes?" Raymond asks me, draping an arm around my shoulder.

I look at them, deciding whether it's worth discussing. They've known Dalton for years and can maybe help me understand why he hasn't mentioned the league, or at least talk some sense into me that it doesn't matter. Then again, Jen devises elaborate strategies for optimum viewing opportunities of her crush. I doubt she'll think I'm acting absurd for merely speculating.

"Do you think it's odd that Dalton hasn't told me about the sand volleyball league?"

They all look at each other. Bristol speaks first. "You think he doesn't want you there?"

"If he wanted her there, he would have asked her to be there." Raymond's voice oozes sass.

"Raymond!" Jen reaches across the bar to slap his arm.

"What? I'm not saying that he doesn't want her

there, I'm just saying that if he did want her there, he would've made sure she was going to be there."

"It still sounds like you're saying he doesn't want her there."

"That's not what I'm saying. Are you even listening to me?"

"Are you sure that's not what you're saying?"

"Seriously, he *should* want her there. He'd gain major points after she sees him spike a few balls."

"Okay, guys," I interject, raising my hands to stop them. "It really doesn't matter because I know you two are going to drag me there anyways."

"Aw." Jen turns to Bristol. "She knows us so well."

However, Bristol keeps her eyes on me, her face morphing into a mischievous grin. "We're going to make him wish he invited you."

"How does that work if she's already going to be there?" Raymond asks. He has a point.

"Can you just shut up and let me do my thing?"

"Your thing?" I ask, and then my mind flashes back to when Bristol ransacked Jen's closet while I sat on Jen's bed in anticipation. Jen's words of Bristol being the fashion and color palette professional echo in my mind. I sigh. "What time should I come over?"

"You're right, Jen," Bristol says, reaching forward to play with my hair, her face suggesting that she's already contemplating a style for me. "She does know us pretty well."

CHAPTER TWENTY-ONE

"Stop messing with it, or I'll have to redo the whole thing."

I immediately retract my hand from the poof of hair on top of my head, which leads to an intricately woven bun with a French braid running up the back of my head. If Bristol does in fact intend to rebuild the coiffure, we'd miss the volleyball match altogether. Besides, I'd rather not have to bend upside down again—this time in public—for her to fix the braid.

I scan the area for Dalton as soon as the sand courts are visible, wanting to prepare myself as I count down the steps it'll take until he sees me. There's no reason to be nervous, really. I'm just not used to high-maintenance hairstyles or wearing makeup—even if Jen did keep it modest with just a touch of mascara and lip gloss—or the feeling of bikini straps rubbing against my back.

I keep my eyes on Dalton, although his back is to us as he peppers with a tall guy with reddish hair that I presume is his teammate. Each court is occupied, some teams sporting color-coordinated shirts while others dress in completely matching uniforms, Dalton's team included. They all wear matching pink tank tops that read "Big Dig Energy" on the front.

Lively music projects through a couple of speakers as we make our way toward the metal bleachers that sit perpendicular to the four courts. Our footsteps clank against the metal stairs as we climb past scattered spectators to take our seats, Jen and Bristol on either side of me. They remove their shirts to reveal bikini tops underneath, and Jen proceeds to lather on a layer of sunscreen. I take that as my cue to do the same, slipping my arms through the holes of my t-shirt and carefully lifting it over my head to avoid disrupting the fancy do.

Things remained bitter between Jay and me for about a day after our argument over the swimsuits, but neither of us can hold a grudge for long, so we gradually resumed our regular routine. The morning after I'd been sentenced to the never-ending dishwashing duty, Raymond exclaimed his relief at the absence of sibling tension. Again, I hadn't even said anything, he could just tell when I arrived that things were back to normal.

"Dupree!" Bristol shouts as one of Dalton's teammates jogs over to the bleachers to squirt water in his mouth. He's short and stalky with dark skin, bushy black hair and a beard, and thin-rimmed glasses.

"Hi, Dupree," Jen also greets him.

"Hello, ladies. Come to cheer us on?"

"You bet," Bristol responds. "And we dig the shirts."

Dupree snorts. "*Dig*, good one." He must have been the mastermind behind the pun on their tank tops. He sets his water down and returns to the court. "I expect to hear you rooting for me out there!"

"Dupree, total sweetheart," Jen tells me.

"I see," I reply, keeping my focus on the court.

"She's in the zone," Jen talks to Bristol across me.

"You're right, we shouldn't distract her," Bristol teases.

"Oh shut up you two." I shake my head, keeping my eyes forward.

Just then the guy Dalton's practicing with spikes the ball to the ground, and it bounces across the sand toward the bleachers. Dalton turns to grab it, briefly glancing up at the small crowd. He does a double take, and I give him a sheepish shrug for showing up to his match without his knowing. I guess Jen isn't the only one who unexpectedly appears where her crush can be found.

I can't quite read the look on his face, eyes wide and lips pressed tightly together like he's hiding a smile, but not the kind of it's-great-to-see-you smile I'd hoped for. It's almost as if he's wincing at the fact that I'm here. But why? I suddenly feel self-conscious about my new look. Our eyes lock over the span of bleachers until his teammate—the one he'd been warming up with—comes over and clasps his hand on Dalton's shoulder.

"Dude, we know your girlfriend's hot, now get your head in the game!" he tells him, his voice teasing as he jostles Dalton's shoulder.

Girlfriend? His words are a torch to my skin, my face suddenly burning red, more than when I heard Dalton referred to as my man at The Wonka Room. This time is way more public, an official label that's never been discussed between the two of us.

"Well, that went well," Bristol says.

A whistle blows, summoning all players to the court. Dalton's teammates quickly jog to the bleachers. Dalton follows them in a reluctant manner. He looks up at me again, pursing his lips and shaking his head. It's then that the rest of his teammates slip off their athletic shorts and fling them onto the rest of their piled gear, each exposing a pair of short spandex underneath, some solid colors, others with vibrant patterns. A few girls cheer nearby, and a couple of the guys wink at them in return, basking in the attention.

As they make their way to the far end of the court, one calls out to Dalton. "Come on, man, the game's about to start."

Dalton lets out a sigh, looking away with an embarrassed grin plastered on his face as he too slips off his shorts to reveal spandex with swirls of purples and blues with white speckles to represent the Milky Way.

"Ow, ow!" Bristol calls out with hands cupped around her mouth.

"Stop," I nudge her, feeling just as embarrassed as Dalton while his teammates join in on the teasing. One of them whistles at him, causing the others to laugh and watch my reaction to his skimpy outfit. I look away.

"I think we know why he didn't invite you," Jen tells me while trying to hold back her laughter.

The whistle blows again, and Dalton takes his position on the court next to the net. His teammate carries the volleyball a few paces past the back line, his brown hair covered by a backwards-facing snapback. He tosses the ball high into the air and runs toward the court, smacking the ball with his palm and sending it straight over the tip of the net. A player on the opposing team deflects it out of bounds. Off to a good start.

When Dalton is set up to spike, he jumps a few feet in the air and either slaps the ball toward the ground or taps it over the net to mislead their opponents. My friends were right, it's impressive. Even in the scanty getup. I holler along with the rest of the small crowd cheering them on.

Now it's his turn to serve.

He twists the ball in his hands, making his way behind the line. When he turns to face the court, he looks up toward the bleachers. I give him a smile for encouragement. The whistle blows, and he tosses the ball high into the air, jumping to meet it halfway on its descent. It sails straight into the net. His hands fist in frustration. He looks again in my direction, pointing at me in playful annoyance.

"Is he blaming me for that?"

"It could be the hair," Bristol contemplates, "in which case he'd be blaming me."

Regardless, I give him a smirk and an innocent shrug. His teammates all gang up to tease him again, roughhousing his shoulders and tousling his hair.

The score remains close the entire match, the opposing team pulling ahead at the very end to snatch the win. After Dalton missed a couple serves, I noticed him avoiding the bleachers altogether, keeping his focus on the game. Now that the teams will swap sides, he won't have to deal with the audience in his line of sight. His team gains an immense lead straight out the gate and keeps it up the entire match, sending them into a third and final match.

∼∼∼

"CONGRATULATIONS," SAYS A GIRL AS SHE LEANS IN TO kiss the guy in the snapback, her dirty blonde hair cascading over her shoulders in thick, voluminous waves. The rest of the guys are sliding on their athletic shorts again. I'm sure Raymond will resent missing out on the game once I give him details of their team uniform.

After slipping my shirt back on, Jen, Bristol, and I

make our way down the bleachers to join the team and the rest of their friends who came to watch.

"Way to go, guys," Jen tells them, and then points at me. "This is Avery."

"Yeah, we know who you are," replies the redhead with a sly smile. He sticks out his hand. "I'm George. This is Dupree, Diego, Melanie"—snapback and wavy locks—"and you already know that handsome fella at the end."

"Okay," Dalton speaks up, cutting him off before he can say more.

"It's nice to meet you all," I tell them as we all start walking away from the courts, Dalton falling into step with me at the back of the group.

"You don't have to lie to them. You can be as blatantly honest and rude as you'd like."

We make our way along the beach toward the pier and JuiSea. Melanie turns to the rest of us girls. "Are you coming swimming with us?"

"Sure," Jen and Bristol respond without giving it a second thought. It's summer and it's hot, the natural thing to do would be to go for a dip in the lake.

Unless your natural instinct is to avoid swimming and unpredictable situations involving people and water at all costs. My pace slows a bit.

"Uh, actually I should probably—" I start before Jen cuts me off.

"Didn't you get the whole day off?"

"Yeah, I—I do," I say, trying to sound casual, "but I—"

"But we already have plans," Dalton cuts in, moving closer to me. There's that same knowing look that Jay gave me when I rejected Dalton's invite to the lunar eclipse gathering. There are only a few people who can give me that look.

"Right," I agree, my voice a tad distant and uncertain. How convincing. At least Dalton is smoother with the justification.

"I mean, unless you want to stay and swim?" he offers. "But I'm not really up for it today."

"Me neither," I agree again. I figure I'll just follow his lead. First time and he's already better at these diversions than I am, and I've had a decade of practice.

"Suit yourself," Melanie tells us. Jen and Bristol fall into step on either side of me as Dalton walks with the rest of his team. They give me cunning smiles.

"That was smooth of him," Bristol says, keeping her voice quiet.

My heart rate quickens. Does she know? It's not that I don't want them to ever know about my past, I just want them to find out from me. But if they already know, then that means someone's been talking behind my back, and there are only two people in this town with that knowledge to begin with.

"What do you mean?" I ask, nervous for her answer.

"I mean you two don't actually have plans, right? He didn't even know you were coming to the game."

"So?"

"So, he's just making stuff up to hang out with you one-on-one. It was smooth." She shrugs.

"Oh. I guess so."

They both nudge me, reminding me of the treatment Dalton received from his teammates when I showed up to the sand courts.

We split ways with the rest of the group upon reaching the pier, the lot of them heading straight to the water while Dalton and I make our way in the opposite direction. I notice Raymond at the shop. When he sees us, he makes a fist and pulls his elbow downward, mouthing the word "yes." He's been encouraging me to hang out with Dalton again outside of working hours. I just didn't know it'd be today.

CHAPTER TWENTY-TWO

THE ORCHARD IS QUIET. PEACEFUL. THE COMPLETE opposite of the lake at this time of day. No bustling crowds or booming music or flying discs that could hit you at any moment. Just the birds chirping as they flutter in the treetops and the scent of apples as they ripen above us.

I push the tip of my foot off the ground, allowing the swing to sway back and forth. It's a bit high—I almost had to jump to sit on it—but then again Dalton has a few inches on me. He fashioned it from scrap wood lying around his garage. I appreciate the innovation. Here I am still trying to piece together my bedroom after four weeks and he just woke up one morning and decided to build a swing.

"Catch."

I look up just as an apple falls from above, rebounds off my lap, and lands on the ground with a thud. Startled by the sudden assault, my eyes frantically look from where the apple hit me to the ground below to the tree above until they settle on Dalton, who's standing on his book-reading branch.

"What the heck?"

He laughs at me and reaches his arm through scattered twigs to pick another one. It isn't as ripe as the first one he hurled at me, but then again most of the other trees won't be ready to harvest for a couple more months. I'm about to step off the swing to grab the apple on the woodchips when Dalton stops me.

"Don't," he tells me. "I'll get it." He jumps down from the branch and lands in a crouching position, grabs the apple, and inspects it before presenting it to me. "No bruises."

I take it from his hand. "I hope I can say the same for my leg. Here I was thinking I'm safe from flying objects, but apparently not."

He takes a seat on the ground with his back against the tree and bites into his apple, creating a loud crunch.

"What are you doing?" I ask him.

"I'm sitting," he responds casually, "and I'm eating this apple and enjoying the moment as I revel in my team's victory."

"No, I mean, why are you sitting on the ground? Shouldn't you be up there in your little nook?" I nod toward his branch, and he follows my gaze.

"I suppose, but now I have reason to be down here." He takes another bite.

"Is that so?"

"Indeed." He nods. "I sat up there for the view. I like seeing all the branches and leaves intertwine and feeling like I'm a part of it. But now I've got a view down here too."

My lip twitches, threatening to form in a dorky smile at his comment. I take a bite of my apple, steering my mind away from the complications of what each bite might signify about my personality. We sit in silence for a moment, aside from our chewing.

"Hey, thanks by the way," I tell him in slight humiliation. He looks up at me. "You know, for saying we had plans and all."

"We did."

"Hmm, I seem to recall you saying that you were busy today."

"Yeah, I usually don't bring the girl I like to come watch me jump around wearing intergalactic spandex."

"No?"

"No," he confirms. "Regular black spandex, absolutely. That way I still have some dignity. But not the ones I had on today."

"So, what you're telling me is that you have more than one pair?"

"Loads," he chuckles. "I have loads and loads of gaudy spandex."

"I can't wait for next week then," I tease. He makes the same expression as before the first match, the one that I couldn't quite read at the time.

"You know, my friends think you made up our plans together just to spend time alone with me," I tell him. "They don't actually know about my...thing."

"What thing? And I do want to spend time alone with you," he tells me, attempting to keep the conversation light-hearted.

I give him a weak smile. He looks at me with those same concerned eyes I saw at the waterfall.

"Avery," he says my name with such compassion. "I'm sure someone's probably brought up this idea before, and I don't want to upset you so please forgive me if I'm overstepping. I also don't want you to think that there's anything wrong with how things are now because that's not what I'm trying to say. It's just that I was thinking about this, and I want to throw it out there—"

"Just say it," I blurt out, having a pretty good idea as to what's coming and wanting to skip over all the disclaimers. He takes a deep breath.

"I think—please don't hate me but I think you could learn how to swim and overcome what's been holding you back."

I stare at the woodchips beneath my feet. It's the same thing Jay was getting at the other night, overcoming my fear, although Dalton's approach is a bit more reserved in nature. I take another bite of my apple.

Dalton tilts his head back against the uneven bark of the tree, drawing in a deep breath and exhaling the words, "You hate me. I just thought that what you did at the pool, jumping in after that many years… It was a really brave thing to do." He shrugs. "I don't know, it just seems to me like there's a more courageous side of you trying to escape from underneath all the guilt you've piled onto yourself." He waits, nibbling at the apple core in his hands.

I think back to the times when I treaded water in our apartment complex hot tub without touching the floor or walls. Treading is the easy part, it's the anxiety and the flashbacks that hold me captive.

"I know how to swim," I assert, although I doubt he'll believe me after pulling me out of the water at our picnic. He nods almost imperceptibly, staring at the woodchips in front of him. "And I don't hate you," I add.

He looks up at me, his smile sympathetic. "That's a relief."

I clear my throat. "So, why only this one?" I gesture to the skirt of woodchips around us. "None of the other trees seem to have this particular landscaping."

"She's special."

"That's what you said the first time we met."

"You mean the first time you trespassed?" he corrects, raising his eyebrows as if I'm a reckless delinquent. Although only half-eaten, I chuck my apple at him, which he deflects with quick reflexes. It bobbles across the uneven woodchips. "Jeez," he laughs.

"Ha-ha," I mimic because of his trespassing

comment. "And now look at me, sitting in a tree with my kidnapper."

"Whoa, slow down." He gapes at me and throws his hands up. "Whatever happened to the Tarzan version of Clark Kent?"

"Ugh," I cover my face with my hands, my next words muffled by the wall of embarrassment. "Please, I don't need to be reminded of anything I said or did that night." I slide my fingers apart just enough to catch a glimpse of his pleased face, and then drop my hands. "Besides, that was after you rescued me from Handsy. I didn't know that you were about to kidnap me and bring me back to your house against my will."

"You have a point. Next time I'll just drag your limp body to the sidewalk so you can sober up by yourself on a deserted street in the middle of the night."

"Next time you can help by making sure I don't drink to begin with," I say, repulsed by the thought of it.

"Deal."

I press my foot off the ground again, swinging gently under the web of branches. "No really though, why is this one special?" I ask, circling back to the tree. I watch as he thoughtfully prepares his answer. He stares into the distance, his eyes soft and his lips curving to the pictures playing in his mind.

"It's my earliest memory," he starts off slow, "yet I can still tell you what color of shoes I was wearing that day, what the weather was like, the way the sun perched high in the sky without a cloud in sight. I was four, my sister Amy was five, and we were playing out here in the orchard, running through the field and dodging trees." His voice mimics the action in his memory.

"We came across a couple apples hanging low in a tree, so bright and mouthwatering, so my sister climbed up the trunk to pick them. It was only mid-July at the time and the harvest doesn't begin until later in the season, so finding apples that perfect that early on," he pauses, sighing at the splendor, "it was like holding the key to a hidden treasure chest. Just, shocking and fills you to the brim with excitement." He laughs. "It was just a couple of apples, but I was only four so back then it was equivalent to a treasure chest.

"We munched on our apples together and I watched as my sister twirled through the field, just over there." He points to an area behind where I'm sitting on the swing. "And when she was done with her apple she marched right over here to a patch of dirt, dug a hole, and buried the core. I remember asking her, 'Won't you forget where it is?' She just continued to pack down the dirt on top of her buried treasure and told me, 'Just because you forget about something doesn't mean it's not there.' And so, we forgot about it.

"It wasn't until our mom did some weeding about a month or two later that she discovered its initial sprouting and showed us all. From that moment on, my sister watered it and sang to it and did all sorts of crazy non-scientific things to care for it. I think she even put on dance recitals to entertain it, thinking she would inspire the tree to grow faster." He laughs. "It continued to grow over the years, and to our disbelief, it grew to be the biggest tree out here. No one knows how or why."

He looks up to where speckles of red peek through the thicket of greenery. "And it seems to blossom months before any other tree, although it only started bearing fruit last summer," he says distractedly. My eyes follow his gaze.

"So, it's your sister's tree."

"Yeah." He smiles, lost in thought as he peers through the maze of branches. "It's my sister's tree."

∿∿∿

THE AIR IS STILL AND SILENT. NO RIPPLE OF WATER NOR rustle of wind, just the soundless landscape. I try to take in my surroundings, but my mind is foggy. I have zero recollection of why I'm sitting in a canoe or how I got here to begin with.

What's going on? *I think, the words blurring together in my head.* Why am I here?

I wouldn't be out here alone, that I know. I couldn't be, but there's no other movement, no indication of life in the vicinity. The water is flat. Even the clouds hang motionless on the horizon.

Yet something tugs at me, prodding at the furthest part of my brain, telling me that there's more here than what meets the eye.

But what? *I ask my instincts.* What is it I'm supposed to be seeing?

I sense that I'm forgetting something, something important, but I can't recall who I am or what I'm doing, if I came here with anyone else or on my own.

Think, think, *I push myself, but no matter how hard I concentrate, the results are unfruitful. I didn't just wake up from anesthesia; I lost my memory altogether.*

A collection of words floats through my head, speaking to me in a feathery voice of a man and echoing through the blank corridors of my mind.

Just because you forget about something doesn't mean it's not there.

CHAPTER TWENTY-THREE

"AND HOW'S MY SWEET RAYMOND DOING?"

"You don't even know him," I remind my mom. How have I become the messenger of an emerging long-distance friendship between my teenage male colleague and my middle-aged, newlywed, Slovenia-bound mother?

"I feel like I know him from all the wonderful things you tell me," she argues. "Did he really think I look thirty years old in that photo I sent you?"

"He really did," I confirm while gazing at my undecorated bedroom wall—although now painted—and trying to pick the perfect spot to hang my bulletin board. Jay decided to make Saturdays a consistent day off for me, so this morning I've been focused on continuing my bedroom transformation before heading to the second week of sand volleyball matches.

"If he wasn't gay, he'd be perfect for you," she says, obviously flattered by the compliment.

"You mean perfect for you? Who wouldn't want their daughter dating someone who thinks her mom looks twenty years younger than she actually is?"

"Seventeen years younger," she corrects. "Honey, I'm not there yet. I still have a few years left before the big five-oh."

I laugh at her. "I wasn't implying that you look old."

She groans. "Fifty's not old. Don't tell me fifty is old."

"Is she calling me old?" I hear Andrew ask in the background.

"Yes, darling, she is."

"No, I'm not!" I defend myself.

"Avery, when you come to be our age, I hope you have a daughter who calls you old too," Andrew calls out.

"And if you don't," my mother adds, "I'll be sure to call you every day from the comfort of my senior living facility to remind you."

"I don't think that's helping your case, Mom."

"Hush. Exploring Europe with Andrew has made me feel younger than ever so I'm not going to listen to another peep out of you if it's got to do with my age, you hear?"

"Fine, fine, you look like you could be my sister. How's that?"

"Better. But if I were you, I'd start taking notes when Raymond's talking about me. He does a much better job at flattery."

"I'll be sure to do that."

"Okay, let's see here...Raymond, Jen, Bristol." She lists off the friends she's already asked about. "Am I missing anybody?"

She is, but not to her knowledge. I haven't quite found the right moment to bring up the maybe-almost-official relationship that's developing. Most of our calls are just quick chats to inform the other person that we're all still alive and well.

"There is one other person I've been hanging out with," I start.

The thing about mothers is that they always know you better than you think they do. "You have a boyfriend. What's his name?"

"Mom!"

"Oh sorry, did I ruin the surprise? Continue with your story, I'll still act surprised when you tell me. Go on," she encourages.

"He's not my boyfriend," I tell her, and then add, "I don't think."

"I knew it," she exclaims. "There's been a slow increase in peppiness to your voice over the last few phone calls. I wanted to wait until you were ready to bring it up, but man, was I dying to ask you about him."

I smile. Do I really sound peppy? I guess I've been

acting a bit livelier lately, dancing more often in my room and finding myself grinning helplessly at random, unprompted moments. Little things keep reminding me of Dalton, like when a customer orders The Fruit Fairy for their child or when I see two people peppering a volleyball near the lake. "Well, what did you want to know?"

"Anything, everything. Oh, come on, honey!" The eagerness she's built up till now finally releases. I tell her about our awkward first meeting and his daily visits to the shop, which have continued over the past week and led to a couple more off-the-clock hangouts as well. And lastly, I share with her the sand volleyball league. She laughs when I mention his team's name and attire. By the end of it all, Dalton has my mom's long-distance stamp of approval.

"Go put a label on it," she encourages me. "He sounds very nice. I wouldn't let anyone else snatch him up. Just be smart."

"Will do."

After hearing her and Andrew's updates on their trip, we say our goodbyes, leaving me with just enough time to hang the bulletin board and photos from the wedding before heading to the sand volleyball courts for another round of impressive spiking and ridiculous, skimpy spandex.

"WAY TO GO, LEVI!" JEN CHEERS FERVENTLY FROM THE stands. Levi flashes her a bright smile from across the sand courts, making Jen's cheeks suffuse with color. This week his team plays against Dalton's, which leaves the loyalty between the four of us—Jen, Bristol, Raymond, and myself—divided.

"I still can't believe you're rooting against Big Dig Energy," Raymond says. "I mean, look at them."

Jen scoffs. "May I point out to you that Levi doesn't wear a shirt when he plays?"

"Well, until he plays in a pair of spandex, my loyalty lies elsewhere."

"You're a bunch of perverts," Bristol states from beneath her cap and sunglasses. "Anyways, you should just root for the players, not a side."

"You sound like a mom with children on both teams," I tell her.

The referee blows his whistle to signal the end of the second match and both teams give high fives as they cross under the net.

Dalton's more confident this time around, not acting nervous when it came time for his team to remove their baggy outer layers and reveal their fitting team attire. Maybe "confident" is the wrong word—it's not as if he's flaunting the get-up, and I still think my presence makes him feel awkward, but at least he's able to follow-up our quick glances with swift serves that soar over the net. And just like last week, his skills leave me speechless.

Through a series of rapid serves and spikes, digs and dives, the third match is over in a matter of minutes with Dalton's team coming out on top. Jen quickly shifted from loud and enthusiastic to still and taciturn just a few points into the match when the momentum seemed locked in.

"Look on the bright side," Raymond tells her. "He might need someone to comfort him after the loss."

She shoots him a cold glare. I look down to where Levi is happily conversing with Dalton's team, a beaming smile plastered on his face as always. "I don't think he's too upset about it," I comment.

As we make our way down the bleachers to join them, Dalton maneuvers around his teammates to stand next to me in the jumbled collection of players and friends.

"Congrats again," I tell him, nudging him with my elbow.

"Thanks for coming again," he responds, nudging me back.

"Ugh," Raymond groans, distorting his face and sticking out his tongue. "Your cuteness makes me want to throw up." Although I know he secretly loves it, I scrunch up my nose, giving him a disgusted look in return.

We shuffle away from the sand courts so the next teams can start warming up and walk along the beach in a huge mob like last week, the pier growing larger in the distance.

"Somebody go long." Dupree punts the volleyball ahead of the group, which veers left into the water. George and another guy from the opposing team immediately toss their shirts onto the hot sand before running into the water, creating splashes and waves in their wake. When the water is thigh-deep they dive in, racing to retrieve the volleyball.

I notice Bristol sliding off her pair of jean shorts so that she too is in her swimwear. The rest of the group follow suit, setting down their bags and taking off their outer layers.

"Could someone please do my back?" Jen asks, holding up a bottle of suntan lotion. I can't help but notice that she's facing Levi when she requests the favor, even if she doesn't direct it at him specifically.

"I can do it," he responds nevertheless, taking the bottle from her and squirting some in his hands. Melanie rubs sunscreen onto Diego's back and neck, and while everyone else prepares for either the rays or the waves, Dalton and I just stand there. The gears in my head start turning, my self-protective instincts kicking in to save me from the situation.

We're close enough to JuiSea for me to escape with a valid excuse. I could tell them I want to say hi to my brother, except Raymond would find that one suspicious. I could run up and make a smoothie. Sipping on something would buy me some time to chill on the beach with the rest of the sunbathers. Heck, I could take a group order and stay busy for a while.

"Avery," Dalton says beside me. I'd been staring at the divots in the sand with shifty eyes as my brain strategizes the most effective escape. "Avery," he repeats.

"Hmm?" I turn to him. He'd been watching me, a concerned look in his eyes that only I understand.

"Did you hear me?" he asks. I suppose I hadn't, considering I'd only heard my name and responded to that already. "I asked if you wanted to get out of here."

"Oh," I say, looking around again. Jen and Bristol lay out their beach towels while the rest of the group wades into the shallow water near the shore. Jay's music projects over us, making it harder for me to concentrate. The newness of the situation has me in a trance.

"Let's go," Dalton says determinedly, as if sensing my mental stupor.

"No," I counter and turn to face him. "I'm not that girl," I tell him, keeping my voice low so no one else can hear.

"What girl?" he asks, confused. Jen and Bristol now jog toward the water, joining the rest of the group.

"I am not the girl who steals a guy away from his friends," I tell him pointedly.

He squints at me in thought. "Is it technically stealing if it's my idea?"

"Yes. As much as you want alone time with me," I tease, "I know you also really want to go swimming with the guys." His expression gives in, admitting that it's true. "Go," I gesture.

As if on cue, Diego calls out to us from the water. "You guys coming in or what?"

"Dude," George scoffs and slaps the surface of the water to splash Diego's face. It's obvious he doesn't want anyone interrupting Dalton and me. A series of splashes erupts after that.

Dalton turns back to me. "You thirsty?"

I purse my lips, hiding a smile as I slowly shake my head in disbelief. Last Saturday he took me to the orchard for my sanity, and this time he's offering to sit out after being told to go have fun with his friends. "What's a girl gotta do to get a guy to hang out with his friends?"

"What's a guy gotta do to hang out with the girl?"

I let out a laugh. "You're unbelievable." He smiles, taking it as a compliment.

"We're going to grab some drinks," he calls to the guys who are still roughhousing each other in the water. Jen, Bristol, and Melanie are all off to the side, avoiding the splash zone.

"Yo, bring me one of those—" Dupree starts, but is cut off by George shoving him underwater.

I copy Dalton as he drops his belongings and kicks off his shoes. "Shall we?" He gestures up the slight embankment, palm facing up. As we walk, I feel his hand brush up against mine, almost too quick to register, but it makes my stomach flutter with excitement.

Just when I'm about to log it away as an accident, I feel him reach his hand around mine, sliding his fingers between my own. His hand feels warm from the sun, rough from the sand, and absolutely right.

There's a whistle chasing after us from someone in the water. Dalton lets out a chuckle and gives my hand a squeeze.

CHAPTER TWENTY-FOUR

WE SLURP THE LAST OF OUR SMOOTHIES, OUR STRAWS noisily sucking more air than sustenance. I reach out to take his cup as he sets it in the sand. Both of our hands grab hold of it like a tug-of-war.

"I'll take them back," I tell him.

He grips it tighter, pulling it away from my hand. "Nope," he declares, now reaching for the empty cup in my other hand. "You're not on the clock today." He sets them down in the sand as far from me as possible, lying almost completely flat before sitting back up. Grains of sand stick to his side and torso. I feel the urge to reach across him and brush them off, but keep my hands at my sides, not wanting to attract more whistles from our friends.

I look out to the water, but my eyes can't find any heads bobbing above the surface where they'd been swimming just a moment ago. My heart kicks into high gear as I frantically search the water. Why don't they have one of those lifeguard lookouts like in the movies? I grab ahold of Dalton's wrist.

"Where'd they go?" I ask, my body tense.

"Hey, it's alright," he grabs my white-knuckled fingers with his other hand. "They just swam to the dock."

My eyes shoot over to the pier and desperately scour where the wooden beams meet the water. I eventually come across an assembly of floating objects and let out a breath that I'd unknowingly been holding.

"What are they doing over there?"

"We like to jump off the dock, see who can do the craziest stunts. It's really just a dare contest," he admits. The way he talks about it—using inclusive words like "we"—sparks a pang of guilt that he's sitting out with me and watching his friends from afar.

"Go show off your daringness, then," I urge him. He raises an eyebrow at me. "You've sat out long enough," I explain, nodding to reassure him that I'm okay. "And I appreciate it. Really. But I hate how often my stupid anxiety gets in the way. Go have fun."

He sighs and stands, brushing the sand off himself. "It's not stupid, by the way," he tells me. "But if *you* think it is and you want to do something about it, I know someone who might be willing to help."

Right, because that ended so well last time.

He speaks with such sincerity that I can't be

annoyed at his offer. Still, I'm not going to take him up on it anytime soon.

"Tempting," I joke.

He nudges my foot with his. First holding hands, now playing footsies. My insides melt.

"Be safe," I tell him, and then add a quick smile to keep up my act. I'm still nervous no doubt—being in this environment always does that to me—but it's not for him to have to deal with.

"I will. We've done this hundreds of times if that helps at all." He shrugs one shoulder, realizing that it doesn't in fact help. My dad had one successful jump under his belt before he slipped on the second.

Dalton heads toward the pier, running the length of the dock to where his friends swim in the water at the end. When they see him approaching, they holler, cheering him on as he picks up speed. I dig my fingers and toes under a security blanket of sand as I grip the ground for protection.

Dalton propels himself into a front flip, the splash creating a slapping noise as he disappears into the water. I hold my breath for the seconds it takes for him to pop his head above the surface again. I exhale, feeling my shoulders relax as I watch him flip his wet hair out of his face. He looks my way, waving a hand at me.

Thank you for the reassurance, but not the attention.

Half of the other heads turn my way.

"Avery," Raymond shouts, "get your pretty little butt over here!"

"Come on, Avery," Jen and Bristol join in, loud enough that I look around to see if anyone else is staring. I extract my hand from the tunnel of sand I'd been digging subconsciously and wave at them, hoping they'll redirect their attention to the rotation of guys climbing up the dock ladder to flip over the edge. Dupree is on the dock with Levi on deck.

It continues like this for a while. Their stunts—flips, dives, cannonballs, and accidental belly flops—and my watching them from afar in a dry bathing suit. But eventually their jumping fiasco dies down, and Jen climbs the ladder to lie down on the dock with her arm and foot dangling over the edge. There's no indication that they'll return anytime soon, and I've grown tired of waiting here like a dog on a leash.

As Dalton mentioned in the orchard, swimming isn't the key issue—it's the apprehension I feel in these situations, and I've been watching them long enough for the nerves to subside. All they're doing now is treading water, so rather than grabbing my stuff to leave, I decide to walk over there, to come face-to-face with my fear.

I stand up, wincing at the pain in my legs from sitting in the same position for so long, and dust off the sand that sticks to the back of my legs. My body feels heavy with tension as I take my first steps toward the pier.

It begins high up the embankment to account for heavy rainfall, allowing me to get used to its width and the spaces between each wooden plank before I'm crossing the water below. Still, I keep to a linear path down the center with a slow pace and watchful eyes that monitor my every step. There are no railings, no benches, nothing. But I'm already halfway to the end, committed to seeing it through.

Jen doesn't see me approach, her eyes shut as she soaks in the sun.

"Hey," I announce my arrival. She lifts her head, opening her eyes to squint in my direction.

"Finally." She welcomes me with a smile and rests her head back down. "What took you so long? Come join me." She pats the spot next to her, but I carefully sit down in the middle of the dock. My body presses into the wood, feeling stiff and tingly.

"Are you talking to yourself again?" Raymond asks Jen from somewhere below.

"No," she replies with sass, glancing over the edge to where the rest of them are still swimming. "Avery's here."

"Finally!" he shouts.

"Hey, Avery," I hear Levi's cheerful greeting.

"You know we don't follow that whole 30-minute post-eating pre-swimming rule around here," Raymond tells me.

I hesitate, taking note of his expectation that I'll be getting in the water.

"Noted," I mutter, if only to say something.

"Uh, why can't we see you?" asks Dupree.

"Yeah, where are you?" Melanie laughs.

Maybe this was a bad idea after all. It won't make sense for me to sit down and then suddenly leave again, but now they expect me to come near the edge so I'm at least visible, and possibly even jump in like the rest of them. What am I supposed to do, say that I'm too comfortable to move a few feet to the side? I rotate my legs and lay flat on my stomach with my elbows propping me up to peer over the edge.

"There she is."

"Come to join the party?"

I see Melanie and Diego swimming near each other, Levi floating on his back, Dupree and George bobbing in the water like buoys, Bristol sitting on the ladder prong that's level with the water and Raymond with his arms draped over her legs as if they're floatation noodles. And then there's Dalton...

He keeps my gaze, his eyes questioning my motives.

"Are you coming in?" Diego asks.

"It's so relaxing," Levi adds, his eyes shut and his voice heavy with tranquility.

"We have to see what moves you've got," Dupree says. "I'll bet she can top Dalton's flip."

"No," I draw out. "No skills in that department, trust me. I'd probably end up in the hospital." My impromptu excuses will need some workshopping if I plan to have a social life for the next month.

Is this what it would have been like to grow up in Nelson? Daily dock hangouts with large groups of friends, working alongside my brother year-round, possibly already dating Dalton? Although if I'd grown up here, my dad's death would have still haunted me. I wouldn't be hanging out by the water with people who can't get enough of it. No, I would have made friends with the coffeeshop type, the ones who read new books every week and play board games on Friday nights. And I wouldn't have had to worry about cliff jumping on a picnic date or being peer-pressured over the edge of a dock.

First, it's George. "What are you waiting for?"

Followed by Melanie. "The water's not that bad."

And then Dalton. "Maybe she doesn't want to swim."

Raymond. "Lame."

Dupree. "Get in already."

Along with Diego. "Come on."

And Levi. "You can do it."

Dalton again. "Guys, leave her alone. She'll get in if she wants to."

With the addition of Bristol. "I can move off the ladder if you want to climb down. Just let me know."

Once more from Raymond. "Avery, stop psyching yourself out and jump in. It's not that cold."

And thankfully Jen. "Don't listen to them."

"It looks higher than it is."

"What are you afraid of?"

"Yeah, there aren't any sharks here. It's a lake."

"Don't make me come up there!"

"Stop it, guys!"

The sight of the lapping water beneath me gives me vertigo as my nerves fire on all cylinders. I try to swallow the lump that rises in my throat and ignore the itch of tears that threaten to spill over. Each comment and laugh rattles in my head, making its way to my innermost self that shouts, *You're a coward! And a liar. Your dad would be ashamed of you.*

I try to focus on my breathing with what little concentration I have left, but there's a tingling sensation in my hands that spreads up my arms and my heart starts palpitating like an amateur drummer unable to keep a beat. My mouth feels dry, and my stomach feels nauseous. Everything in my surrounding fades to muffled commotion, the voices that rise from the water now obscured and meshed together. Only one stands out due to proximity.

"Hey." Jen's concerned voice penetrates my barrier as she touches my wrist, leaving a prickly sensation in its wake. "Are you okay?"

The dock shakes. There are still people shouting, but I can't make out what's being said or why it feels like I'm experiencing a minor earthquake.

Jen's hand disappears from my wrist as she lets out a shriek, followed a second later by a splash. My head whips up to see a tall figure with broad shoulders, reddish hair, and a pair of large hands reaching down to grab me.

The feeling of being heaved off the dock and slung over his shoulders zaps me from my shocked state and thrusts me into survival mode. The world spins upside-down, the only steady focal point being the center of George's back. His wet skin glistens in the sunlight, and the smell of sunscreen clogs my nose.

I scream at the top of my lungs, violent and animalistic, as I thrash my arms to be freed.

"You're going in whether you like it or not," he says, clutching my legs and spinning around to disorient me. Blood rushes to my head, but I continue to scream and flail, slapping as hard as I can against his exposed back and subconsciously hoping that I leave distinctive red handprints. I can only imagine the looks we're getting from the beach.

George's grip on my legs loosens and he flings me forward, unpeeling me from his slimy back. I brace for impact, expecting the water to suck me under and envelop me in its suffocating embrace. I expect to feel disoriented and unsure of which direction to swim in. I expect another panic attack, and perhaps another rescue mission, this time in front of a crowd of people.

What I don't expect is the feeling of a hard surface against my feet, and then my butt, as I stumble backwards onto the dock.

"Jeez, can you calm down?" George asks me angrily, reaching a hand around to rub his lower back. "It's not like you would've died."

At this point, Dalton emerges from where the ladder meets the dock. He climbs onto the wooden planks, water pouring off him.

"What the hell was that?" he bellows, marching up to George with such vigor that I almost feel sorry he tried to throw me in.

Almost.

"Whoa, calm down, Dalton." George raises his arms, claiming innocence. They're standing so close that their chests are barely separated. The height difference doesn't seem to faze Dalton in his state of rage.

"Don't tell me to calm down! You can tell me what the hell you were thinking." He shoves George backward. George takes the blow without retaliating, but the infuriated look on his face shows no promises if Dalton goes in again.

"What's your problem?" George yells back, teetering on the edge of throwing a punch in return. Levi appears, and then Diego, who both hedge their way between Dalton and George, facing either of them.

"Everybody calm down," says Levi in an attempt to smooth things over.

"Yeah, everyone's alright," Diego states, directing it more toward Dalton than George. "He was just having a bit of fun."

"Fun?" Dalton scoffs. "I didn't realize having fun meant picking up a girl against her will and throwing her off the end of a dock when she *clearly* doesn't want to go in the water. Since when did it become fun to disrespect someone like that? Huh?" He doesn't hold back any fury.

Bristol's suddenly at my side, with Jen and Raymond

in tow. She kneels beside my sprawled-out body and wraps her arm around my shoulders, helping me to sit up. "Are you okay?" she asks.

I nod, keeping my eyes transfixed on the chaos in front of us and the fact that it blocks the only dry exit from where I sit.

Now the whole group is on the dock—Dupree, Melanie, all of them sopping wet and finding a spot either between Dalton and George or by my side.

"Do you want to leave?" Jen asks, worried. The last few minutes have made me so flustered that I don't even acknowledge the tears that slide down my face. I look to Dalton who throws his hands up in frustrated surrender.

"You know what, forget it," he says, turning his back on everyone that stands between him and George. He takes a few steps to where I crouch on the ground. "Let's go," he tells me, still fuming, but able to suppress some of it when speaking to me.

He wraps his arms around my waist and helps me stand. It feels humiliating receiving his help in front of everyone, but once I'm upright, I realize that the numbness and tingling sensation still courses through my body, and I'm suddenly grateful for his support. I probably would have died from embarrassment had I stood up and fallen into the water on my own accord.

"Avery." Both Jen and Bristol try to get my attention. I can see them and Raymond trailing in my peripheral as Dalton leads me back down the center of the dock.

Jen wraps her arm around me as well. Raymond stops when he reaches the other side of the group.

"That wasn't cool, man," he tells George, taking his chance to stand up for me before following us down the dock.

In the distance I hear George and the others questioning what just happened. I keep my eyes fixed on the land ahead of us, wishing I was far from nearby witnesses and my confused cluster of friends.

CHAPTER TWENTY-FIVE

"Can you build me one?" I ask Dalton as I sit on the wooden swing and pluck the last of the splinters from my foot, which had jammed into a jagged piece of wood when George hurled me off his shoulder. The farther we got away from the scene, the more the little suckers obstructed my ability to walk, not that I was well off to begin with.

When we'd reached the outside perimeter of JuiSea, the five of us—Raymond, Jen, Bristol, Dalton, and I—paused our escape and instead turned it into an overwhelming Q and A session featuring yours truly. Dalton remained quiet, letting me sift through their questions regarding if I was alright and why I freaked out. No longer was I going to keep the secret from them, but after all the commotion on the dock and the shock that my body was in, I knew I needed a calm place to unwind before giving them an explanation.

Luckily, they were still looking out for my best interest and didn't object when I promised to explain everything later.

Now it's just Dalton and me in the orchard, sitting in our designated spots: me on the swing and him on the woodchips with his back against the apple tree.

"You want me to build you a swing?" he clarifies. "And hang it where?"

"I don't know," I shrug, letting my foot slide off my knee. "I'll ship it home and find a different orchard to trespass in."

"Or maybe you can think of something a little less bulky than a swing. You know, something you can carry with you."

"Do you have a catalog I can look through?"

"You'd be surprised at how many things I've made."

"Like the clothes rack next to your bed," I mention, picturing the wooden piece of furniture in his room.

He smiles. "I almost forgot you've been there."

"So, what else have you made besides furniture and swings?"

He reaches his arms above his head, the backs of his hands rubbing against the bark as he stretches in thought. "Coasters, a couple cutting boards, picture frames, a longboard, a birdhouse..." He trails off at the end to indicate there are more.

"Impressive."

He drops his arms. "Nah, just a hobby I mess around with. I'm more interested in machinery. I've always imagined myself becoming a mechanical engineer."

"Why don't you go to school for it?" I ask, rocking back and forth on the swing. "I know you mentioned sticking around for the harvest, but can't your parents hire seasonal help so you can go get a degree?"

"Um—" he hesitates, running a hand over his cheeks and mouth. "There's something I, uh, haven't told you." He takes a considerable breath, letting the air escape through tight lips and puffed-out cheeks. I swallow, unsure if I should respond or wait.

He clears his throat. When he finally speaks, his voice is void of its naturally lighthearted tone. "Almost a year ago, when my sister left for college, she was in a head-on collision."

I let out a quiet gasp.

"And she," he continues solemnly, "died on impact."

He picks up a woodchip next to him and twists it in his hands. I remain silent. After all these years of hearing people tell me how sorry they are about my dad, I know apologies don't help the heartache. They don't change the facts, only reaffirm how unfair life can be.

"That's why I decided to stick around this fall." He flicks the woodchip and grabs another one. "I didn't want my parents to have to deal with the distance or the thought of me in that same scenario if I left for college too."

I look at him in astonishment. This tragedy

happened less than a year ago and already he's able to respond in such a way that puts his parents' emotional wellbeing above his own ambitions. I try supporting my mom and brother in ways a daughter and younger sister can, but even after eleven years I still seem to recoil into my pit of anxiety and remorse, letting myself be the one who needs the most support.

My heart aches for him, constricting with the sadness that only losing a family member can invoke. I feel a powerful urge to slide off the swing, kneel beside him, and wrap him in my arms, like a hug might ease the pain. And although I know an apology won't fix anything, my sorrow is too great to hold back.

"I am so sorry, Dalton," I tell him, sitting on the now motionless swing that hangs lifeless from its branch. "If it's any consolation, I think what you're doing is really admirable, postponing your education to be there for your parents. It's a perfectly sound reason not to go to college right away."

He clicks his mouth in acknowledgement, examining the unique shape of the light tan woodchip in his hands. "Thanks," he responds, and then sighs, dropping the piece of wood.

"Really," I press on, earnestly seeking eye contact so he understands how amazing he is. He looks at me, giving me a half-hearted smile. "I don't think I'd be handling it as caring as you are. I mean, I probably wouldn't go to school either, but it'd be from my own distress holding me back."

I think about my own mourning and how I let my feelings build up an impenetrable fear. "The guilt and the blame I feel for my father's death—it's suffocating. It seizes my chest and crushes my lungs, like it wants me to feel what he felt." My voice cracks. And then, realizing the direction I'd taken the conversation, I clear my throat. I didn't mean to turn it around on me after he had opened up about something so deep and heart-wrenching.

He pushes himself off the ground, wooden pellets scurrying away from the movement, and looks at me with a sudden intensity—eyebrows furrowed, lips twisted in disbelief, like he's troubled by what I said.

"Avery, what happened to your father wasn't your fault," he tells me, stern with increasing passion. "It's painful watching you beat yourself up over it." He strides about the area with hands shoved in his pockets.

The sun won't set for hours, yet it's darker than usual. The late afternoon storm clouds cover the once-blank canvas of the sky, as if intentionally setting the mood for our conversation.

"I was the only one who could have prevented it," I remind him, feeling a bit irritated that he can't just accept what I'd failed to do that day and let me deal with the consequences. "That makes me the person responsible."

"No!" He practically cuts me off. "Do you know any kindergarteners?" He watches me intently, waiting for any indication of my experience with little kids. "Would you expect a kid that age to act heroic and save the life of a full-grown adult, even a family member, if they were suddenly thrown into a situation that trau-matizing?"

Dalton and I stare at each other, my eyes tentative while his penetrate deep into my soul. I bite the inside of my cheek, trying to picture a small child in the canoe where I'd sat. Normally guilt and shame dominate over notions like self-forgiveness and grace, concepts so foreign to me now that I've learned to live without them. But today, replacing the child in the canoe unveils a small part of me that understands Dalton's view, why he's adamant about the way I treat myself.

He steps forward until we're only a foot apart. He looks down at where I sit with my legs dangling over the swing, ankles crossed, and elbows hooked around the ropes for balance. Perhaps all my apprehension could have been prevented had I shown myself a little compassion. Maybe I would have had enough emotional capacity to deal with my fear and work through the trauma instead of always putting myself down.

"I wouldn't be afraid," I mutter, my posture defeated as I stare lazily off in the distance. And then, realizing he didn't hear my train of thought, I add, "If I didn't blame myself."

"Maybe not," he agrees sympathetically, his voice gentler now as he nudges the tip of his shoe into the ground. "Either way, you can't let fear keep you from moving forward." He states the words carefully, softening the offense at how I've lived my life up till now.

"Whether it be forgiving yourself, trying something scary..." He pauses, fingers fiddling at his sides as his eyes dart back and forth between mine. "Or taking a risk," he breathes, and then his lips are on mine.

His hands clutch the ropes so quickly that my arms shake loose from where they'd been keeping my balance. He must notice too because he slides one of his hands between the rope and my waist and presses it firmly against my lower back, his strength sending heat waves through my entire body. The familiar scent of cedarwood and citrus encircles me, the one I've come to take comfort in from the moment he lent me his t-shirt.

His soft lips part from mine briefly before moving in again, a magnetic force drawing us together. There's so much more than physical attraction fueling us. There's a deeper connection, a bond welded together by the similarities of our pasts.

I unravel my ankles and hook them around his calves, inviting him closer. My fingers run through his hair, which he must take as a hint because he brings a hand to my neck, the other one still the only thing keeping me from tumbling over the back of this swing.

We're interrupted by a crash of thunder so earsplitting that our heads yank apart as quickly as they'd come together. I grab the ropes to secure myself, frightened by the sound. Dalton's hair is frazzled, parts of it sticking out of place. Raindrops start to fall, although we can't feel them yet under the umbrella of tree branches.

He laughs and turns to face me, and all I can think about is kissing him again, this time in the rain. I look down, wanting to conceal my flushed cheeks.

He reaches a hand in my line of sight, palm up. When I lift my gaze to him, he's smiling, obviously pleased by the recent events. I bite my lip and place my hand in his, letting him pull me off the swing.

Together we dash across the orchard and through the tall grass by the fence. Fat raindrops spatter on my head and shoulders while thunder roars overhead. Dalton hops the fence in one swift movement before relinking hands to help me over. The storm quickly turns into a torrential downpour, and with our fingers interlocked, we scurry down the puddled pathway to seek refuge.

CHAPTER TWENTY-SIX

BY THE TIME DALTON'S HOUSE COMES INTO VIEW—A haven gleaming in the distance with a barn attached to one side—we're completely drenched, the storm having chased us through the forest with an artillery of pummeling raindrops and hail pellets. We don't slow as we burst through the front door and slam it shut with such vigor as if to laugh in the storm's face for failing to defeat us.

"Oh, my!" a woman exclaims from the kitchen. She's thin and pale, with most of her brown hair clipped back, leaving only a few strands down to frame her delicate face. Upon seeing us, she swiftly sets down the knife she'd been using to slice bell peppers, moves around the kitchen island, and disappears down a hallway.

Sally, Dalton's golden doodle, barks in excitement as she trots over to greet us, tail wagging.

"Hey, girl." Dalton ruffles her face. She licks his hand and then proceeds to lean against my legs.

There's a dining area to my right, the kitchen straight ahead, and a living room to my left. It's cozy—blankets drape over the backs of sofas, a bowl of fruit and colorful placemats cover the dining room table, and décor featuring inspirational quotes hang on the walls. The woman returns a moment later with a stack of towels in her arms.

"Oh, sweetie, you must be freezing," she says as she approaches us. I assume she's addressing her son since we've never met, but when she reaches us, she hands the stack of towels to Dalton and shakes one loose to drape around my shoulders.

"You must be the lovely Avery," she says, wrapping me in a warm embrace. Not some half-hug to be polite, she really doesn't mind the fact that my clothes are sopping wet and my skin is frigid to the touch. She squeezes me tight anyway. "I'm Leeann. It's so nice to finally meet you."

I glance sideways to Dalton, taken aback by the welcome. Obviously, he's mentioned me to his parents, but his smile shows no sign of embarrassment by his mother's affection.

"It's nice to meet you too," I respond, and she pulls away. Up close, I can see the creases and bags that outline her eyes.

"Let me find you some dry clothes to change into," she says, her face thoughtful and her hands still on my arms. She turns to her son. "Dalton, why don't you show Avery how to work the shower faucet and get out a clean towel for her to use?"

I can see where he gets his hospitality from.

"Thank you," I tell her before Dalton grabs my icy hand and leads me to a door just left of the kitchen. On the other side is his room: abnormally large, uncommonly tidy, and unquestionably familiar from my second night—or more accurately, my second morning—in town. I hadn't noticed that his bedroom was an actual barn since the last time I was here I bolted away without looking back, but it's the structure I noticed attached to the side of the house as we ran toward the front door just a moment ago.

Dalton leads me to the bathroom at the far end of his room, the stench of cleaning products the only thing missing from my previous visit. He grabs me a clean towel and twists the shower handles to release a sputtering stream of water. When he turns back to me and notices my teeth chattering from standing in wet clothes, he leans down to give me a kiss.

"Don't be long," he says, both of us not wanting to separate from each other.

"I'll be out before you know it," I respond and playfully nudge him out the door.

⁓⁓⁓

I've never seen anyone cut up an apple as efficiently as Leeann. One second she's holding a whole apple, the next she's sliding a plate in front of me with a dozen perfectly shaped slices on it. Had I blinked, I would have missed the whole thing. I take a slice.

I'm seated on an elevated cushioned chair on one side of the kitchen island while Leeann continues to chop up various fruits and vegetables on the other. I hear the faint running of water from Dalton's shower. Sometime during my own, Leeann must have slipped in to grab my wet clothes and leave a pile of dry ones behind: Nelson High School sweatpants with the number twenty-four printed on them and a t-shirt that says, "It takes courage to grow up and become who you really are."

Upon my return to the kitchen, Leeann promptly asked how I was enjoying my summer, to which I told her it's been great. I left out the part about her son playing a major role in that. Her inviting presence makes me miss my own mom and her tender nature.

The front door slams shut behind me, and I whip around in my seat to where a man in the doorway—tall with thin, greying hair and spectacles—shrugs out of a raincoat.

"E.E. Cummings," he muses, his voice rich in wonder. He hangs his raincoat on a coatrack and joins us in the kitchen. "Your shirt," he clarifies, glancing my way. He gives Leeann a kiss on the cheek. "She always did love his work, didn't she, honey?"

"She did indeed." Leeann smiles and proceeds to introduce us. "My husband, Robert."

Robert reaches a hand across the marble countertop to shake mine. "I was wondering when Dalton might bring you around here. I didn't think we were the embarrassing type, did you?" he asks Leeann.

I chime in. "Most kids think their parents are the embarrassing type, no matter how cool they actually are. Although you might be the exception—Dalton speaks highly of you both."

"Well, that's reassuring," Leeann responds.

"Honey, she called us cool," Robert adds.

Leeann smiles and leans into her husband. Their affection is a delight to witness, one that starkly contrasts the sorrow etched into their features.

When Robert leaves the room, I ask, "What did he mean about the E.E. Cummings quote?" I take another apple slice as Leeann slowly wipes her hands on a dish towel.

"Our daughter," she finally responds, her weary eyes courageously finding mine. "That was our daughter Amy's shirt. One of her favorites, actually. She wore it all the time."

My body tenses to the sudden pang of feeling like an intruder.

Sensing my shift in demeanor, Leeann speaks up. "It's nice to see someone wearing it again. It makes the memory of her much more tangible. I can almost hear her laughter. Or the way she'd run in here with a bounce in her step to read us an eloquent passage in one of the dozens of books she treasured." Leeann lets out a laugh as she pictures it. "Now Dalton's trying to read that same stack of books, always disappearing into the orchard with one tucked under his arm."

"I'm really sorry for your loss," I console her.

"It's the worst pain a mother can feel," she chokes, yet her composure remains strong. "One of the worst parts," she continues, "is seeing how much it affects Dalton. Watching him deny opportunities for his future, choosing not to go to college…"

She resumes chopping as if she needs a distraction from the pain. I think back to what Dalton said about not wanting to leave his parents behind, of sheltering them from the possibility of losing another child.

"I really admire that he's willing to postpone college to help with the harvest and everything," I say, hoping that it will provide some comfort in the situation.

She freezes mid-chop and gives me a quizzical look. "He's not postponing college," she explains. "He doesn't ever want to go. He feels so responsible for the accident and fears something similar would happen if he left home."

I'm unable to reconcile what she's telling me with what Dalton shared at the apple tree. Amy's apple tree.

"Wait, you said he feels responsible?" I question, trying to make sense of it all.

"Oh, yes." She resumes her meal prep as she dives into the story I'm sure she's recited many times over.

"Robert and I had said our goodbyes to Amy earlier that day, thinking that she and her friends were driving straight to Palmerston College to move into the dorms. We weren't aware of the going-away party some of her high school classmates were throwing that afternoon here in town. They decided they'd swing by for a couple hours and drive to campus that evening.

"Since Dalton was in the class below her, he was invited too, and when it came time for Amy and her friends to leave, Dalton was there to wish her off. He sensed that the friend driving had been drinking because she reeked of alcohol and tripped on her way to the car. Dalton questioned her, but of course she denied it.

"The news of their deaths tore us to shreds, but when the biopsy showed that the driver had been drunk," she pauses to steady herself, her face replaying the events of that day, "Dalton shouldered all the blame. He'd known she wasn't capable that night and he so desperately wishes he would have stopped her. Stolen her keys, slashed the tires, anything.

"Now, not only is he scared of something terrible happening if he did go to college, but he doesn't think he deserves the opportunity. He's completely closed the book on that chapter in his life before even giving it a chance. Robert and I would bring it up, talk about scholarships, bring home pamphlets for different engineering programs, but the more we brought it up, the more adamant he became about not going. So, we eventually dropped it altogether."

Leeann doesn't look up when she finishes, knowing full-well there's no easy way to respond to a story that tragic. I don't know what to think. Logically, it makes sense, and I can relate all too well. But the connection I felt with Dalton in the orchard because of our pasts was only the tip of the iceberg. Did he plan on ever revealing the rest?

Dalton's the first person I've opened up to in years, the first I've let my guard down around. He's been a consistent source of encouragement for me to overcome my fear. I even feel like I've been taking small steps outside of my comfort zone and making minor shifts in the way I think about my past and what that means for my future. I now realize that his role in supporting me has been a front to hide behind his own guilt and shame. Heat burns inside me as I discover the deceit behind his words. If he's unable to bring himself to go to college, why should I listen to him tell me to face my fear? He has no right to tell me how to deal with my past.

Something wet strokes my hand by my side. I look down to see Sally greet me with sloppy kisses. She'd been behind Dalton's closed door, which means—

I look up as Dalton joins me at the counter, his wet hair falling into his eyes. He tries to wrap his arm around my waist, to which I reflexively pull away. His uncertain eyes question me, and then glance between me and his mom across the kitchen. His expression softens into a smile.

"Oh, it's fine. She doesn't care."

She might not, but I do, I think.

Dalton tries wrapping his arm around me again, but I pull back another time and face him with a stern look I can't seem to shake.

"I should get going," I declare, sliding out of my chair. The last thing I want is to have a confrontation in front of his sweet mom after she told me her heart-wrenching story.

"What—" Dalton starts.

"You're more than welcome to stay for dinner," Leeann offers as she drizzles oil into frying pan and turns on the stove.

"Thanks, but I think I'd better go while there's a gap in the storm," I tell her.

"Dalton can drive you later," she counters, moving the chopped vegetables into the pan.

"That's alright. My brother's probably wondering where I am anyways." Dalton keeps his eyes on me, and I suddenly wish he didn't know about my habit of lying to get out of uncomfortable situations.

Leeann grabs a landline from its receiver. "Why don't you give him a call, so he won't worry where—"

"Mom," Dalton interrupts her, his voice decided. "Maybe next time."

She looks back and forth between us, her demeanor sagging as she gives in and puts the phone back. A pang of regret seizes me as I realize I'm running away in her daughter's favorite t-shirt, that me wearing it brings back memories Leeann will never have the chance to recreate with her daughter.

"You're welcome back anytime," she tells me as she moves around the counter to give me another warm hug.

"Thank you," I respond, breathless as I reach my arms up to return the embrace. I avoid making eye contact with Dalton, although I can feel him staring. He walks me to the front door and opens it.

"I'll see you later." I try keeping it short, still avoiding his gaze. How did we go from a passionate kiss in the orchard to this?

"I'll walk you out," he responds, gesturing for me to step outside. As soon as the door clicks shut behind us, he reaches for my hand and asks if I'm alright. I yank it away, shooting him a look. If he believed any part of my lousy façade before, that's well over. I begin walking in the direction of Jay's house.

"Is it something I did?" He follows.

I want to laugh. And scream. And tell him how his encouragement and lies make me feel after finding out the truth. But I remain quiet.

Dalton takes the opportunity to prod some more. "Is it something my mom said?" he questions, still just a couple strides behind me.

I stop and close my eyes, squeezing my hands into

fists at my sides. *He lost his sister,* I tell myself. *Show him some grace.*

I grit my teeth while trying to tame my thoughts and give him the benefit of the doubt, but I can't help the irritation I feel toward him for deceiving me. *You've lost someone too. You know how it feels.*

But losing a family member doesn't give someone permission to give hypocritical advice, to give me false hope about my life while covering up the truth of his own.

"What did she say?" He tries again.

I whip around to face him. "A lot more than you," I say pointedly, unable to restrain my anger. I continue to clench my fists, trying to maintain my composure.

"I," he stutters, "I don't understand."

"I don't expect you to," I scoff, turning my back on him to continue my walk home.

"Whoa, wait a second." He leaps forward and grabs my arm to spin me around again. "Please talk to me. Tell me what's going on," he pleads, his voice frantic as his bewildered eyes search my face for an answer.

"Let's see here." I cross my arms, a gesture he responds to by sliding his hands into the pockets of his jeans. "You completely misled me about how your sister passed away, you lied to me about why you're not going to college, and you had the audacity to tell me to face my anxiety and overcome my fear despite you wallowing in your own."

He opens his mouth to speak, but no words come

out. He just looks past me into the orchard. We stand in silence, and it takes everything in me to wait for his response and not fire off more accusations. His timid eyes find mine again, but he doesn't say anything.

"Really, nothing?" I ask, exasperated.

"What do you want me to say, Avery?" He yanks his hands from his pockets and gestures in a helpless shrug. "I didn't lie to you about how she died, and I *do* think you can overcome—"

"Telling me about something that happened and withholding a major part of the story doesn't constitute as the truth in my book, Dalton—" I interject, my words spewing quicker than my thoughts can follow.

"You're one to talk about lying. And besides, it's not up to you how much or how quickly I open up to you—"

"It's up to you how you mislead someone and how you make them feel about something incredibly sensitive—"

"I'm not responsible for how you interpret my perspective of your whole water issue. I'm sorry you respond so negatively to my encouragement—"

"You're a hypocrite!" I explode. "You feel guilty about letting your sister ride off with that drunk driver and you're shouldering the blame of her death and letting that hold you back from a huge part of your life. You're telling me all these things about my situation, but you're blind to your own reality!"

"Well maybe despite what happened with my sister,

I think it's a little pathetic how much you've let an experience that happened to you a lifetime ago affect every single day of your life since," he bellows.

I freeze, my words catching in my throat as tears tickle the corners of my eyes. The sternness in his face softens when he sees the impact of his remark.

"An experience?" I repeat, the anger in my voice replaced with despondency.

"Avery," he steps forward, placing a hand on my arm.

I don't pull back, but I trust my eyes and voice to convey that my heart is already miles away from him.

"I didn't mean—" he tries, his tone gentle.

"Stop," my weak voice cuts him off. A tear escapes down my cheek. "Just stop."

Raindrops drizzle on us. I stumble backwards and turn to walk home.

"I didn't mean that," he calls after me, knowing better than to follow again. "I'm sorry," he continues.

I ignore him, my mind shutting down after the emotional overload, but before I'm out of his sight, I turn to him. "Can't let fear keep you from moving forward?" I echo his words from the orchard before he kissed me.

I don't have anything to back them up with, no witty jab or wisdom to impart. I just shake my head and turn to make the lonely journey home.

CHAPTER TWENTY-SEVEN

THE METAL SWINGS SCREECH AS THE FOUR OF US SWAY back and forth in the humidity. The scent of rain hangs in the air alongside our somber disposition. After giving myself a day to process my emotions about the quarrel on the dock, the kiss in the orchard, and the argument—or was it a breakup?—outside Dalton's house, I asked Jen, Bristol, and Raymond to meet me at a local playground, a place where I could share my story without the prospect of running into Dalton.

"Heavy," Raymond states the obvious.

Jen slides off her swing and wraps her arms around me. Bristol and Raymond follow suit, creating an entanglement of limbs and metal chains from the swing I'm still perched upon.

"I'll punch George for you the next time I see him," Raymond offers, his voice indignant. I doubt he'd follow through with it, making his proposal entirely dubious.

"Me too," Bristol seconds, although softer.

"Me—" Jen pauses, contemplating the favor. "I'll have Levi throw my punch for me."

I smile, soaking in the warmth of their embrace and my newfound support system. How have I let myself go on for so long without this?

"Thanks, you guys," I tell them, and they slowly peel away from our huddle. After sharing the details of my dad's death and the repercussions it's had on my life, I feel as if I can share anything with them. The dam I'd built up that has kept my past and my fears hidden from the world is finally torn down and there's nothing left to keep my flood of thoughts from flowing out.

"I'm just so frustrated with myself," I admit. More than the panic and fury George ignited, and more than the insecurity and deception Dalton inflicted. "I'm the one that let it get this far. I'm my biggest hurdle. If I didn't allow myself to hide out in my own personal bubble, the scene on the dock or my fight with Dalton never would have happened."

I look around at their half-smiles and sympathetic gazes, but not one of them hides their agreement.

"Wow," I chuckle. "I was kind of hoping one of you would tell me I'm wrong, that this isn't my fault."

"What kind of friends would we be if we idly watched you sit tight in your comfort zone for the rest of your life? If we didn't support your personal growth?" Bristol inquires.

"It's true," Raymond adds. "If it wasn't for these two supporting me," he nods to Jen and Bristol, "I'd maybe still be in the closet."

Jen smiles softly and nods along, proud of Raymond's journey.

"I'd be a lot safer there, free from criticism and judgement," he continues. "But I also wouldn't feel like my fabulous self. I'd feel like a watered-down version of me, like I'm missing out on something bigger, even if that Something Bigger," he says with air quotes, "is just proving to myself that I could do it, that I could overcome my fear and show the world who I really am."

I sigh and stare ahead at the bright yellow tube slide on the playground. "I don't even know where to begin."

"Look for an opportunity that feels most secure to you while still taking that first step," Jen offers. "Start there. Baby steps will still move you forward."

"With someone you trust," Bristol adds pointedly.

"But sometimes you just gotta dive in."

We all turn to Raymond, eyebrows raised. He glances around at our quick reactions.

"What? I'm just saying that sometimes—" His face morphs from defense to culpable understanding. "Oh, yeah maybe diving in wasn't the best metaphor to use in this situation."

"You think?" Bristol shoves his shoulder.

I think of my mom at our community pool when I had my first diving lesson.

Hands up. Jump in. The butterflies in your stomach are what something new is all about.

It's time I find that out again.

~~~

A LINE OF BLENDERS WHIR IN UNISON, TRANSFORMING their ingredients into violet, coral, and forest green concoctions. The steady stream of customers is fitting considering the scorching mid-July temperatures. Taia slams a crateful of cups onto the counter and reaches up to wipe the sweat from her brow with the back of her wrist.

"And this is only the east end," she tells me, her breathing labored. The hairs that have fallen from her bun stick to her neck. "I'll collect the rest in a moment, but until then if anyone asks, I'll be in the freezer."

"I'll tend the west side," I tell her, pouring all the smoothies into their respective containers. I've already reached my imaginary limit on freezer visitations for the hour anyway.

"Clutch," she responds faintly, grabbing the crate again to head to the back room.

After distributing the smoothies and ringing up the customers, I grab an empty crate from the end of the bar and step off the wooden planks of the shop. I concentrate on not flicking up blistering grains of sand as the heat claws its way up my ankles.

There are fewer sunbathers than normal, most having retreated into the water to stay cool. Even people walking along the shore have their feet shuffling in the tide.

I reach the sand volleyball courts and collect a slippery pile of abandoned cups, condensation clinging to their sides. The sand on the courts is dark as they've been hosing it down every half hour to keep it cool for the players.

Despite its inconvenience, the heat has been a helpful distraction from me replaying my conversation with Dalton on repeat and wishing I'd handled it differently. Or worse, longing for another kiss.

I tuck my fingers into the slots on either side of the crate to lift again.

"Heads up!" a man calls out in warning, and I release the crate in surprise as a volleyball sails just past my head. I glance over to see George jogging my way, looking just as shocked to see me as I feel from the sudden sporting assault.

"Oh, hey Avery," he greets me awkwardly.

"Hi."

"You, uh, seen Dalton around?"

"No. Sorry."

It's clear that neither one of us wants to mention what happened last weekend. He's probably still confused by it, and I'm definitely still embarrassed.

"Well, when you talk to him, can you tell him we missed him at practice? He said he'd be here."

"Sure." *Not sure when that will be, but sure.*

"Thanks."

The hesitancy in his voice mirrors the jaggedness in his movements, as if he's debating whether to bring up the incident or return to his friends. I think back to what my friends told me at the playground about not wanting to idly watch as I sit tight in my comfort zone, so despite my reluctance in bringing it up myself, I have to try.

"About last week," I start, and George's face goes uneasy. "It just brought up a past wound for me, which is why I reacted the way I did." I fidget with the crate in front of me, trying to ground myself in the present so I don't run away from the situation. "It's something I'm trying to work on, but I have a long way to go."

George contemplates this for a moment before responding. "I was a dick."

A surprised laugh escapes me. I don't know what I was expecting—him lashing out in unresolved anger, a half-hearted apology, perhaps just awkward silence?

I smile and shrug, unable to deny it. He mirrors my shrug and I feel like there's an unspoken truce between us. Without the need to complicate things, I pick up the crate to signal the end of our interaction, and he picks up on the hint.

"Well, I'll let you get back to it, then." He grabs the

volleyball and jogs back to the courts, sending the ball sailing over the net as he approaches.

Dalton's friends must not know that we haven't spoken in almost a week. His absence around the shop has become painstakingly obvious. I miss the way his visits broke up my long shifts.

Upon returning to JuiSea, I copy Taia by slamming the crate onto the counter and taking a deep breath, thankful for the ceiling fans that send a slight breeze through the shop. My shirt grips my skin, making me squirm. Jay's manning the bar with ease, so I take the crate to the back room to catch up on dishes—and to stand in the freezer again.

Taia takes notice as I enter the back room and meets me halfway to relieve me of the crate. Her sudden benevolence strikes me as uncharacteristic, but I'm not complaining.

"What?" she snaps, popping the bubble of altruism.

"Nothing," I respond, careful not to irritate her any more than the heat already has. I continue with caution, "It's just, you've been acting different this week."

"I might be apathetic most of the time, but I'm not stupid. I know you two broke up," she states pointblank.

I blink a few times, hoping that the heat rising beneath my cheeks is mistaken as a sunburn. "I don't know if I'd call it—"

"Oh please, you two were dating. He was here every day and now he hasn't stopped by in a week." She turns to the sink and begins spraying down the crate of silicone cups. I move toward the freezer where delectable cool air still lingers from the last time it was opened.

"If it wasn't a breakup, then what's going on between you two?" she pries.

I'm surprised by her curiosity. Our relationship typically consists of quick work-related one-liners. Besides, I have no concrete answer for her, and I don't plan on rehashing every detail of what happened that day, so I give her the simplest response I can think of.

"We had a disagreement."

She huffs. "Must have been an intense fight for it to go on this long," she deduces, shooting me a look. I shrug. "Unless it wasn't a fight and in fact a breakup."

"It didn't feel like a breakup," I object, but the inflection in my voice questions the idea. I sigh. "I guess I just wish I knew what happened to Amy a lot sooner."

"Amy? Why?"

"It would have saved us from some misunderstandings."

Taia ponders this as she washes the dishes. "You remind me of her, you know. Of Amy." She turns to face me, drying her hands on her JuiSea apron. "You're both quiet and look out for others. Some would call it empathy; I just think it's a people-pleasing act to gain acceptance because of your lack of self-confidence."

A noise bubbles out of me, almost like a laugh. I'm taken aback by her candidness but amused at how she's approaching the touchy topic of my potential breakup.

"Have you stopped to consider how he might feel about your breakup—or whatever you want to call it—after losing the person he was closest to only a year ago? He shut down for months after she passed away, and now he finally had the courage to get back out there only to feel like he's losing someone again. I wouldn't be surprised if he's experiencing the grief of her death all over again or if he feels like he doesn't deserve you because of how Amy died. He's probably losing his mind trying to figure out why this keeps happening to him."

I'm stunned by her analysis. She may not know what caused the argument, but she has known Dalton—and his sister—a lot longer than I have.

"I mean, I know Amy was his sister and all, and you're, well, you," she jabbers on, having resumed the dishes. "But who knows, maybe it's hitting him harder than it would someone else."

I click my tongue, realizing there's probably a degree of truth laced in her words. Does he think he's lost me for good, just like he lost Amy forever?

"Again, not stupid."

"Only a bit less apathetic."

"Exactly," she shoots me a smirk over her shoulder. I chuckle, grabbing a heap of clean cups to restack the bar.

CHAPTER TWENTY-EIGHT

JAY AND I HAVE RETURNED TO OUR RHYTHM OF operating the shop by day and occupying the couch by night, managing to create a dent in the collection of movies we had queued up for the summer.

When Saturday morning rolls around, I find myself alone in the house with no plans. With Jay at the shop, Raymond on shift, Bristol at her college campus for internship interviews, and Jen hanging out with Levi before and after his sand volleyball game, the busyness I'd felt since arriving to town has come to a standstill.

To help pass the time, I cook breakfast rather than snatching a Pop Tart or piece of fruit, clean part of the house to contribute to my staying here, shower and force myself into clothes that aren't my pajamas, and work on the final touches to my room. Soft music plays as I pin up the string of lights that I bought on my first day here. Once they line the perimeter of the ceiling, I plug them in and stand in the center of the room to appreciate the new space.

Sunshine pours through the open window, diminishing the effect of the twinkling lights, and most of the walls still remain blank, but the paint job turned out better than expected and the bulletin board above my desk is covered in the photos from my mom's wedding. One corner of my desk holds a stack of scarcely touched books while the other is adorned with a little jade plant given to me by Jen as a room-warming gift.

The simplicity of it all puts me at peace, if only for a moment.

My eyes find the stack of borrowed clothes balancing neatly over the rim of my laundry basket. If I hadn't been given such meaningful items, I may have contemplated not returning them, hoping that my "forgetfulness" would be forgiven. However, my stomach churns with unease because of the significance the clothes carry and what I know must be done.

Before I can persuade myself otherwise, I throw the stack of clothes in an empty Arrowbase bag and head for the door.

˜˜˜

My heartbeat quickens at the sight of Dalton's house as I emerge from the forested pathway. I could cup my hands together and create a pool from my own perspiration. Suddenly I wish I'd skipped breakfast altogether—my stomach isn't thanking me for it now.

I will myself to the front door, unsure if this entrance or the door to the barn is more appropriate, and knock. Stepping back in anticipation, I cradle the bag of clothes awkwardly in front of me like a peace offering.

I linger longer than necessary, reluctant to do this all over again if no one answers. A minute passes. Then two. Disappointed, I turn to retreat down the dirt path. Just as I reach the edge of the trees, I hear a creak behind me, followed by a delicate voice. "Avery?"

Leeann's wearing a loose t-shirt and cotton pants, her dark hair pulled up in a large clip and not a trace of makeup on her splotchy face. Her eyes look swollen, the skin underneath them puffy and red.

"Hi," I greet her, clutching the bag against my torso as I approach the door again.

"I'm sorry," she tells me, and I suddenly feel like I've intruded. She shouldn't feel sorry about the obvious distress she's under. If anything, I should be the one apologizing for dropping by unannounced. "He's not here," she continues, and I realize she's sorry about my timing, assuming I'm here to see Dalton. I wonder if she knows.

"Oh. No, I'm not—that's not why I'm—" I hesitate and then extend the bag of clothes to her. "These are yours." Well, Amy's I suppose, but I don't feel comfortable mentioning the name of her late daughter, especially given her visible grief.

Leeann takes them from me, her arms thinner than I remember from a week ago. I wonder what she looked like before tragedy struck her life. She unravels the handles of the bag, which I had twisted and tied up nervously on the walk over here. She peeks in the bag, a sad smile pulling at the corners of her mouth, and looks at me again with those inflamed, melancholy eyes.

"I don't know where he is," she tells me.

I'd rather not discuss my relationship with Dalton with his mom. I'm not even sure if she's aware of what's going on between us. Heck, I'm not even sure if I know.

"That's fine," I tell her. "I was just dropping off the clothes."

"I don't know where he is," she repeats, her voice defeated. "I mean—" she falters, swallowing hard. "Today marks a year since Amy's passing." I suddenly wish I'd picked any other day to drop off the clothes. She continues, "Dalton—he, um—he's been having a hard time I think, not acting the same as usual lately."

Leeann's words are underlined with a hint of desperation, and I'm reminded of how she and Robert would bring home college pamphlets to encourage Dalton to pursue a degree. I can't imagine what other subtle ways she's tried supporting him, always treading a fine line between giving her son space to grieve and urging him to keep living the life his sister would have wanted for him. How many hours of sleep has this compassionate woman lost trying to care for the well-being of her only living child, to save him from himself?

"I know he carries a lot of guilt," she presses on without my prompting, "And he hides it well from others, but I think today it might be heavier than usual."

She steps over the threshold, rests her hand on my shoulder, and draws in a deep breath to tell me one last time, as if pleading with me. "I just don't know where he is."

〰〰〰

TINY YELLOW AND RED FINCHES GLIDE THROUGH THE forest, their twittering melodies overlapping my labored breathing. Following my concerning exchange with Leeann, I retraced my steps toward the apple tree, checking to see if Dalton was hiding out in its branches. The next logical spot would be the sand volleyball courts—also void of him—and the surrounding lakefront. I even stopped by the shop despite his recent absence. And finally, this ill-frequented hiking trail, which seemed like the only outstanding option.

When I'd arrived at the sand volleyball courts, Dalton's team was in the middle of playing. I frantically searched the court for him, but his band of spandex-clad friends were missing their star player. Scanning the metal bleachers, I found Jen and Levi, their fingers intertwined as they sat close together. Jen spotted me across the way and perked up, waving for me to join them.

"Where's Dalton?" I mouthed to her, hoping she could at least read the unease on my face if not the exact words from my lips.

She pursed her lips and shrugged, answering my question. "Sorry," she mouthed back.

I took one last look around the area and sighed at the dwindling possibilities. I turned to Jen again, whose eyes hadn't left me, and felt her love and support for me radiate across the sand. Little did I know at the start of the summer that I'd discover some of my closest friends here.

"Good luck," she offered, her bright eyes full of hope. I could almost hear her optimistic voice as if I'd been sitting right beside her.

After experiencing the recent support of friends who know about my past—all my guilt, fears, and insecurities—I want to offer Dalton the same. If this summer has taught me anything, it's to let people in over suffering in solitude.

Deep down, I know Dalton is okay. He must be. He wouldn't do anything reckless. But here on the trail, my heartbeat pounds in my ears, drowning out the sound of rushing water. I see the trees begin to thin and I slow in anticipation, worried that I'll arrive at an empty beach, the only movement being the flow of cerulean water as it cascades over the rock formation where

Dalton and I had our picnic. I take the last few steps into the open area.

There, sitting in the middle of the shore, is Dalton.

He's facing the water, though staring at the blanket of pebbles in front of him. His forearms are perched on his knees, one hand grasping the other wrist, motionless.

I have no heartening speech prepared, no consoling words for his situation. I only have my presence to offer, so I take the first cautious step toward him.

The pebbles protest loudly beneath my feet, but Dalton doesn't look up. When I reach him, still motion-less, I can see the mourning etched on his face—taut jawbone, twitching lips, and laser-focused eyes on an irrelevant spot in front of him.

I lower myself beside him, cradling my knees to my chest and stealing small glances at his somber face. His gleaming eyes flicker in my direction, acknowledging my presence but averting eye contact. The twitching in his lips increases to that of a quiver, his jawbone tight-ening even more to fight against the inescapable pain.

All at once, his face scrunches up in emotional release as he lets out a guttural cry and drops his face against his arm. One moment he's unnaturally still, the next he's overcome with tremors that seize his entire body.

I place my hand on Dalton's back, and he lets his weight fall against me, unable to hold himself up anymore. My arms wrap around him as his hands move to conceal his face and the flow of his tears. I recognize the complexity in his cries, the battling emotions that only intensify the longer they go unresolved. Harboring so many unwanted sentiments manifests in the rawest of breakdowns, the ones that completely engulf you, leaving you incapacitated and exhausted. I let out a breath, unaware that I'd been holding it in.

Dalton's vigorous shaking shows no sign of stopping—he has wholly surrendered to his emotions. I wrap my arms tighter around him and nuzzle my cheek against the top of his head.

I'm here, I think. *You're okay. I'm here.*

I enter this space with him, allowing myself to feel what he feels to my fullest capacity. Grief. Guilt. Self-loathing. Dalton has no doubt held onto these feelings for the last twelve months with minimal relief, much longer than someone in his situation should.

Much longer than any six-year-old girl having witnessed her father drown in front of her own eyes should.

CHAPTER TWENTY-NINE

IT'S A RESTLESS NIGHT. I TRY TO SLEEP BUT FIND MYSELF buzzing with a need to right a wrong that has taken up residency in my life for far too long. After a couple hours of half-conscious sleep followed by a couple hours of tossing and turning, I drag myself through the open window onto the rooftop for some fresh air, hoping to reset my pestering mind.

The lake is black and unmoving. A single streetlamp hums and flickers, emitting a yellow-orange ring of light on the empty lakefront boulevard. The waning moon looks farther away than usual, leaving me with a heightened sense of solitude in my nocturnal hideaway.

My mind can't shake the image of Dalton—strong and charismatic Dalton—collapsing into my arms under the weight of his grief, his tear-streaked face buried in the crook of his elbow. Or the way he kept pounding his fists on the ground in unshakable frustration. The unrestrained agony in his bloodshot brown eyes.

The visual representation of the loss he feels would be heavy for anyone to witness, but I can't help but think back on my own story and see the similarities between what he's giving up because of his contrition and how I've done the same. I want to tell him that what happened to his sister doesn't have to deter him from what he wants out of life. He can still enjoy meaningful relationships and pursue ambitious dreams. He can find peace in the present, forgiveness in the regret, and fulfillment in living each day to its broadest potential.

But when I search my own heart, I know I'm the last person he should listen to.

Dalton's words echo in my mind.

Can't let fear keep you from moving forward.

Can't let fear keep you from moving forward.

Can't let fear keep you from moving forward.

My stare bores into the lake until my peripheral fades and the darkness of the intimidating water is all I see. Before I'm cognizant of it, my body moves from the roof to my room to the staircase and out the front door. I don't bother grabbing shoes or a sweatshirt as nothing seems to matter other than the repetitive words pulling me forward as if in a trance.

I traverse the barren street and amble through the shrubbery that borders the shore. I stumble forward, each step sinking into the cool, rough sand as I approach the shadowy water. I stop just a foot before the land meets the sea, face to face with the adversary of my nightmares, my Achilles' heel.

I breathe in the fresh air of the night, and it brings me to the present. I'm keenly aware of the negligible distance between me and the edge of my comfort zone, separated only by a slight step, the first step to redemption.

The first step into the unknown.

I take the last stride forward, crossing the barrier of my asylum.

Cold water bites at my toes, but I don't pull away. It envelops my ankles, freeform and weightless. I let out a deep breath, close my eyes, and turn my head toward the sky. The stillness of the night and the water gently lapping my feet brings me back to that night, all alone in the canoe. The feeling of helplessness when there was nothing I could do to save my dad and no one I could turn to for help. I've done everything in my power to keep that situation from repeating itself, seeking control by evading situations in which I could lose it.

This is me taking back control.

It's not too late.

It was never too late.

CHAPTER THIRTY

I HOLD MY GROUND UNTIL STREAKS OF GOLDEN LIGHT peek over the horizon. A couple of early risers take to the streets, getting in their morning strolls. I collect my thoughts and trek the short distance back to the house, determined not to lose focus of my quest. After hours of uninterrupted pondering about the prospect of this endeavor, I'm ready to take action.

I sit at my desk, open my laptop and an internet browser, and search every key word and phrase that comes to mind. I'll need a portfolio to refer to when I'm tempted to change my mind. After extensive research, I send a few articles to Jay's printer and gather up the paper into a neat stack. I hear the shower faucet turn off and know I'm running out of time before Jay and I head to the shop.

I wait for Jay in the kitchen, perched on the edge of a stool with my hands gripping the paper in anticipation. I hear the creak of a door and footsteps emerging from the upper floor. Jay whistles as he bounces down the flight of stairs. I slide off the stool and turn to face him, his carefree expression coming face to face with the timid eagerness of my own.

"Morning," he greets me, and then promptly picks up on my hesitation. He eyes the stack of paper in my hands, the front page turned away from him, creating speculation. "What's that?" he inquires.

I hold out the stack to him. Jay fingers the corners of it, flipping through to catch the headline of each article.

Redefine Yourself: Steps to Reclaiming the Life You Lived Before Trauma.

Rewiring Your Amygdala to Better Respond to Fear and Anxiety.

Chasing Freedom: 7 Steps to Overcoming Your Fears.

He flips to the last article.

Conquer Your Fear of Water.

The cheerful attitude that accompanied Jay into the room is replaced by seriousness. I see the concern on his face, his protective instincts kicking in. He probably never expected this day to come. But I also see his concealed optimism in the way his eyes search mine and his hands clutch the papers in anticipation, just as mine had moments before.

He keeps his gaze steady, his voice even more so. "Are you sure about this?"

My lips turn upward in a nervous smile. I nod, eyes tickling with tears as I envision a new future for myself.

~~~

"HERE YOU ARE, JOEY." I SLIDE HIS SMOOTHIE ACROSS THE counter.

"Hey, how much longer will I be seeing your smiling face around here?" he asks, his voice gruff as usual. Each one of his visits is the same: thin black sunglasses, bare chest to show off his exceptional tan and muscular build, and his extra-large Peanut Butter Punch.

"Only a few more weeks," I respond, taken aback at how quickly the end of summer is approaching.

"Who needs a high school diploma anyways?" he counters. "You should move here full time, work your way up the corporate ladder, and eventually buy out your brother's business from under him."

I return the protein powders and Greek yogurt I'd used in his smoothie to their respective spots, amused by his proposal.

"Given that there are only two rungs on this corporate ladder, I suppose I'm halfway there."

"Exactly. So, I'll be seeing you around, I presume?"

"I wish, but I'll be back to visit when I can."

"You'd better. Something about the way you make this drink is a whole lot better than the guy who claims to be the mastermind behind it. Can you believe that dude owns the place?"

"It's that extra scoop of peanut butter," I tell him, my hand cupped around the side of my mouth to keep it our little secret.

He lets out his signature raspy chuckle, delighted by my deviation from the Blender Bible. As he departs from the bar, I see Bristol approach.

"Just a sec," I tell her, collecting up all the used blenders and empty fruit containers. I pass Raymond in the doorway to the back room and his face shifts into a grimace as his eyes roll into the furthest caverns of his head.

"No," he whines, drawing out the word. "The worst customer is here. You deal with her."

Bristol has a habit of taking twenty minutes to decide what to order, which always results in her go-to smoothie—our trendy Lemon Lavender—or telling us to "just make whatever."

I glance back in time to catch Bristol mock Raymond's grimace. "You know, one of these days you'll be grateful for all the quality time I create by my indecisiveness."

"Or one day, I'll find myself in line at a grocery store between two families with screaming babies and think to myself 'It's okay, I've had to practice patience for more painful situations than this.'"

"Fine then, just make me whatever!" she declares.

"Oh my gosh, the clouds have parted. I can see a glimmer of heaven shining through," Raymond exaggerates melodramatically. "Ladies and gentlemen, we thought this day would never come, the day that Bristol decides on her order—albeit not exactly—in a normal amount of time."

"Yeah, yeah. Are you going to make my smoothie or what?"

"Eh, maybe in twenty minutes," he retorts.

Bristol reaches across the counter to smack him on the arm.

I set my stack of dishes in the sink and grab more ingredients from the walk-in freezer. The flow of customers has dwindled despite it being the weekend. When I return to restock the bar, Bristol has taken a seat on one of the stools.

"How'd the interviews go?" I ask her. She must have just gotten back from her campus visit this morning.

She collapses over the bar, forehead against the counter, and lets out an aggravated groan. Her mood defies the atmosphere around the pier where carefree visitors meander and upbeat music projects from the rooftop speakers.

In response to Bristol's outburst, Raymond asks me, "Yo, do we have any more of that mood booster supplement I can dump in this thing?"

I shoot him a look before consoling Bristol. "I'm sure it went a lot better than you think."

"It's not that," she moans, her voice muffled by the countertop. She lifts her head to face me, her forehead vaguely indented by the wood grain. When she speaks again, her voice is full of longing. "I really want it."

"Want what, the internship?" I question. "I thought you didn't want to work your first semester."

"I didn't," she agrees, passion accelerating her speech. "But this internship, this company, it—" she falters, unable to find the right words to express her fervor. Instead, she lets out another noise to try to convey the importance of this prospect.

"Must be some position," I tell her before asking a walk-up what smoothie he'd like. The ability to multi-task between serving customers and keeping up conversation has grown easier over time.

Raymond sets Bristol's mystery smoothie in front of her, but her preoccupied mind doesn't register its presence.

"It is!" she exclaims. "I'd be shadowing a substance abuse counselor for youth in the foster care system that have a propensity to use drugs as a coping mechanism for the terrible stuff they've had to go through. It'd be perfect, like actual good work that genuinely makes a difference."

"That's incredible," I affirm, closing the lid to a blender and securing it on the machine. "I mean, it sounds like it could be really heavy at times, but I think you'd be great at it."

"You think so?" Her voice slips back into nervous longing.

"Absolutely. When will you hear back?" I hand the silicone cup of the Berry Blue Skies to the customer and ring him up at the cash register.

"Probably not for a couple weeks. The internship won't start until a month into the semester so—"

"Sip," Raymond interjects.

We both turn to him, confused by his sudden and succinct utterance.

"Take a sip, woman," he tells Bristol, gesturing to the smoothie she's successfully managed to forget.

She sucks on the bright orange straw, the flavor melting away her nervous tension. "Thanks, Raymond. Which one is this?"

"I'm calling it the Lemon Lollygagger after all the time you've wasted trying to decide on what to order."

"Not a fan of the name if I may say so myself," she shoots at him, and then turns to me in all seriousness, "but I'd add it to the Bible." I grab a pen and sticky note sitting next to the cash register and hand them to Raymond so he can write down the ingredients of his new creation for Jay's consideration.

"Yeah, I'm not sure if 'gag' in the name will be appealing to customers," I agree. I take the sticky note back from Raymond, covered in almost indecipherable penmanship, and stick it to the inner cover of the Blender Bible.

Laughter floats through the air from the beach, shouts of amusement from a group of kids jumping into the lake from the pier. Ever since this morning and my decision to overcome my fear, I've been keenly aware of what summer pastimes the lake has to offer. I've been so caught up in the dangers of water activities that I've become a total stranger to all the delights they can bring as well. There's an entire world that I've been missing out on, one that I'm finally ready to explore.

"I really hope you get the internship, Bristol," I say, knowing all too well what it's like to long for an envisioned future, one full of new opportunities—some heavy, although mostly rewarding. "I really, really do."

CHAPTER THIRTY-ONE

Dawn peeks over the horizon, suspicious of our new sunrise activity. My friends had recommended I start somewhere I feel secure and with someone I trust. That's why I now find myself at a shallow part of the lake with Jay by my side, a canister of hot coffee in his hand. We've been coming out here every morning. At this time of day, and at this specific location, it's unlikely we'll come across any unwanted onlookers as I learn to navigate this new terrain.

I've managed the sleep deprivation with ease, energized by the bizarre combination of determination and nervousness as the vision of my goal comes into focus. Although Jay rubs his eyelids about once every minute during our early morning missions, he never complains.

The first morning we spent two hours out here and

I only managed to go in far enough for the water to reach halfway up my calves, a couple inches farther than the night I came alone. Minor progress, but progress, nonetheless.

Each morning since, we've seen major strides in my ability to go farther into the water. Although some mornings I can't even think straight unless Jay is within arm's reach, and my only focus on those mornings is to just sit with the unwanted feelings and process all the ugly thoughts around my fears, each time I survive another rising panic attack, the better I get at the exposure therapy (or self-torture as my mind likes to think of it).

Today my goal is to go far enough where I can remove my feet from the security of the sand and the sensation that I'm still on land. I keep reminding myself of all the times I treaded water in the hot tub at our apartment complex. I've done this before. I can do it again.

I remove my shorts and t-shirt—the swimsuits I'd bought with Jen and Bristol finally getting their proper use—and tie my hair up in a bun to avoid getting it wet. The water nips at my legs as I slowly wade into the lake at a sloth's pace. Jay proceeds a couple steps ahead of me, leading the way while remaining close enough for contact in case I have a harrowing flashback or feel like I can't breathe. His calm demeanor invites me forward. Never demanding or impatient, he waits for me to acclimate to the new depth and the sensation of buoyancy that accompanies it. It's a slow-moving process.

Meanwhile, Jay casually sips on his canister of coffee that he keeps above the surface. I find myself jealous of his comfort. He moves with the water as if the water and he are one, completely unaware of the intricacies in my mind and how every step for me is escorted by a multitude of memories.

With each step I take, I focus not only on the physical newness of the situation, but on relinquishing the blame I've been harboring since the incident. The bulk of our time here at the lake is that of mental transformation. The physical act of getting in the water and swimming seems straightforward enough. It's the psychological blockades that prevent me from advancing with ease. I repeat in my mind what I've come to learn over the last several weeks about that day in the canoe. That it wasn't my fault, that there wasn't anything I could have done to save him, that I'm entirely blameless.

I am a victim of my father's death, not a perpetrator.

Jay dips his head into my line of sight, checking to see that I'm still with him. Amid trying to rewire my brain, I'd frozen in place, the water flat all around me. I look up at him and smile, taking my next step and realizing this depth would be enough to tread if I bend my legs and tuck my knees in.

"This is good," I tell him, placing my palms on the

surface of the lake. I lower myself into the water until it sweeps across my shoulders. My toes, having dug their way into the sand, release their hold and my arms glide back and forth through the water with cupped hands to keep me afloat.

I release an airy laugh through my staccato breaths, trying not to let my pride hinder my focus.

"Look at you go," Jay encourages.

I place my feet back on the sand and stand up, goosebumps scattering across my arms in the chilly morning air. Somehow with my entire body wet, I feel slightly more at ease with the water's movement.

"Congratulations," Jay tells me, his face beaming with joy.

"Don't congratulate me yet," I riposte. "I still have a long way to go."

"You gotta celebrate the victories along the way."

I smile and shrug in acceptance, taking a deep breath.

Here we go again, I think before lifting my feet, spreading my arms, and letting the water envelop me.

※※※

"I can't believe today's the last day of the sand volleyball league," Raymond muses as we meander from JuiSea to the sand volleyball courts. It's late in the after-noon, the final game of the day.

"I can't believe the Harvest Festival is only two weeks away," he mopes.

We walk along the shore, my feet almost skimming the water. A couple weeks ago, I wouldn't have walked within a few strides of the lake's edge. It doesn't bother me now, but Raymond doesn't know of my progress yet, so I keep my feet dry for the time being.

Raymond stops dead in his tracks, eyes bulging as he looks at me. "I can't believe you go home in a few weeks!"

I can't believe it either. It's one of the reasons I've been so determined to overcome my fear this quickly, outlining objectives for each morning's swim. I know that once I'm home and I don't have the same access to a body of water, I might give up on the whole endeavor. It's now or never in my mind.

I reach my hand back for Raymond to take and pull him along.

"It's not like we'll never see each other again," I remind him. "It's not like I'll never visit my brother."

"True, but work won't be the same without you."

"Maybe I can convince Jay to hire a cute, young, single guy as my replacement," I suggest, giving him a guileful grin.

"Still wouldn't be as good."

I release his hand and drape my arm around him. Any future visits to Nelson wouldn't just be to see Jay. I've created a second life here, with new friends and an entirely new me. I suspect that I'll be back more frequently than people expect.

We find Bristol and Jen waiting in the bleachers next to a couple of empty seats they saved for us. With the summer winding down, more people are out trying to soak in as many activities as they can.

"Where's Levi?" I inquire. "I almost didn't recognize you without him."

Jen beams at the observation, happily content with the idea of her and Levi being attached at the hips.

"He's dorm shopping with his mom," she responds. "Now that he's met his roommate, they're divvying up what each of them is going to bring."

"Are you nervous about him moving away for college?" Bristol asks.

Jen contemplates this, her glossy lips pursed. "I'll definitely miss him, but I'm so happy I can't imagine that long-distance will be an issue."

"So, it's official then?" I ask, indulging in the relationship gossip.

Her shoulders sag at the question, lips turning from pursed to pouting. "No. He hasn't brought it up yet."

"He might already think it's official," Bristol consoles. "You may need to just bring it up yourself. It's obvious you two are a thing. The conversation won't scare him away."

"Absolutely," Raymond agrees. "Boys are completely oblivious. Next time you see him, just walk up and declare, 'I am *your girlfriend.*' And if he doesn't pick up on the hint, then I say ditch him."

"I wouldn't consider that a hint," I interpose.

Raymond swats his hand in my direction.

"You're right," Jen sighs. "I should just say something."

Dalton arrives at the courts, jogging to throw his stuff down and join his team who have already warmed up and stripped down to their matching attire. I was beginning to wonder if he planned on attending this one, considering he missed last week's game.

He notices me in the stands as he sets his bag down. We lock eyes for a moment, and although we haven't spoken since his breakdown at the waterfall a week ago, I feel like any tension between us has been replaced by a mutual understanding. The things that upset me before, I finally understand. I get why he wants to conceal part of the story about how his sister passed away, I get how something so heart-shattering can cause someone to deviate from an expected path, and I get how it can make someone lie and act uncharacteristic at times. My lashing out at him in retrospect was really just me exploding at the parts of myself I see reflected in him.

The volleyball match spans three games resulting in a loss for his team. They were long games with endless volleys, but in the end, it came down to a bit of bad luck. As usual, the game is followed by a conglomeration of players and spectators.

I try not to watch as Dalton pulls his athletic shorts over his spandex and replaces his tank top with a normal t-shirt, but his haste makes me question if he's about to take off before I can reach the bottom of the clanking metal steps.

As our two groups merge to form a social circle, however, I see him glancing my way. He moves to stand next to me and I'm surprised at how natural it feels to be near him again.

"Sorry about the game," I tell him, deciding it's best to stick to small talk for now.

"It's alright." He shrugs, making a face to show it doesn't matter, although I've seen his competitive side during the games and wonder if he's secretly upset over the end of their winning streak.

Our group of friends busy themselves in conversation, discussing notable blocks or spikes and formulating plans for the evening. Dalton takes a step away from the crowd, motioning with his head for me to follow. The familiar scent of cedarwood and citrus fills the air between us.

"I just wanted to say thanks," he mentions, his voice low to avoid any eavesdropping. "You know, for the other day."

I shake my head, hoping to convey that it wasn't a burden whatsoever. "There's no need to thank me. If anything, I was returning the favor."

He gives me a half-smile as he recalls when our roles

were reversed on that pebbly shore. "Regardless, I really appreciate it."

"Anytime," I tell him, and I mean it. I don't know where he and I stand—if we'll resume our connection or if the end of summer also implies the end of our relationship. Either way, I'll always be there for him when he needs me.

"It sounds like they're headed up to Shepherd's Point if you want to join, but I understand if you don't—"

"I want to," I cut him off. He looks surprised, and I quickly follow up with what I actually mean. "I mean, I would want to, but I'm pretty tired." My new swim schedule has made it so that I'm in bed before nine each night.

He narrows his eyes. "You don't have to do that around me."

"Do what?"

"I understand if you don't want to go."

I realize he thinks I'm making up an excuse to avoid the location. He doesn't know about the progress I've made around water or that I truly feel inclined to check out the famous Shepherd's Point after a couple months of living here. Hanging out with a group of friends next to the water? Bring it on.

I could tell him, explain to him why I'm sticking to my routine rather than hanging out with my friends so close to when I'll be leaving Nelson. But a part of me wants to keep it a secret for now. I still have a lot of ground to cover—or water to tread—and I don't need people asking for updates or distracting me from my mission.

I smile in gratitude, even though he's way off the mark. "I know."

As I say my goodbyes, I realize it's the first time I've declined a water invitation for a reason other than my fear. And hopefully the last time I'll ever need to decline a water invitation altogether.

CHAPTER THIRTY-TWO

A FEW DAYS LATER, SAME MORNING ROUTINE, ALTHOUGH this time I let Jay watch from the shore. If I'm really going to overcome my fear, I can't rely on Jay to guide me out of my comfort zone every step of the way. It's time I escort myself out.

I've been in the water on my own the last couple mornings, and today's goal is to hold my breath underwater for thirty seconds. I want to work my way up toward diving down to the bottom of the lake or even jumping in from the pier, but today's exercise will suffice for now.

Now that the initial seriousness has waned a bit, Jay feels comfortable bringing humor into the mix. It's sometimes in the form of made-up songs that tell the tale of my triumph, but more often than not, it's his sportscaster commentary as he watches from the sidelines.

"She ramps up for the plunge," Jay narrates, his pace portraying an intense competition between two athletes. "This is the moment we've all been waiting for, the move she's been building up to in her career as a professional water wader."

I turn to scoff at him. I've already dunked my head under a few times in the last several days, getting used to the feeling of being completely engulfed by the water's shapeless form, but only staying under for five seconds apiece. This next one is it. Thirty seconds on the clock.

I take a deep breath in, expanding my lungs to their fullest capacity, pinch my nose—I don't want to risk inhaling water again after the waterfall incident—and lower myself beneath the surface, letting the water rush over the top of my head until I'm surrounded by shadows.

One, two, three...

I count the seconds, hyper-focused on maintaining a steady cadence if only to keep my mind from wandering elsewhere. Perhaps this is what it will take to participate in social settings that involve water, an acute awareness of the present, an intense focus on something steady, rhythmic, and reliable.

Eleven, twelve...

Yet, despite my attempt to keep my mind from wandering, I can't help but notice the specks hovering in the murky waters and think to myself that I've been here before. It's all too familiar. Among the shadows that extend for miles into darkness, I see a figure. It's far enough away that I can't make out what it is, but it moves closer with every second I count.

Nineteen, twenty...

And then it hits me. It's him, my father. The view underwater is familiar from all the nightmares that have haunted me for as long as I can remember. Of course I'd see him here. I'm usually pulled off to the side of a river on a canoe, but he's always been here for these moments. Always.

Twenty-nine, thirty.

My legs push against the sand, and I emerge from the water, gasping for air. I jolt my head back, whipping my wet hair out of my face.

"And she's done it!" Jay announces with his hands by his mouth to act as a microphone. "We have just witnessed history being made, folks. Avery, age seventeen, has broken the record for the longest underwater solo apparatus." He imitates a crowd going wild.

Despite the slight breeze raising goosebumps on my skin, I feel a warm sensation inside of me, the overwhelming feeling of accomplishment. Every morning I set out with a concrete goal in mind, and every morning I manage to check it off the list. I never dared to dream of this day, never imagined it was possible. I smile to myself, looking out over the lake and envisioning all the possibilities that my future holds with this new, courageous side of me.

~~~

IT STARTS WITH OUR LAUGHTER, THE DIFFERENCE IN OCTAVES blending harmoniously together. Then the sunlight and vivid colors slowly fill in the world around me. We're weaving our way through the winding streams in our two-person canoe.

He maneuvers the vessel into a secluded alcove surrounded by jagged rocks and towering trees. We're sandwiched between chirping magpies above and darting minnows below.

The scene is broken up into snapshots of the past: my father plunging into the water, me jumping and giggling as he emerges to spook me, him exploring the rocky shore, me watching him from the safety of the canoe, and him climbing up the embankment.

He braces for his second jump.

I hear the sharp crack and watch as his body slaps the surface of the water.

In my panic, I hurl myself over the edge of the boat, my soaked sundress suctioning to my skin. But I'm no longer six years old. It's the present day.

"Dad!" I cry out to him, swimming as fast as I can toward the spot where he'd landed. "Dad!"

I finally reach him, pulling him into my arms as I brace myself against a nearby boulder. His body is limp, his head drooping.

"Dad, can you hear me?" I plead, frantically searching his face for a sign of consciousness. His eyes open gently, delicate

as they find mine, his gaze like looking in a mirror. I cradle his head above the water, willing him to take deep breaths.

"It's going to be alright," I assure him, but it's really an attempt to comfort myself. "You're going to be alright."

His calming gaze is coupled with a contented, soft smile.

"You can let go now, Avery," he tells me in a mellow voice that exudes peace and love as if he's trying to pass those sentiments onto me. "Let go."

His eyelids slowly drift shut as if falling asleep.

Tears escape down my cheeks, but I refrain from crying out. He's called me to a higher response, one of love and peace and acceptance. They don't negate the pain, the feelings of loss and abandonment, but they're powerful enough to surpass them.

My eyes flutter open, the rest of my body heavy against the mattress. My thoughts aren't racing like usual. My heartbeat remains slow and steady. There isn't an ounce of panic within me.

It's pitch-black out with no sign of dawn arriving anytime soon, but I rise from my slumber and make my way across the dimly lit street, crickets speculating as I pass by.

It's time to lay down my past once and for all.

Still clothed in my shorts and baggy t-shirt that I wore to bed, I wade into the water. This time I don't pause after every step to acclimate.

"I'm sorry, Dad," I whisper over the water. "I won't let it hold me back anymore." The water rises up my legs, gradually slowing my momentum. "Your memory deserves more than that."

I leap forward, hands up, headfirst, diving beneath the surface as if I'm diving into a pool of freedom that's been waiting a lifetime for my arrival.

CHAPTER THIRTY-THREE

THE TUNNEL OF TREES BLURS PAST ME, MY FOOTSTEPS creating a steady rhythm against the dirt pathway. Now that I no longer need to occupy the empty lakefront at daybreak, I've returned to my roots. With only two days left in town, it feels right to come back to where it all began.

I slow my pace as I approach the apple tree that Dalton and I frequent. The unkempt grass almost completely conceals the wooden rail fence now. I push my way past its wayward growth and rest my forearms against the upper plank of wood to take in the orchard. It's hard to imagine a time before I knew this sliver of bliss existed.

Dalton's swing hangs above the skirt of woodchips, his craftiness still impressive to me. As I appreciate the scenery that I've grown so fond of over the last couple months, something seems off. As I look to the branches,

I notice their bareness. Each tree limb is void of the apples that once immediately caught my eye by the sharp contrast in complementary colors.

Excitement bubbles in anticipation of the Harvest Festival later this morning. It seems to be the highlight of the summer around here with an endless array of mouthwatering foods, exciting contests and prizes, live music from local artists, and of course the sand volleyball playoffs. JuiSea will be teeming with customers, but Jay scheduled his staff to work in shorter shifts so that we'll all have a chance to enjoy the lineup of today's events. I scurry home to get ready for the festivities—never have I been so eager to head to work.

When I cross the street, I turn to catch a glimpse of the special day. Groups of people are sectioned along the perimeter of the lake as far as I can see, raising canopies, unfolding tables, and mounting signs to display their goods. Just like how Arrowbase felt like a Super Target on steroids, the Harvest Festival might measure up to the greatest farmers market I've ever witnessed.

∼∼∼

THERE'S A PEP IN MY STEP AS I SERVE THE ENDLESS FLOW of customers. Despite the sadness I feel for leaving the shop, knowing it's my last day motivates me to excel at every aspect of the job. It certainly helps that every customer today has a dazzling smile and friendly demeanor.

The clock strikes noon and it's time for me to clock out. As I remove my apron, Jay slowly steps around the archway, his weight sloped against the wall. He's holding a cup filled to the brim with a violet-color smoothie.

"As a thank you," he says, presenting me with the drink to take as I cruise up and down the line of booths.

"Thanks," I take it, sucking on the neon orange straw that sits next to a bright yellow paper umbrella. Rich chocolate and citrus flavors—and perhaps a dash of spice—dance on my tongue. I raise my eyebrows at him and tap my free hand against the one holding the cup, applauding gently for this new masterpiece.

"Very nice," I tell him. "What is it?"

"That right there," he emphasizes, "is the latest and greatest addition to our menu. It's called The Bravery." He pauses before adding, "It's your smoothie, Aves."

"Hmm?" I question, distracted by another sip of its complicated, yet delectable taste.

"I figured you weren't the type to want your name on the menu board, so I had to find a way to incorporate it into a different name for the smoothie. And besides, I think it's rather fitting given the last few weeks."

I set the cup down and pull him into a hug to show my appreciation.

"Yeah, yeah." He quickly returns the hug before

pulling away again. "Now get off me. You're all sweaty and I have a shop full of customers to attend to." He juts his chin toward the lake. "Go. Have fun."

I turn to leave JuiSea but stop short when I see Raymond standing at the edge of the shop, having just arrived for his shift. His eyes glisten as I walk the length of the bar to meet him.

"You better make this quick because my eyeliner is on point today and I can't have you messing it up." His voice is laced with false bravado as he tries to conceal his emotion for what could possibly be our last in-person interaction for the foreseeable future.

I don't respond right away. I simply pull him into a tight embrace and squeeze as if it's the last time I'll ever see him. "I had no idea when I first moved here that I'd find my best friend."

He lets out a quiet whimper. "Well now you've done it."

I pull away and see a tear escape down his cheek. He quickly wipes it away and looks to the ceiling with wide eyes blinking rapidly to prevent his makeup from smudging.

"You're my favorite Warren," he tells me, giving me a sad smile. "Until Jay gives me a raise. After which point, I can't make any promises."

I laugh and shove his shoulder. "I expect you to visit me in Colorado. Wait, scratch that. My mom expects you to visit her in Colorado."

"Ooh, girl you know I'll be visiting you and Denise,"

he agrees and we both nod, knowing this isn't a final goodbye. We'll be seeing each other again.

Raymond sniffles and gives me one last hug before we part ways.

I wander leisurely past each booth, stopping to chat with eager vendors about their offers—homemade soaps, edible bamboo shoots, crafty cards covered in calligraphy, salsas ranging from subtle to setting your mouth on fire. I try samples and purchase a few souvenirs starting with a reusable bag that says "Nelson Harvest Festival" on one side and "We Lake Having You Here" on the other.

A flash of bright hair catches my attention and I step around the next booth to see Jen and Levi browsing a selection of homemade jewelry in the shade of a canopy. Levi picks up a pair of jade earring studs and holds them next to Jen's face. She smiles, tilting her head and lifting her chin as if modeling the selection.

"These would look pretty on you," he compliments.

"You think?" Jen responds.

"Yeah, just a second." He turns to an elderly lady sitting in a lawn chair overseeing the booth. "Excuse me, ma'am, how much for these?"

I step underneath the canopy to join Jen.

"I'd say it's pretty official if he's buying you jewelry," I keep my voice low.

Jen turns to me in surprise, almost whipping me in the face with her long ponytail, and gives me a hug. "It is," she gushes, unable to contain her enthusiasm. She holds onto my forearms, not quite separating from the hug.

"We were at the McCormick's booth, the one with all the huge hibiscus flowers, and we were just looking around when Levi mentioned that he should buy me some flowers, and that's when Mrs. McCormick said what a cute couple we are—" she rambles on excitedly, "—so I hesitated because I didn't know how he felt about us being called a couple and if the term couple meant boyfriend-girlfriend or what." She finally takes a breath before continuing. "So, I fumbled over my words and that's when Levi spoke up and told Mrs. McCormick that he's lucky to have me as his girlfriend! Apparently, he's already been thinking that for weeks now. He could've let me in on it." She laughs at the miscommunication between them.

"I'm happy for you," I tell her.

"Here you go, Jenny," Levi presents a little white box with a pink ribbon tied into a bow on top. The lady must have wrapped the earrings for him. "What's up, Avery?" he greets me cheerfully.

"Hey Levi, how'd your team do this morning?" Unfortunately, I couldn't attend the sand volleyball playoffs because of work, but I've been waiting to hear the outcome.

"Not bad. We didn't make it to the championship game, but Dalton's team got first."

Not bad indeed, I think. I make a mental note to congratulate Dalton later.

Suddenly, Bristol bursts into the canopy, grabbing both Jen and me by the shoulders.

"I got it!" she exclaims. "I got the internship!"

"That's awesome! Way to go."

"I knew you would."

"I just got off the phone with them and not only did they offer me the position, but they also want to move the start date up and said there's potential to be hired on part-time after the semester ends."

"So much for an easy first semester," I tease her.

"Forget that." She motions her hand in front of her as if pushing away the idea. "It's going to be amazing."

The elderly lady running the jewelry booth enters the canopy, crowding the already cramped space. It's obvious she wants us to move along if we aren't interested in buying anything else.

We continue walking along the shore, watching the vendors from afar to see if anything catches our eyes. A bright-colored beach ball soars in front of us and lands in the water. I quickly retrieve it and toss it to the owner. When I turn to rejoin my friends, their eyes bulge in surprise.

"What?" I ask, their confusion spreading to me.

"You just—" Jen stutters.

"You got in the water," Bristol says in shock.

A meek smile spreads across my face. "Oh. Right. That."

"Since when?" Jen asks me ardently, prodding for details.

"I've been working on it in the mornings. Jay's been helping me."

"That's huge!"

"We're so proud of you!"

They embrace me from either side, reminding me of our previous huddle when Raymond, Jen, and Bristol all consoled me rather than congratulated me.

The music from JuiSea has faded, replaced by a melody from an alternative rock band on stage in a grassy field. We linger to listen, but when I glance farther ahead, I finally spot the booth I've been searching for and make my way over to it. Leeann and Robert busy themselves, getting change for their teeming customers and stocking large paper bags with apples from the truck bed parked behind their tent.

"Avery," Robert calls out, waving his hand for me to come around the tables. He nudges his wife, pointing in my direction. She sets down a bag of apples on the nearest table and rushes over, throwing her arms around me. I'm not sure if it's because of the festival or my final few days here, but I've lost count of how many hugs I've received today.

"Oh, Avery," she lets out, sounding almost relieved. "I'm so glad you're here. Have you had a chance to talk to Dalton yet?" Her voice is infused with delight.

"Not yet, but I was hoping to congratulate him. I heard about the big news."

Her eyes shine brightly, proud of her son. "I think

he's still with his team, but if I see him, I'll let him know you swung by."

I pull out a folded-up piece of paper from my back pocket and hold it out to her. "Could you give this to him for me? He'll know what it means."

"I'd be happy to. Here." She reaches for a bag of apples, handing them to me in return. "Take these. For all your help. You have no idea how much it means to us."

I'm not quite sure what she means by it, but I thank her for the gift, and we say our goodbyes. As I depart from their tent, I think back to what I'd written out for Dalton earlier that morning. My final feat.

A recipe to make
A leap I chose to take
Steps I dare retrace
Meet me in that place

CHAPTER THIRTY-FOUR

I watch as Dalton emerges from the end of the trail. He glances around for me. I've been perched halfway up the embankment that leads to the top of the waterfall, hugging my knees to my chest and watching a few twinkling stars blink into existence as the sky turns from pale blue to deep indigo.

"Looking for someone?" I call out to him over the roar of the waterfall. He snaps his head in my direction, his dimples making an appearance as a smile spreads across his face.

"I dunno," he responds. "I received an anonymous poem that led me here."

"Interesting. I once received a recipe for a picnic that led me here as well." He shakes his head, still embarrassed about that move despite it propelling our relationship to the next level.

He makes his way to where I sit. "So, what brings

you to this hidden waterfall on the evening of the most popular day in town? You know you're missing out on all the festivities."

He takes a seat beside me and peers over the rock wall, probably shocked at how close I am to the edge. Our arms brush against each other and I long for him to come closer. I take a deep breath, trying to conceal my giddiness as I anticipate what's soon to happen.

"Two things," I preface. "First, I owe you an apology for the other day."

"Avery—" he interjects, shaking his head as he takes my hand in his.

"No, please," I insist as I try to remember the words I'd practiced a hundred times in the mirror to prepare for this moment. "I let my deep-seated emotions get the better of me, blinding me to what you've been going through. I of all people should know better, and I'm sorry I didn't understand at the time. I do now, and I'm here for you, whatever that looks like."

"You were right, though." He gives me a sorry look. "I was acting hypocritical. I think I was just projecting onto you all the things I wanted but didn't know how to give myself."

I nod, knowing there's healing and growth to be had on both sides.

Dalton sighs and gives my hand a squeeze. We sit in silence for a moment, and then he gets a puzzled look on his face and asks, "What's the second reason you brought me here?"

I don't respond right away, instead biting my lip and letting my eagerness build before I reveal why I've beckoned him all the way here.

"I want to show you something."

He furrows his eyebrows in suspicion. "And you had to bring me all the way here to show me?"

I nod gleefully. "Yeah. I did."

"What are you talking about, Warren? You're making me nervous. You know that?"

I know he's likely kidding, but I still find it ironic that he's more nervous in this situation than I am. I've never not been nervous at times like these, but this time it's manageable.

Without further ado, I push myself into a stand and remove my tank top and shorts to reveal my mauve one-piece.

"What are you doing?" he asks, skeptical of my actions.

The butterflies in your stomach are what something new is all about, I remind myself of my mom's words, shooting Dalton once last smirk before jumping over the edge.

Water rushes over me as I plunge into the pool. When I emerge and look to the spot where I'd jumped from, Dalton is nowhere to be found. I tread for a couple seconds, looking up the embankment for him before I hear splashing coming from the shore.

Dalton, who must have sprinted down the slope and thrown off his shirt on the way, runs into the pool until the water is high enough to dive in. He reaches me within seconds, stretching his arms around me in an attempt to save me. I let him cradle me in his arms but I try to catch his gaze so he can see that I'm calm, that I'm okay.

"What were you thinking?" he asks, flustered by the sudden change of events.

I wait for him to understand, swaying my arms through the water around me.

"What are you doing?" He takes in my behavior, my level of composure. He hesitates, unsure of how to proceed, before simply asking, "How?"

"I wanted to show you that I did it. I did what you said I could, and it was the hardest thing I've ever done." I pause only because I can't contain my beaming smile. "But I did it."

He gawks at me, his hair dripping into eyes that are full of amazement. He smiles back at me, and then whispers, "I knew you could."

I lean into him, soaking in his embrace. As my arms snake around him, I notice he's wearing a small wooden pendant around his neck, tied on with thick, black string.

"I like this," I comment, gesturing to the necklace.

"Oh, yeah," he lights up, taking the pendant in his fingers and pulling the string up and over his head. "I made it for you." He places it in the palm of my hand. "The design represents growth, strength, peace, and new beginnings, which"—he chuckles—"fits the moment perfectly."

I turn it over in my hand, caressing its intricate spiral figure.

"It's beautiful," I whisper in awe. "Much better than trying to fit an entire wooden swing into my carry-on."

He lets out a laugh. "That's all I was going for, the convenience factor," he jokes.

I reach up to slide it over my head, pulling my hair through the black string.

"I love it. You should sell your woodwork at the festival next year. It'd be a huge hit."

"Not a bad idea," he ponders. "But I don't think I'll have enough time to make stuff."

"Why is that?"

His eyes dance back and forth between mine as he contemplates how to answer. "Say, do you think I'd look good in green and white?"

My face contorts in confusion at the arbitrary question.

"I'm thinking of attending LHU in the spring," he tells me.

I freeze, thinking I may have misheard him. I look at him intently, trying to pick up on any sort of kidding. When he smiles again and gives me a slight nod, my chest explodes with a kind of joy I've never experienced before.

I wrap my legs around his torso and press my lips against his, unable to contain my excitement. He kisses me back and I can feel his smile intensify, both of us reveling in each other's successes.

There's a loud sizzling sound followed by a thunderous boom, the start of the firework show. I pull away to look at him again, streams of pink and blue reflecting in his eyes from the explosives disappearing into the night sky. I want to express how I feel, but the words get lost in the fireworks of my own mind, so I kiss him again.

This must have been the big news Dalton's mom was referring to, not his team placing first in the playoffs.

I pull away again. "I'm so proud of you, Dalton," I tell him, breathless.

"It's nothing. *You*," he emphasizes, "*you* should be proud of yourself. I know I am."

We watch glimpses of the firework show over the treetops, holding onto one another as the steady stream of water pours over the mossy rock wall, the noise reverberating all around us. No longer will I miss out on moments like these. The fear may not have completely dissipated, but it won't hold me back any longer. And for now, that's something worth celebrating.

ACKNOWLEDGMENTS

This book would not be in your hands if it weren't for the support of several friends and family members. It would be amiss not to thank them here. First and foremost, my parents, for always encouraging me to pursue my dreams and pushing me to become the best version of myself; my sister, Courtney, for helping me cultivate a love of writing and for providing invaluable feedback on a desperate draft of my manuscript; my sister, Stephanie, for always believing in me; Gracie, for being my first and most enthusiastic reader back before it was Shattered Streams; Oksana, for your kind words and steadfast encouragement; Hanna, for your helping hand as I learn how to navigate these waters (pun intended); Sierra, for your gentle guidance in my self-development and overcoming my own fears; my editor, Jessica Powers, for your keen insight and writing wisdom; and finally, Stacey Nicholls and Ethan Gaskins of Quill and Quality who made it possible for this book to reach the hands of my readers. For all of you, I am immeasurably grateful.

ABOUT THE AUTHOR

KELLY POLLARD resides in Loveland, Colorado. When she isn't writing, you can find her in nature, traveling, or cozying up with a book and her two cats, Athena and Cleo. Shattered Streams is her first novel.

Visit Kelly at www.kellypollardbooks.com.

⊙ instagram.com/kellylaurapollard

www.ingramcontent.com/pod-product-compliance
Lightning Source LLC
Chambersburg PA
CBHW052016240626
47153CB00006B/1841